Girl in the Making

Anna Fitzgerald was born and raised in Dublin. *Girl in the Making* is her first novel.

Girl in the Making

Anna Fitzgerald

SANDYCOVE

an imprint of

PENGUIN BOOKS

SANDYCOVE

UK | USA | Canada | Ireland | Australia
India | New Zealand | South Africa

Sandycove is part of the Penguin Random House group of companies
whose addresses can be found at global.penguinrandomhouse.com.

First published 2024
001

Copyright © Anna Fitzgerald, 2024

The quotation from 'Fern Hill' by Dylan Thomas, from
The Collected Works of Dylan Thomas (Weidenfeld & Nicolson), is reproduced
by kind permission of the copyright holder, The Dylan Thomas Trust

The moral right of the author has been asserted

Set in 13.5/17.75pt Perpetua Std
Typeset by Jouve (UK), Milton Keynes
Printed and bound in Great Britain by Clays Ltd, Elcograf S.p.A.

The authorized representative in the EEA is Penguin Random House Ireland,
Morrison Chambers, 32 Nassau Street, Dublin D02 YH68

A CIP catalogue record for this book is available from the British Library

HARDBACK ISBN: 978-1-844-88647-0
TRADE PAPERBACK ISBN: 978-1-844-88648-7

www.greenpenguin.co.uk

For my daughters

PART ONE

Sparrows

(1966–1975)

Three

there she is there she is

I can stand under the giant yellow tree at the bottom of my garden where I am not allowed to go – no he says no – and then I am in the golden honeypot I can stay quiet there I can look up at all of the golden honey floating down on me and I can see a little piece of blue sky and I can look for balloons there in the piece of blue sky that is high up from the honey come and play with me Winnie the Pooh because I am in the honeypot too and I want to play with someone but Tom shouts there she is there she is but I want to stay here and wait for Pooh bear I will stay here until someone comes to play with me then he says come here come here why BECAUSE I SAY SO my shoulders go bump at the lion's voice hide in the honey tree Pooh the lion is coming

Four

I do not like worms

When she goes out I am afraid very afraid when she goes out but I don't know what I am afraid of but I am afraid and I think it's important to be afraid if I want to be safe I do not like worms in our grass so I do not sit on our grass and I do not like it when he jokes I do not like his magic tricks when will she come home I have to listen hard for the sound of the car and the flash of the lights as it turns into our driveway and the lights fly across my *Alice in Wonderland* paper that she put on my walls but I am scared of the Mad Hatter and she does not know I am tell her tell her no I can't tell I lie still and stiff because I can hear quiet sounds and not just quiet when I lie still and stiff listen hard for her to come home listening makes her come come come take me with you the next time please the next time because I do not like the worms in our grass I do not like his magic tricks I am afraid when you are not here take me with you the next time don't go without me any more I do not like it when I am in bed and I hear the front door shut when you pull it quietly behind you and you go to see your own momma out in the dark night all by yourself and the car might crash and you might not come back and then what will happen to me I am too small and I cannot hide because all the flowers have fallen off the honey tree and Pooh bear is so frightened that he won't come out to play with me Pooh used to hide sometimes and I would call for him and call for him at the honey tree Pooh Pooh but now Pooh is hiding all the time there is no one to play with

Five

I Wanna Hold Your Hand

The birthday candles were so bright. Momma whispered that she had always wanted a girl and that she was so happy that I was born. I thought, *It is good that she wanted me*. Everyone should be wanted by somebody. Then I blew out the candles.

We went to the zoo after that. But Aunty Ida couldn't come. 'There is no room in the car,' HE said. 'I will stay here and wash up,' said Aunty Ida. It was hard to cross the big road in the park. Momma pushed our new baby twins in the pushchair and Cissy stood on the brake bar. HE held Tom's hand. The cars whirred past, really fast. It was very loud. I was worried because there would be wild animals in the zoo. They could escape and eat me and Cissy and Tom and Momma and the twins. Momma kept looking right and looking left. Looking right and looking left. We waited for ages. 'Hold Jean's hand, Edmund,' said Momma. I held my hand up and HE closed up my wrist with his tight fingers. At last we crossed. HE dropped my wrist as soon as my shoe was on the grass verge. 'Run on,' HE said. 'Go on, run on.'

Six

There May Be Trouble Ahead for Tom

Tom needs to learn this for tomorrow. There will be trouble from the teacher if Tom does not know this tomorrow. Tom is afraid. Momma is afraid. HE is afraid that Momma is mixing Tom up.

> *'The Owl and the Pussy-cat went to sea*
> *In a beautiful pea-green boat . . .'*

'Very good, Tom.'

> *'They took some money, and took more money —'*

'No, Tom. No. Stop, you are confusing him. Shhh, be quiet. Try again, Tom.' Poor Tom, he cannot remember.

> *'The Owl and the Pussy-cat went to sea*
> *In a beautiful green-pea boat,*
> *They took some money, and plenty of honey —'*

'No, Tom, no,' HE says. 'You are confusing Tom,' HE says. 'Go in to the babies.' Momma has to go. The noise is mixing Tom up. Tom is mixed up. 'Start again, Tom.'

> *'The Owl and the Pussy-cat went to sea*
> *In a beautiful pea-green boat,*
> *They took some honey, and plenty of money,*
> *Wrapped up in a five-pound note.'*

'Good, Tom, good. Tom's got it. Clever boy, Tom. Keep going, Tom.'

> *'Pussy said to the Owl, "You elegant fowl!*
> *How charmingly sweet you sing!*
> *O let us be married! too long we have tarried:*
> *But what shall we do for a —"'*

'Can a pussy marry an owl?'

'Jean, you stupid girl. Tom is mixed up again now. That's your fault. Get out of the room. Out now. Out. Go help with the babies. Try again, Tom.'

I am afraid there may be trouble ahead for Tom. Think, Tom, think.

Listen, babies, I will say it for you:

> *'They sailed away, for a year and a day,*
> *To the land where the Bong-Tree grows*
> *And there in a wood a Piggy-wig stood*
> *With a ring at the end of his nose,*
> *His nose,*
> *His nose,*
> *With a ring at the end of his nose.'*

Seven

The Cheater

It was hard on Thursday nights. I did not like Thursdays. It was the night to learn our spellings for the big tests on Friday. Tom and Momma worked hard as soon as we came home from school. Momma just tested me once. Mine were easy. Tom's were a bit harder because he was in second class, but we were in the same classroom because Mr Burke had first and second class together. I watched Tom. I listened to Tom. We all worried about Tom's spellings, even though Tom was the cleverest in the house. It was a worry because if Tom scored under six out of ten, Mr Burke would hit Tom. 'Everyone out,' HE said when he came home, and he and Tom worked very late.

On Friday mornings, early because our minds were sharpest early, Mr Burke said, we had our spelling tests. Sharp little minds. A good time for spelling tests. Mr Burke was very cross a lot of the time and it was lucky that I was good and quiet and polite and very careful all the time. Sometimes he hit the whole class, even the good ones like me, if anyone talked when he left the room to go to the head's office. I think he hid outside the door to catch us out so that he could hit us, because he came back so suddenly. He threw open the door just when no one was expecting it. I never spoke or whispered or moved when he went out, because when he was about to leave he said, 'Don't speak, don't move.' I usually sat on my hands, that was the easiest way not to move and not to fiddle with things and it was what Mr Burke made us do. But it made no difference because some boys would always speak, and some would always move. They would not sit on their hands like me.

I sat near the door. That was my place because I was good and I could open the door and let messengers in. Owen Hogan sat beside me because he was not good. He picked his nose and rubbed his snot on the wood of our desk. It made me feel sick. He always moved and made noise. Then on Fridays the test would begin. It was worrying but I always knew my spellings and got ten out of ten because there was no other way to do it if you didn't want to be worried all the time.

This Friday, which was a very bad day in my life, Mr Burke called out the words and I wrote them slowly and neatly because he gave us so much time, but Owen kept sniffing and picking his nose and his head kept jerking up and down and turning from side to side and he kept looking up at Mr Burke. Twelve English words were written down and then twelve Irish words were called out. Mr Burke said, 'Jean Kennedy, *bailigh na coipleabhair*,' because I was good. Everyone folded their arms and Mr Burke kept a lookout for cheats. I brought the collected notebooks to his desk and I put them down carefully. Then he said, 'Open your workbooks on page eighteen,' and he sat back in his chair with his very big body and his very angry face and his eyes which could see everything and his ears hearing everything.

I bent my head to begin my work and I did not look at him again until he roared, 'Jean Kennedy, come up here. Owen Hogan, come up here.' I was very surprised because I was so good. But Owen was not surprised. We went and stood in front of Mr Burke. 'Hold out your hands,' he said and he came from behind his desk with his stick. I did not know why, but I am obedient so I did hold out my hands, but I did not know why I had to. Then he hit my hands and then he hit Owen's hands and the tears stung in my eyes and just fell down even though I did not want them to, even though I tried to stop them. Very, very hard I tried. Because it was so embarrassing. And then he took my spelling notebook, which was crispy and clean with no mistakes, and he took Owen's, which was dirty and smudged, and he wrote a word in both and he held the notebooks up to our faces. He pushed mine into my face and it said 'CHEAT'. Then he put my notebook in the dirty wooden square bin full of apple cores and sticky jam paper and pencil shavings and then he said, 'Now I don't know which of you copied which – but I do know this: girls are more inclined to cheat than boys. Jean Kennedy, go stand in the bin. Owen Hogan, go stand in the corner.'

I had never stood in the bin before, though lots of other people had. It was hard to climb in and I thought the bin would fall over and all the apple butts would spill out and then there would be trouble. But I got in it and Mr Burke said, 'Face the wall,' so I did. And there I stood in the bin, very afraid that I would wet my knickers. What would happen then? And when Momma came to collect us and asked me how was school, I could not say a word. I was too mixed up and too sad and I was afraid that if I spoke a single word I would burst out crying because it was so unfair. And even though I hadn't cheated and always got every single spelling right, I knew that everyone had stared at me and everyone thought I was a cheat. Cheating and lying go hand in hand — that was what Momma said. She said it when Tom told her that Willie Furlong cheated him in a comic swap. 'No one likes a cheat' — Momma often said that. And I was afraid that no one would like me now and that Mr Burke would never trust me again. And that he would think I was a bad speller.

Eight

The First Very Sad and Very, Very Grey Day

I do not know why I woke very early one Sunday morning in summer when it was almost as chilly as a winter morning. And I do not know what woke me. I woke even before Cissy and the twins and even before our baby Cecil, who always woke everyone up really early. I dressed in my shorts and last year's sandals because I did not have this year's yet, and because last year's were only a bit tight, and I went very, very quietly downstairs. I had never been alone like this downstairs before. The quiet was strange and it made me feel guilty. I thought I had better find a way to break it. Whenever I found myself with nothing to do I liked to walk the walls of our back garden, even when they were wet and slippery, as they were that day. I had become so good at it and I knew all of the dangerous chips and bumps so that I never fell off, and when the O'Malleys walked the walls with me I would shout back to them, 'You are coming towards the uneven bit.' I had not fallen off since I was seven and a half and that meant that I held the record but I did not say that to the others. No one likes a show-off.

I dragged a kitchen chair to the back door and stood on it so that I could pull the bolt. It was always stiff but I managed it at last. It was just the kind of morning that I did not like. A drizzle so light that you did not realize you were getting wet until your bare legs began to itch. The grey concrete garden walls were dark from the wetness that clung to them, and the grey sky just hung over our back garden and would not move. One day I had said to Momma when she was painting our front door white, 'Can we paint the back walls too?' But she had said, 'No. You can't paint concrete walls.' I thought for a moment of going back inside but then it occurred to me that maybe the O'Malleys had woken early and would see me on the wall and come out to play. So I stuck the tip of my sandal into a little crevice in the wall and pulled myself up with my hands. Then I spat on my hands and rubbed them together to stop the stinging. I always did that. I started walking slowly, to get the balance and rhythm right. Always start slowly. I would teach this to Cissy and our twins when they were ready. I had completed eight laps exactly, which was my exact age, when suddenly I began to feel a little like the sky myself. I sat on the wall with my legs dangling into the O'Malleys' side and I hoped they would notice me. I sat for ages, but I was getting very wet, which might get me in trouble, so I went inside. I dragged the chair to the back door again and pushed the stiff bolt across. I carefully returned the chair, tucking it in under the table for neatness.

By mistake I wandered into the sitting room, where we were not supposed to go in case HIS records got scratched. It was almost total darkness with the heavy red curtains still closed and the air still smelly with HIS cigarette smoke from the night before. I stared at the telly. I was not good at turning it on and off and I was not good at changing the stations. I usually left that to Tom. This morning I would try, even though I was very worried that I might break it. I knew I had to find a way to get this grey sky off my body. It had stuck on to me like the drizzle stuck to my bare legs. The telly turned on quite easily. It was just a button. I had picked the right button and I felt very pleased with myself. Maybe the telly was not as hard to operate as Tom said. Changing the station, though, looked more difficult. I knelt down and examined the buttons: RTÉ, BBC. I pressed RTÉ but there was only the test card because it was so early and it was Sunday. So I pressed BBC.

A man sat in his big overcoat in a rowing boat on top of a raging sea. His hair was blowing everywhere and he struggled with two huge oars. And then I saw the two poor girls, who were big girls and looked about fifth-class age and must have been very sorry that they had gone out on that boat that day. They were sitting on the floor of the rowing boat, clinging to each other. The poor man in his overcoat struggled and fought to keep the boat steady as the sea threw them around. And then a mean whip of wind made the boat sail up off the water as easily as a balloon slips away from you on a blustery day as soon as you step out the door after a birthday party, and the poor man's oar was ripped from his hand. One of the girls' ribbons was ripped off too, but I don't think she even noticed because she was so afraid. It was a terrible thing to see but I kept watching because it would probably be okay because it was telly, and Momma always says that we could expect happy endings on telly, and whenever I cried at something sad on telly she said, 'Just wait till the end, it will be fine,' and then at the end she would say, 'All's well that ends well.'

Suddenly the little wooden boat was upside down in the water and first I saw the man clinging to it and then I saw that the girl whose ribbon had been ripped off was gasping and trying to keep her face out of the water. The poor sad man, who must have been their daddy, saw her and was swimming towards her, which must have been hard in his big winter coat. But when he was halfway towards reaching the girl, he heard the cries of the other girl, who was nearer to him now, and his face looked so terrible at that moment that I cannot describe it, but it was much worse than poor Momma's had been when Mrs Gleason from next door knocked on our front door to tell us that poor Momma's own daddy had died in the night of the flu. That was before we got our phone. The waves were crashing over the man's head now and sometimes I could see the first girl but sometimes the water covered her up completely. The poor man pulled the second girl over to the upside-down rowing boat and placed her arms over it, and then he looked out to where the first girl had been. But she was gone now. The poor man raised his head up towards the sky and shouted and shouted, but the roaring sea would not let anyone hear what he said. I didn't know if he had tears because he was already so wet. Anyhow I didn't know if fathers had tears.

Why did they put this on the telly? I wondered. Then the programme switched from the sea to a television studio which was quite like the one in *Blue Peter* but without any animals. Six grown-ups sat in a half circle talking about the poor man and the poor girls. But mainly about the poor man. And I wondered why they were not crying. I was crying by then, but quietly in case I got in trouble for turning the telly on by myself. Most of them were wearing priest collars, but one of them just looked like a very serious man with a normal tie. He was the one asking the questions. There was only one lady. They talked about the poor man and the first girl at the bottom of the sea and the second girl who had been saved, and I began to see that everything was even worse than I had thought. Even greyer than the grey that had already stuck itself onto my body. I listened to the men talking and then I figured it out. The man had brought the girls out in the boat for a treat. The first girl, who in the end had sunk to the bottom of the sea, was his own girl. He was her daddy. And the second girl was her friend, who had gone with them for a nice day out. They talked about whether the man should have carried on swimming to his own girl and saved her. Or had he done the right thing by swimming back to the girl who was not his own girl? It was very mixed-up. They talked for a long, long time and I think they were still fighting about it when the programme ended. Especially the men in the priest collars, who spoke very poshly like the BBC newsreaders. The lady hardly said anything at all. I don't know what they decided in the end and I did not find out what the right thing for the poor man to do was. But I would always worry about it and I would never be able to forget the poor man's own poor girl who would be for ever and ever at the bottom of the sea. I wished that the daddy had saved his own girl, and then I felt mean about the other girl's poor momma. And I wondered if the daddy had preferred the girl who was not his. Even in the playground, whenever I skipped and we all sang, '*A sailor went to sea sea sea to see what he could see see see, and all that he could see see see was the bottom of the deep blue sea sea sea*,' I would sing in my head that extra line: '*just like the poor drowned girl*.' I could never get that line to stop coming.

Afterwards I went back outside and I walked the walls and the grey from the sky and the walls stuck onto me even harder and I knew that I would never be able to get it off me and that it would always be on top of me.

Nine

What I Did on My Summer Holidays

For weeks Momma sat, bent over her Singer sewing machine, making the dresses. One would be for her, one would be for Cissy and one would be for me. The fabric for mine was mainly blue and red, a mixture of different-size red and blue stars all scattered across a whitey cotton that Momma said was more like ivory. If it had had stripes going down it, it would have been a bit like an American flag. When I said that to Momma she said with a big smile, 'Oh, you're quite right, love.' Momma, of course, had a more grown-up shape to her dress because she had a grown-up-shaped body while we had little-girl bodies; mine was nine and Cissy's only six and a quarter.

Momma pulled the sewing machine out into the middle of the sitting-room floor each afternoon. I hated that. Everything was cluttered; spools of thread everywhere, no space to sit down, and her head was constantly bent down away from us. I had to keep threading the sewing-machine needle because her eyes were not good in such a shadowy room and I hated that too, but I did it patiently because I loved her so much. By then she already had her glasses and she said they were like medieval torture to wear, digging into her face.

She may have been afraid that they ruined her beautiful brown eyes, and it is quite a sad thing to say but they did a little bit because they squashed up her eyelashes, which were really long and black. Though she was still the most beautiful lady I have ever seen.

I did not know until later that the dresses would be for the holiday. Momma did not tell us we were going until closer to the time, because I would not have been able to sleep, she said. Butlin's Mosney Park, the only Butlin's in Ireland. Redcoats and cabins, an outdoor swimming pool, all our dinners and breakfasts served to us. It would be like America. I knew what it all meant because I was the second eldest, and also because I had a really strong feel for America back then.

Momma said that Butlin's was why, instead of buying me the red anorak that I really wanted straight away, she had just put a deposit on it that day when I had waited outside Keveney's shop, holding on to the pram and minding the twins while Momma and Cissy had gone inside. I was not good at waiting and I wanted that red anorak so much. It is so hard to wait.

Watching her head bent over the dress, her foot hovering over the pedal of the sewing machine, I sat and waited and waited. I watched so carefully, waiting for a needle to snap so that I could fetch her a new one. I helped her to find the scissors when the thread hid itself, like a little demon Momma said, disappearing beneath layers of paper patterns. And I played with the others so that Momma could get on with the dresses, though sometimes I would rather have read

Five Run Away Together or walked the walls of our back garden. I tickled them and pretended that I could not see them when they hid behind the coal scuttle, wrapped themselves in the curtains or lay flat in the dust and lost pieces of Lego and Tom's American and Japanese plastic soldiers under our couch.

Momma thought I was excited about the dresses. But I was not excited about the dresses. I was excited about going to Butlin's. That week piles of wet clothes sat in basins until they grew hard and HE got cross with Momma and said that they reeked of an awful damp smell. That was because it had rained and rained and rained for days and there was no point in hanging them out. Our beds were never made; they grew crumby and the blankets slipped to the floor when we got in. We did not grow bored though, even with all the rain and the Singer sewing machine plonked in the middle of the sitting room, because there was something in the air, a feeling that the world was about to change. I caught the excitement from Momma's dedication to making perfect dresses, with the stars on mine remaining whole except around the seams, and the little ones caught it from me because I was high, in my American mood.

It was cold even though we had been wearing our summer clothes for weeks. The paraffin heater was turned up high. It made us all a bit sleepy, Momma said. And it was hard to keep Baby away from it. So Momma and I and Tom dragged the table with the Singer sewing machine across the carpet so that she could sit directly in front of the paraffin heater, blocking the little ones from it. I would have made Momma tea, but I was only nine and it was hard for me to reach everything and to turn on the gas. But I would have liked to make her tea. I mashed bananas with sugar for Baby and for the little ones. Momma said I was really good, her little helper. And I was being really good. And so was Tom. But then who would not be good when we were so lucky?

She worked so hard. She was so tired. When Aunty Ida came she said, 'Oh no, Tess, you are very strained with all of that sewing.' I did not say anything but I had been thinking the exact same thing as Aunty Ida: Momma was just not cut out for sewing. It seemed to worry her a lot. I held Cissy's dress up to her while Momma put pins in and then I tried mine on. But I did not like it. I dreamed of American clothes – an American look, my big cousins called it – sneakers and jeans with wide bottoms and a cotton T-shirt, and maybe even a baseball cap like cute American tomboys in films. And I might even wear it backwards. I felt bad that I did not like my dress. That is why I said, 'I love it – I'm going to wear it every day in Butlin's.' And every time I said that, a terrible worry fell over me, for how would I climb walls there in a dress, and how would I run fast, and I would be so easy to catch if I could not run fast.

I knew the time was near when the kitchen table was piled with heaps of clothes. HE and Momma were having a grown-up conversation, one of their last-minute disagreements. It was always hard to get out because there were so many of us. She said we could not arrive in Butlin's without proper suitcases. But HE said there would be no space left in the car if we brought even one, and that black plastic sacks were fine and we could sit on them. HE said that we could carry them into the chalets at night when it was dark and no one would see. Momma did not like the idea, and I thought privately that it was un-American, but she began to place the piles of carefully ironed clothes into the sacks. I wrote each of our names on a piece of white paper and Sellotaped them onto the sacks so that we would know which was which. That seemed to cheer her up a lot. I was so pleased that I got the markers from my school bag and on each label I drew a picture of that person's favourite thing: so a rose for Momma, a football for Tom, little teddies or cars for the little ones. I did not draw anything on HIS label because I did not know what his favourite thing was. I thought for a minute about drawing an Irish flag but my orange marker had run out, and anyhow sometimes HE said that America was the land of promise and Ireland the land that never kept its promises, so I just left his blank.

Of course, you will guess that I could not sleep the night before. I heard their alarm go off, their whispering, and then the rustling of the black sacks as they were carried down-stairs. I got up and went outside to help. But no, HE said. It would be better if I stayed in the bedroom in case the little ones woke up and attempted to escape out the front door. So I watched them packing from the upstairs window. Fitting all of the sacks into the car was difficult and HE kept putting them in and taking them out again. Then Momma threw her hands in the air and went inside while HE stopped and had a cigarette just staring at the sacks on the ground. After a few minutes HE walked to the gate and back. HE looked like he was thinking hard. I was growing very anxious because I thought perhaps HE was changing his mind and we would not go at all. Momma came out then and started placing the sacks on the back seat and flattening them down by lying on top of them.

Then I was a little bit bad because I started to make noise so that the little ones would waken up. It worked well and a few minutes later we were all in the kitchen. 'We're all ready,' I said, but Momma said that clean faces and brushed hair would be expected. It was not going to be like last year when we had gone to Dunmore East to the caravan. So the little ones sat across the kitchen table and with a lovely warm, soapy facecloth she washed their faces and their knees. But we still were not ready because our hair was not combed. This could not be left because when we arrived we might have to go straight to the dining room. She brushed everyone's hair and smoothed the boys' hair down with a bit of spittle, and put the royal-blue ribbons in my hair and red ones in Cissy's. Momma had given me two ponytails, high on each side of my head. I felt really clean and like I belonged to a very important family.

It took a while to arrange us in the car. In the end Tom sat at the window, Baby Cecil sat on Momma's lap in the front. I had one twin on my lap, and Cissy and the other twin sat in the middle. There was lots of squabbling, except of course for when Momma sang 'Feed the Birds', because when she sang that there was no one in the world who would not listen.

Our car reversed out of the driveway and we seemed at

last to be on our way. When we got to the corner of our road, there was Aunty Ida just turning to come up the hill. Momma called, 'Stop, Edmund.' Then Aunty Ida noticed us passing her and she started to wave madly at us. But HE kept going. HE did not even slow down. Momma opened her window and leaned out, waving and madly blowing kisses: 'God bless, God bless!' I turned round and waved and waved. And Aunty Ida stood with her bags on the ground, waving and waving and blowing a million kisses. Momma was annoyed and said, 'Why didn't you stop?' HE said, 'For God's sake, you saw her two days ago,' and then he drove faster.

When we were ten minutes away, Momma remembered that the dresses were still on the back of the sitting-room door. I had felt for days that we would never leave, that it was never really going to happen. That Rose Finnerty in second class was right and that no one, including us, could afford to go to Butlin's because it cost as much as going to America. And now we were turning back. When we got there, Momma passed Baby Cecil to HIM and ran into the house and came back with the dresses. They argued over where to put them. In the end they were hung across the window on my side of the car, and the head of the little one on my lap was blocking the view straight ahead, so that I could not see out. I would have liked to see out, to trace our whole journey to Butlin's with my eyes. But it did not matter. I had lots to think about.

It was a long journey and we had to stop a couple of times because Baby Cecil was sick on Momma's clothes, probably because of the motion, Momma said. She said she was in no state to arrive in Mosney and that she should go behind a bush in a field at the side of the road somewhere so that she could change her dress, but HE said that he was fed up stopping and starting and stopping and starting and no one would notice Momma's clothes. Momma did not talk for ages after that and I could tell that she really did not want to arrive smelling of sick. I thought I would try singing. So I started to sing, '*We're all going on our summer holiday*,' which I knew everyone liked because we sang it almost every day with Momma in the last days as she finished the dresses. But my voice sounded thin and small and watery and no one joined in. Then Tom reached behind the little ones and thumped me on the back. I leaned forward and looked across at him to see what he wanted me to do, but he had already turned away and was looking out his window. I stopped singing then because Tom always knew the right thing to do.

When we pulled into the car park we all went strangely quiet and sat still for a while, even the little ones. I think we were all nervous. A few feet away there was a painted wooden chalet with a sign outside in the shape of an arrow which said 'OFFICE'. HE said that that was where we collected the keys. And so we all peered through the windscreen in silence, staring at the office. A couple of people went in and came out again after a few minutes, but still we sat in the car and by now the windows had become steamed up. My legs were sore from the weight of the little one on my knee and my thighs were stuck to the plastic sack I was sitting on.

After a while HE said, 'Why don't you go in and get the

keys?' But Momma was worried because she smelled of sick. HE said he was not going because he was feeling headachy from driving and from all the squabbling in the back. So we sat another while, until HE suddenly flung open the car door and got out, slamming the door shut and wakening Baby Cecil, who started to cry. We watched HIM walking up the gravel path and into the office. HE was in there for ages and other people went in and came out again before he did. Each time we saw the office door being pushed out, one of us would say, 'Here he is,' and someone else would say, 'No, I knew it wasn't him.' I was worried that there would be no chalets left for us because we had arrived so late as a result of all the stopping and starting, but I did not want to ask Momma in case it turned out to be true. So instead I just waited quietly until my face felt like it was burning and I knew that if I looked in the mirror it would be completely red because that is what happened to my face when I worried. And Momma's was the exact same.

When HE came out I thought I saw a little smile on his face and he was definitely walking faster than he had walked when he was going in. HE looked towards us and then down at the gravel again. Tom got out of the car first and ran towards him. Tom always knew the right thing to do. They walked back together then and HE stuck his head into the car and said, 'What are you all waiting for?' Then we opened our doors and climbed out on our legs that were numb, and stiff, and sticky.

HE said to leave the suitcases until later and we all remembered the plan and agreed that we would because we were even surer now that this was not the kind of place to arrive at with black plastic sacks instead of proper luggage. Momma said, 'Yes, let's come back for the suitcases.' She said it very loudly, not like her own voice at all, in case there were people listening, I think, but I could not see anyone around except for us. HE led the way along the gravel paths, which were lined with flower beds, and he kept looking down at the two keys in his hand and then up at the numbers on the chalet doors. We were numbers 71 and 73, which turned out to be miles away from the car park, past lots and lots of beautiful chalets, some of which had open doors, so that I could see inside. That was when I caught a glimpse of bunk beds. But you should never get your hopes too high. We kept walking along the straight gravel paths for ages and we kept very close together and I did not speak as HE led us. Even the little ones only whispered. I was so pleased, there was a smile sitting on my face all the time, which I wished was not there because the children we passed might see it and think I was silly and overexcited. The chalets were painted white, with red or yellow or blue trim. The beautiful gravel paths crunched beneath our brown sandals, and there were plants with big shiny leaves which must have been brought over from Hawaii or somewhere. I had never seen plants like these before, except maybe in *Tarzan*. And I thought, *We are not in Ireland now. This is America.*

Numbers 71 and 73 were not beside each other. Another chalet sat between them, but that was our own fault because we had been late. HE asked Momma very crossly if she had really had to go back to get the dresses. But I knew that she had had to. HE had not seen all the work she had done to make them and how her slim fingers had shaken with excitement when she held them up to show me that they were finished. Number 71 had a big bed for HIM and Momma, and also a cot and a bunk bed. The cot had wooden balls in its sides in different colours, which Baby Cecil could turn with his little fingers. And there was a big sticker of Bambi at the end of the cot. But one of Bambi's legs was half gone. The window was small with a wooden frame and red and white gingham curtains. There was a comfy chair for Momma to sit in when she was singing 'Feed the Birds' to Baby Cecil to get him asleep. HE lay on the bed because he was so headachy after all the squabbling and the stopping and starting, and Momma took us into number 73. Two sets of bunks were the first thing I saw, and I was so relieved. Tom could have a top one but so could I. I climbed up onto my bunk and lay down, but only for a moment. The little ones wanted to see, so I pulled them up to have the experience. But I held on to them tightly. Tom would keep the key for number 73 because he was nearly eleven and because he was a boy, so he had pockets. Even my shorts did not have pockets.

We were playing a game of jumping ships, leaping from one top bunk across to the other, when we heard a really loud siren. We all got such a fright, and Tom and I took the little ones by the hand as calmly as we could and went into number 71. On the way Tom said, 'Remain calm,' and I knew he had learned that from watching the *Titanic* film on the telly, so that was a bit worrying. We went into number 71. HE said, 'Why the invasion?' and then that there was nothing to worry about, it was just the dinner siren. Momma brushed everyone's hair really quickly and not very well because HE was annoyed and said it was unnecessary and we would be late again because we were late for everything. But we weren't always.

When we walked out of the chalet, lots of other families were heading in one direction so we followed them. I thought some of the children had American accents as they sped past, but I could not be sure. We felt a bit strange, I think, and so HE walked slower than usual so that soon all the other families were miles ahead and we were the very last. At least we could still see them in the distance and we could follow them, because HE did not seem to know where we were going and all the avenues of chalets looked the same, though later we would learn that each row had its own name.

When we reached the dining room they were about to close the double doors which led into it. There was only one table left and it was right in the middle of the very large room so we had to walk through the gaps between other families to reach it. And then there was no highchair for Baby Cecil, so poor Momma had to stand and swing him to stop him crying while we waited for the highchair to be brought. HE was looking at Momma quite crossly. HE did not want the family embarrassed by our baby crying in a dining room as expensive as this.

The large round table we sat at was very fancy and I had really only seen something like it in films like *My Fair Lady* and *The Sound of Music*. There were white cloth napkins folded like swans, glass jugs of water with slices of lemon floating in them, glistening glasses and white side plates with the letters *BM* stamped on them in blue. It was exactly the same blue as my ribbons. We all sat very quietly and HE kept looking from one of us to the other while Momma bounced Baby Cecil on her knee, hoping that he might get into the highchair any minute and not stiffen his little body when she tried the next time. I would like to have held him on my lap because I always felt better when I had a baby in my arms. Momma and I are the exact same about this.

Then a pretty waitress in a white dress and black apron and with a high bun on her head came over smiling and gave us three baskets of toast, which wasn't really toast but something much nicer which we had never had before. It was very crunchy and crispy, and the boys dived into the baskets and the waitress smiled and said, 'Ye are starving,' so it was okay then and HE did not look so cross. Momma gave a piece to Baby Cecil and he sucked it happily with his eyes gleaming and moving from one of us to the other. It was like he had won a prize. So Momma tried to put him in the highchair again and, delighted with his toast, he slid agreeably down into his seat. Baby Cecil chewed and chewed on his toast and grunted and said, 'Me! Me!' and stuck out his tummy when he wanted more and Momma put big wads of butter on it. He was so happy that he turned round in his highchair and gazed happily at the other families. But none of the rest of us turned round to look at the other families, because it is rude to turn round in your chair and it is the height of rudeness to stare.

Then the pretty waitress came back and HE lit a cigarette

while he was ordering his dinner, and he smiled at her, and she seemed to cheer him up greatly. It was good that she did because none of the rest of us was ever able to cheer HIM up the way we could all cheer Momma up so easily. Then Momma made the mistake of asking the pretty waitress what the toast was. 'What exactly is it?' she asked. HE glared at Momma so angrily, and I did not know what she had said wrong. 'It's French Melba,' the pretty waitress said, and she did not seem to mind the question at all.

Next melon cut in the shape of a rowing boat arrived. We had only ever had melon once before, in a hotel for Tom's communion, but that time it had not been in the shape of a rowing boat. And I thought, *This is because we are near the sea.* There was a cherry on top, which we all ate first. I ate the melon with my fork because I was not sure if you could pick it up. You could shake cinnamon on it, but HE said not to because we wouldn't like it and he remembered at Tom's communion how none of us had finished our melon because we had put cinnamon on it and it had been a terrible waste. Actually I had finished mine because I liked the cinnamony taste, but I did not want to rock the boat so I said nothing and I did not put any cinnamon on mine.

They kept bringing us more food and water and whatever we wanted and the pretty waitress smiled at all of us and she didn't just smile at HIM. But HE smiled at her a lot whenever he saw her coming towards our table. I noticed and I thought to myself, *Whenever HE sees her he wants a cigarette.* And I wondered what made people want to smoke. I looked at Momma and she was so happy and I watched her eating the chicken with the white sauce on it, but I stopped watching when a little bit of the sauce stuck to the corner of her mouth because looking at that made me feel so, so sad. And I don't know why it did, but I knew straight away that I would never forget that feeling about Momma and how the sauce clung to Momma's poor lip.

Then we got ice cream and jelly with wafers cut into the shape of sails. And I thought, *This is because we are near the sea.* And the pretty waitress said, 'They'll enjoy that.' And Momma said, 'It's the height of luxury for them.' And HE glared at Momma and lit another cigarette.

At the end they brought out coffee in a pot with cream and milk and sugar lumps in a little white dish, brown and white lumps. Tom took some of the sugar lumps and put them in his pocket. I would like to have taken some too, but I just had to hope that he might give me one later on. Momma tasted the coffee and said that it was probably freshly ground and not instant Nescafé, but HE said no because he had had freshly ground and it had a distinctive flavour. And this was not it. Momma looked disappointed. Then something happened. I had not expected it at all, and I got such a fright.

A man in a red blazer came to the table and told us to come into the hall for all the games. The little ones got up straight away, but I hesitated and by the time I was ready to stand up, it was too late. They had already disappeared with the man in the red blazer through the double doors. I think I must have looked very worried about the little ones because Momma said, 'They're Redcoats. They play with the children while the mammies and daddies have a rest.' So it was okay then. Then HE said that I had to go too because I was the only child left in the dining room and I looked ridiculous. And when I glanced around, I saw that HE was right and my face grew very red, and I knew that I had to go. I was so afraid. I got up and began to walk towards the door, but just at that moment Baby Cecil started to cry and HE said, 'Take him.' I was so relieved, and I pulled Baby Cecil out of his highchair, untrapping his little feet in their bright red sandals, and walked across the room. Baby Cecil stopped crying because he loved it when I carried him. When we got outside I gave him so many kisses.

Outside the dining room there was a lady Redcoat who was wearing beautiful white runners, and I wanted to ask her if she had got them in America but I didn't of course and I felt annoyed with myself later. The Redcoat pointed me in the direction of another set of doors not far away. It was drizzling now and I walked quickly so that Baby Cecil would not get too wet. When we got to the other set of doors the sound of loud music came through them. I knew that I did not want to go in there, but where else could I go? I pushed one of the heavy doors and went through. I almost fell into the hall because the door was so heavy and so was Baby Cecil. There were lots and lots of children and lots of Redcoats. Some were men and some were ladies, and I noticed that they all wore the same blazers and the same white American runners. They were the nicest clothes I had ever seen. Everyone was singing '*Oh, hokey pokey pokey*' and holding hands as they put their right leg in and their right leg out. It looked like a great game and lots of fun, but I was glad

I had Baby Cecil and would not be able to play. Baby Cecil and I watched for a while and he twisted my hair in his gentle little fingers, which I always found so soothing. That was his way of loving me. Then a beautiful lady Redcoat came up behind us and placed her hands on my shoulders and led me to a chair at the side of the room. I was glad because Baby Cecil was heavy now and my hip bone hurt, but I was not happy to be so far away from the door we had come in. In case I wanted to go out.

After the Hokey Pokey game ended, one of the Redcoats, who looked very like the prince in the *Sleeping Beauty* book that I loved when I was little, jumped up onto the stage and said, 'Now, boys and girls, the mammies and daddies will come for you soon, so I want you all to sit on the floor or lie down before I sing you a very special song.' So all the boys and girls made a great rustling and rumbling sound as they settled themselves on the floor. For the chorus of the prince's beautiful song, some of the lady Redcoats got up onto the stage and joined in. Then the mammies and daddies came. Momma took Baby Cecil from me and said that I could go to the bar where HE was, and she said Tom had already gone and we could both stay up a while because we were quite big now. I did not want to, but Tom did. He stayed with HIM.

The first night in the top bunk was a bit frightening for me because Tom and the little ones fell asleep so quickly and left me in the silence. I did not like quiet and I always tried to find a way out of it, which usually was not hard because there were so many of us. I hoped it might rain heavily, because that would be a sound to block the silence. I think

Americans are lucky because they have the sound of crickets at night. I tried to distract myself by thinking about all the other boys and girls I had seen that day. I especially thought about the ones with American accents, and I came up with some plans of how I might talk to them and play with them the next day. Then I would ask them what America was like, but I would say it in such a way that they would think that I was not that interested, so that they would tell me more. I fell asleep then and I had a terrible nightmare. I dreamed that we had all gone to America but when we got off the plane, it turned out to be the same as Ireland. The exact same. The houses were not white and wooden after all, and the gardens were not enclosed by white picket fences but by the same grey pebbledash walls of my own back garden in Dublin in wintertime, when there were no leaves on the trees and no lanterns on our laburnum tree. I felt that I had nowhere to go now. When I grew up. And I cried. But softly because if Tom heard me he would say, 'Crybaby, dreams aren't real.' And Tom would be right.

I put on my shorts the next day and every day after that. We did not wear the dresses Momma had made. One day I said, 'Will we put on the beautiful dresses you made, Momma?' But Momma said, 'No. Not yet.'

In the evenings, when we were going to the dining room, Cissy and I were told to put on the yellow dresses with the puff sleeves that Aunty Ida had got for us for Easter. She had picked them for us because they were the exact same as the one the girl wore in the film she had taken us to. Aunty Ida had no little girl of her own. And no little boy either, because she had no husband. But she had a job. She said she was lucky to have us. But I said, 'No, we are lucky to have you.' And that was not just because she bought us so many things.

There would be everything you could want in Butlin's, Momma said before we went, and there was. There was even a cinema. On the third day we went to it, but Momma could not come because of Baby Cecil. We queued for ages. There were two queues. One was for *Chitty Chitty Bang Bang* and the other was for *Mosquito Squadron*. Momma said *Chitty Chitty Bang Bang* was the only one suitable. In the poster it looked really good. I liked the look of the flying car and especially the look of the man who was the same one from *Mary Poppins*. I thought we were in the wrong queue. I looked up at HIM a few times, but I did not tell him.

When we got back to chalet number 71, Momma said, 'Was the film good?' And HE said, 'She was fidgeting round and I could hardly concentrate.' Momma said, 'Which one did you go to?' and HE said, '*Chitty Bang Bang*.' And then HE winked at Tom.

On the fourth day, the sun came out for a while and me and Momma and the little ones went to the beach to catch it. HE stayed in the chalet because he had a headache. Momma asked if she could leave Baby Cecil with HIM and he said okay because Baby Cecil was already fast asleep in the cot after Momma had given him baby aspirin for his gums. We walked through the woods and the sun was in and out of the leaves high up over us. The light was sort of silvery and shaking on the path and then suddenly it opened out onto the strand and in the distance we could see the blue sea with big white waves breaking on the sand and the rocks. The little ones made sandcastles with rivers round them and I did too. But then I went to check on Momma. In case she was lonely without me. Momma was lying down in the sand. Her eyes were closed. She was completely still except for her hands, which were stretched out on each side of her. She was picking up the sand with her hands and letting it fall through her fingers. And she kept doing that. I watched her for a while. She was like a little girl. It was nice to watch her. Then she opened her eyes. She stared at me for a moment and then she pulled me down beside her on the sand. She tickled me for ages. I felt nearly sick from laughing, so she stopped. I lay in her arms then with my head on her shoulder. She leaned over and she kissed me on the forehead. Then she said, 'My very own girl.' We lay like that for ages and ages. That was the only day the sand was warm.

The Redcoat and I got to know each other quite well – the one who looked like the prince. He knew that I did not want to be in the Hokey Pokey game too much. So he just asked me if I wanted to sit down or to join in. He asked me that each night after dinner. Mostly I said I wanted to sit down. I really wanted to join in and for him to hold my hand in the game. But I just couldn't say it. Sometimes I say no when I really do want something. I don't know why I do that. One time we were walking to the dining room and he was walking the other way. He looked down at me and winked. He only winked at me. He did not wink at the others. I was very surprised. I wished he was my daddy.

Knocked Out in the First Round

When the sixth day came, Momma said, 'This is the day to wear our dresses.' So we put on the dresses, Momma and Cissy and me. It was a rainy day, so we all went over to the ballroom, and it turned out there was a band and a long row of red velvet seats on the stage as well. Momma said, 'I have to sign us in. Come on, girls.' Suddenly I knew something fishy was going on. Then the girl gave Momma two cards, one big with the number 07 written on it and the other small with the same number. And we got into a queue at the side of the stage and Momma gave the small card to me but there was no card for Cissy. And she said, 'You will have to share it.' First I held it at the height of my tummy and then I moved it and held it in front of my face. 'No, not like that,' said Momma, and I had to hold it at my tummy height again. Then the music stopped and the queue of mammies and children started to walk up the steps onto the stage. And then I saw that everyone else had a number too. Some Redcoats helped us to spread ourselves out across the stage, and they walked up and down the neat long semicircle of mammies and boys and girls, looking at us carefully. And then we just stood like that for ages. And some women and men came and sat in the red velvet chairs. I said very quietly to Momma, 'Why are we up here?' and she said, 'Don't worry. It's lovely,' she said. 'It's a Mother and Child competition.'

I looked down from the stage and lots of people were coming in and sitting at the round tables or getting themselves a drink at the bar. And Tom was there, and HE was there with the little ones. They were all getting drinks, except for me and Cissy, who were stuck on the stage. And Tom got crisps as well. Then everyone went very quiet and looked at us lined up on the stage. And we three were wearing the home-made dresses. Then a man with some paper stuck onto a piece of cardboard walked along the line of mammies and children. He stopped and looked at each of them carefully and he wrote down their numbers. Then he came to us. And by now I was redder than I had ever been in my whole life. I needed to go to the toilet. My face felt like it was crying. Like it had the shape and feel of crying. Like it was folding up. Then the man with the cardboard and paper leaned into Momma and he said, 'One child only.' Momma looked disappointed but she agreed that that was the rule. And so she leaned down to me and she took the card from me and gave it to Cissy to hold up high and she whispered, 'Go and sit down with Daddy.' So I did.

I went down the steps to where they were sitting. And every part of me was burning red. Especially my ears and my neck. Tom was sitting there, putting stickers on his new Matchbox model car, and HE said to Tom, 'Go up to the bar and get Georgy Girl a bottle of Coca-Cola.' I could not believe I was getting a bottle of Coca-Cola, because I had already had one the day before. And I did not know why HE called me Georgy Girl. HE thought it was funny though, and whenever he was in a good mood for the rest of the holiday he called me Georgy Girl. It can be a sign that someone really likes you if they give you a nickname. HE called Tom Tombo. But it is not always the best sign.

Momma and Cissy did not win. And Momma said it didn't matter. But I think it did, because we all had to go straight back to the chalets. HE said to Momma, 'There's no cheering you up today.' But anyhow it wasn't my fault because I was knocked out in the first round.

Something Very Rude

The next morning, Tom and I were allowed to go to the beach on our own before breakfast as long as we kept together. We walked down the lovely path between the trees, and the sun was coming in and out of the big summer leaves which were bright and clean and shiny because we were so near the sea. We each had a stick so that we could whack the bushes on either side of us. We both loved sticks. 'Watch out for the snakes,' Tom said. 'There's no snakes in Ireland,' I said, and I got a little shiver in my back. 'That's what you think!' said Tom.

When we got to the beach we threw some stones in the water for a while and then we sat down on a dried-out log that I thought looked like an Apache's canoe. We sat beside each other but Tom moved away a bit from me. Because boys are like that. I stared out to sea and so did Tom. And then I saw a terrible bird standing on a huge dark rock. He was bigger than any bird I had ever seen. Much bigger than the seagulls who were standing in rows at the water's edge. His body was really long and it looked like he was wearing a Dracula cape and his head was enormous and mean-looking with strands of stiff pointing-up hair and his head had a big jutting-out forehead like Frankenstein's and he had the longest beak I had ever seen which could swallow a whole fish or even a person in one. He was facing out to sea, his long neck craned, his head still, and then suddenly he opened his wings, each in a V shape, as though he was getting ready to do some terrible thing, like call in the sea monsters to attack me and Tom or even eat us himself. 'What's that bird called?' I asked Tom. He glanced up from chipping away at a rock with a sharp stone. 'That's a black demon bird,' he said. I pretended not to be frightened and I said, 'There's no such thing.' 'That's what you think,' said Tom. We were quiet for a while then. Tom did not like talking to me very much, probably because I was a girl. And I looked across the sea and after a while I said, 'I can't believe America's over there.' And Tom laughed so much that he had to stand up because his tummy ached and he said, 'That's not the Atlantic. It's the Irish Sea. England is over there.' And he laughed really loud for ages and kicked a bit of sand at me and walked off with his stick.

I just sat and looked across the sea. I sat like that for ages, all the time keeping an eye on the black demon bird. The sea was grey and green and black, and rain began to fall on it like a billion fishes biting the surface of the water all at the same time. But it was not dangerous and the sea came in and went out, came in and went out, as softly as someone's tongue licking an ice-cream cone when they want to make it last. Then it started to pick up the stones and the pebbles and sweep them back and forth, back and forth, like a giant underwater sweeping brush, and the sweeping was like the sound of Spanish castanets at first, but then it got louder and was like lightning crackling and the waves were as loud as thunder now. I glanced at the black demon bird. He was still standing there on one leg in the same place. But Tom was gone.

Then suddenly the wind made a whipping sound and echoed round my ears and blew my hair across my face and the sun went behind the clouds. And I knew that the sea could change its mood. I stood up and the wind whipped away my blue ribbon. It had flown up, across the sand dunes, and there was no point chasing it. I looked around in every direction for Tom but I could not see him, and then the blue ribbon whipping off my hair reminded me of the poor man and the poor girls in the rowing boat on the Sunday morning when I had got up too early. And I was afraid that while I had been looking in the wrong direction for America, the wind might have whipped Tom into the sea. I shouted and shouted for him. I thought I would run back and get help. So I started running back to the path in the woods and I ran and ran. And it was hard to run because my sandals were wet and heavy and the wind was blowing me back towards the beach. I ran and ran and I still called Tom's name. It had grown so dark and a voice came into my head and said, 'The world is ending.' And I ran and ran to be with Momma for the end. Then I stopped suddenly because there was a man standing against a tree. It was a Redcoat. I don't know why I stopped. I should have just kept running. But I stopped. His back was facing me. And then he must have heard the squishing of my sandals as I tried to walk past him as quietly as I could, because he turned round. It was the prince in the red blazer. He was doing something rude that I had never seen before. He looked at me and he said, 'Come a little closer, honey.' But I got brave and I started running again. I ran and ran and he shouted after me, 'Are your knickers wet?' Which was so rude. I ran and ran.

I ran all the way to the dining room because HE had said, 'Come straight to breakfast.' I walked over to my family and it was lucky because most people didn't notice me and there was a lot of chatting so my squishing sandals could not be heard. And there was Tom, sitting at the table, eating his sausages and rashers. That was lucky. And Baby Cecil grinned at me when he saw me coming. Baby Cecil loved me so much. But then HE turned round in his chair and saw me. HE heard the squishing of my sandals and he looked down at them. Then, as I passed him, HE grabbed my arm and pulled me towards him. HE slapped me hard on the back of my thigh. I was wearing my shorts. People heard the sound. Then HE pushed me down into the chair beside him. I kept my head low and I could see my thigh was red. Momma's face, when I looked up at her, was the same red, hot colour that I knew mine was. Everyone was looking at our table. I was not hungry. Tom took the rashers off my plate. Momma said, 'Don't, Tom.' HE looked at Momma and said, 'Serves her right.'

Goodbye, America

When we were all packed into the car, sitting on the bumpy black sacks full of our dirty clothes, Momma said, 'All good things come to an end.' Tom started to sing, '*We're not going on our summer holidays.*' HE laughed but Cissy did not like it. I was secretly glad to be leaving America. It had not turned out to be the place I thought it was. Then Momma said, 'We are going to have a baby. Another little angel.' HE opened the window and threw his cigarette butt out. I was so happy to hear about the baby. 'What will we call it?' I asked Momma. 'If it's a boy, then John Fitzgerald, after the poor president, and if it's a girl, then Jackie.' We were all quiet for a while then until Cissy asked me, 'Who did you like best on the holiday?' I said I liked the American girl. 'But you never played with her,' said Cissy. 'But I liked her,' I said. 'The American girl?' said Tom. 'What American girl?' 'The one called Laura – with the twin brothers,' I said. 'Americans!' Tom said. 'They were from Belfast!' And he could not stop laughing. He had to hold his tummy because it hurt so much. And Momma said, 'Well, a Belfast accent can sound American – if you're not used to it.' 'That's what you think,' said Tom.

Changing My Favourite Colour

A few days after we got home, Momma said, 'We can collect your red anorak on Monday.' I said, 'I do not like the colour red any more, Momma.' But Momma said, 'Oh no, I have already paid the deposit and I can't get it back. Daddy will be cross.' Tom had a good idea. 'It could probably be used to buy some clothes for Baby John or Baby Jackie,' he said. 'That's not a bad idea,' said Momma. Tom always knew the right things to say.

I felt sad about the way America had turned out and was worried that the real America would be the same when I went there when I was grown up, and I sat on the windowsill in my bedroom and scrunched my body up small. I was very still and quiet, just lying my head on my bent-up knees. I was tired. For a moment I turned round to look at Cissy's bed. Cissy was only downstairs, but I felt really black inside, like she was gone forever. But then I turned back again because I thought I saw something from the corner of my eye. A little bird was sitting on my windowsill. I looked closely at its light grey feathers that I knew would be really soft if I touched them, and I thought it must be a young baby just trying life outside the nest and I wondered if its mother was looking for it. It had a little yellow breast and it looked like a bird in the film *Snow White* when she is lost in the woods and then feels better when all the little birds start flitting about her and joining in her song with their whistling and tweeting. Then it flew off and I thought, *I will never see that little bird again*. But I sat very still and after a few minutes it came back and peered into my window. It showed me all of its yellow coat this time. That is the day yellow became my favourite colour. And I don't know how that little yellow and grey bird knew to stop at my window that day. But he did know.

A Very Clean Ford Escort

Then I got lucky. A new family moved into the house with the swallows on the gates that was four doors down from ours. They were a small family of only one girl, one cat, and a dog which belonged to the girl only and not to the whole family. The dog's name turned out to be Skippy, after the kangaroo, and the girl's name was Caroline. The moment I set eyes on Caroline, I thought, *She is going to be my best friend*, because we were opposites and Aunty Ida always said, 'Opposites attract.' She had middling-length gingery hair, and I had long dark hair. Her eyes were brown, and mine were blue. She was fattish and short for her age, and I was thinnish and medium for mine. And she smiled and smiled all the time, never stopping even when we were bored and there was nothing to do. I frowned a lot. I knew that because Momma was always saying, 'Stop frowning.' She was worried I would get early wrinkles, and sometimes she would run her cool hand back and forth across my forehead to rub the lines away. So, from the beginning, from the first day when Caroline jumped off the back of her removal van with her roller skates in her hand a week after we came home from Butlin's, we were friends. She later said that from the moment we first skated up and down our hill – passing each other as we skated in different directions, and only saying 'Hi' each time for ages until eventually we said things like: 'Is that your house?' and 'Nice skates' – she knew we would be best friends. And later she agreed with me that opposites attract. Sometimes, though, I wondered if Caroline was really smiling or if it was just the way her teeth stuck out over her bottom lip.

Caroline had a very nice daddy whose teeth stuck out over his bottom lip just like Caroline's, and sometimes I wondered if he was smiling or not too. But he was very nice. When we played in her back garden, which we did a lot, because she had a shed that could turn into anything we wanted, he would bring us a plate of sausages and toast and two big tin cups of sugary tea with the words *I love my garden* on them. I did not usually like tea, but he made it taste so nice with its sugar, and it was so good with the thickly buttered toast and the plate of sausages, especially on cold days when we played in the shed for hours. Sometimes Helen from the middle of our road played too but it was always better with just me and Caroline. We had the same ideas about what made a good game, and we both loved America and everything American, so we could make up any game as long as it was American and as long as we could both have an American accent and neither one of us was stuck with being Irish.

I hardly ever went inside Caroline's house. And I hardly ever saw her momma outside. She was a small woman with long, curly, dark blonde hair. She was so small that when you went into Caroline's sitting room you would not even think that there was anyone sitting in the big armchair at all. The room smelt musty, like the whole house, but it was really tidy. The radio played quietly beside Caroline's momma's chair, so quietly that I guessed she only wanted it so that there was a sound in all the quiet, like the way Aunty Ida left hers on whenever she went out so that when she got back home her house would not feel so silent. Sometimes when we crept into the room, Caroline's momma seemed to be asleep but then would open her eyes all at once. Sometimes her feet were tucked in under her short legs, and a blanket was wrapped round her, and she looked like half a person. Sometimes she really was deeply, deeply asleep and we could even watch telly and she would not waken up. Even in the mornings. I thought she must be sick, but I did not ask Caroline in case it made her sad or worried. If she ran out of cigarettes, Caroline and I would walk to the shop to get her forty John Player's, and sometimes we collected her medicine from the chemist's. She always told us to spend the change on sweets or whatever we wanted. She said very kind things like, 'You have lovely eyes,' and when Momma cut my hair she said, 'I love your fringe,' and then when Momma pinned my fringe back with a hair slide because my eyes were itching, Caroline's momma said, 'I love your hair back. Now we can see your pretty eyes.' I used to love to stand in front of Caroline's momma as she looked up at me from her big armchair and said nice things. And I loved her accent, which was so soft and came from County Kerry, Caroline said. But Caroline was always nervous and cross when we were in the room with her momma. And she would pull me out of the room to hurry me up, and then pull me down the hall and upstairs to her own bedroom.

Caroline's daddy was so nice, especially in the summers when he took me and Caroline to Silver Strand in his Ford

Escort, which was always spotlessly clean and had a warm leathery smell and a small nodding bulldog on the dashboard with a daisy in its mouth. He kept a cloth which he called a chammy on the dashboard and kept wiping over the steering wheel and the controls when we were stopped at traffic lights. He had a little cassette player which he kept on the front passenger seat and he played the same two songs over and over as we drove to the beach, which was a very long journey. For Caroline he played 'Sweet Caroline', and for me he played 'Daydream Believer', because my name was Jean. And on these trips, he always called me Sleepy Jean and never plain Jean, and when he shouted up the beach for us to come – 'Oh Sweet Caroline, oh Sleepy Jean' – we both felt like Californians. He brought a basket of food to the beach and he just kept giving us more and more things out of it. Apples, crisps, sandwiches, cake, a huge jug of orange which never seemed to empty. I never felt as safe as when I sat on the beach like that, or on the way home with sand all over his lovely car.

One day, Helen from the middle of our road was playing with us in Caroline's house. And Caroline said, 'No one goes beyond the kitchen door.' She was in a bad mood. That was fine and I understood that Caroline did not trust Helen the way she trusted me. I stayed in the kitchen with Helen while Caroline went upstairs to get stuff from her room. But while she was gone, Helen sneakily dragged a chair from the table over to the cupboard and climbed on top of it. I thought that was so rude. And she reached into the top of the cupboard and held up a cane and showed it to me. She raised her eyebrows as though to say, *So now you see.* Then she put it back, climbed down, silently tucked the chair back under the table, and said, 'That's what he uses to beat his wife. Because she never gets up for Mass.'

Ten

The Other Georgy Girl

Whenever she visited, she would say, 'Sorry I'm a bit early,' or 'Sorry I'm a bit late,' when usually she wasn't either. Sometimes HE was nice to her, sometimes he was not. Sometimes HE laughed at her. And sometimes HE would say, 'Sure, stay. It's too late to get the bus now.' She was not as pretty as Momma and once HE said, 'She's a bit of a whale, your Ida.' Momma said HE was so rude, and he said, 'I'm only joking and who's the one who drives her home late?' So Momma said, 'You are right.'

We never knew which days Aunty Ida would come, especially before we got our phone. She did not have a phone but there was a phone box where she worked, and she could use that. She always came dressed for winter and always for rain. She always wore galoshes. HE laughed at that and he said to her, 'Dressed for the weather, I see.' Whenever HE spoke to her, her round face went red and it did not stop getting red for ages. And she would say, 'Oh yes, Edmund.' Then she would sit heavily into the chair and I would bring her a glass of water because even if it was cold out she was thirsty because our house was almost at the top of the hill and a long walk from the bus stop. And she would drink it in two gulps

and pat me very, very lightly on the head and say, 'Good girl.'
You never felt such lightness as the lightness when she
touched you. Then she would start to take out of her bags all
the nice things she had brought for us. You never knew what.
Comics or sweets or things that you badly needed and somehow she always knew what — like whistles or torches or sets
of jacks. And Momma would say, 'That's too much.' And HE
would say, 'For God's sake, Ida.' And she would say, 'Oh,
sorry, Edmund. You are quite right, Edmund.' But the next
time she would bring us just as much! Then Momma would
make her a lovely cup of tea with plenty of biscuits. And the
two sisters would chat away. Some days when she arrived,
she looked very worried and sometimes she whispered to
Momma, 'I think the fellas in work are laughing at me behind
my back.' But Momma would just say, 'It's a pity about them
that they have nothing more important to do,' or she would
say, 'You're only imagining it, Ida.' Sometimes Aunty Ida
would ask Momma in a whisper, 'Do you ever think the
Troubles will come down here?' And Momma would say,
'Shhh.' And then say quietly, 'I very much doubt it.' Then
Momma would always make her feel better and distract her
and the next thing she would be laughing in her shy little
way. The twins and Baby Cecil and me and Tom and Cissy
would always stay in the room when the two sisters were
together because of the happy feeling they brought to it. But
Aunty Ida was not as pretty as Momma. HE said, 'The two
of you don't look like sisters at all.' And then HE would say
more quietly, 'That's the luck of the draw.' 'Oh yes, Edmund,'
Aunty Ida would say. Momma might look at him crossly and

sometimes she might not. I think sometimes she was just so tired that she did not notice things.

A few weeks before Christmas, HE said, 'Is she coming again this year?' And Momma said, 'Yes of course.' And HE said, 'She'll eat us out of house and home.' At that moment I thought maybe HE would not let her come and I thought, *It will not be Christmas without her.* But Momma loved her too much to let that happen and she came.

She came for Christmas Eve because Momma said, 'No one should be alone on Christmas Eve.' I looked quickly over at HIM when she said that, and he said, 'Well, I'm not collecting her.' And I thought, *I hope I get married and Cissy too because we don't want to be alone on Christmas Eve. Or ever.* So she came. I was clipping some holly branches off Mrs O'Malley's bush – which was so frosty and Christmassy – when I looked down to the bottom of our road and there she was, coming up the hill, with a kind of aura round her like the smoky light around the picture of Jesus in our classroom when he is standing on the rock just before his Father resurrects him. Her head was bent down, and her shoulders were leaning forward. She was carrying more bags than I had ever seen her carry before. I don't know how to describe the feeling of joy inside me at that moment when I saw her coming up the hill. No one should be alone on Christmas Eve. Or ever. So I dropped Mrs O'Malley's holly and I ran down the hill towards her. When she looked up and saw me, her light brown eyes lit up and I think she probably thought the same as me. She thought, *I don't know how to describe the feeling of joy inside me at this moment when I see her coming down the hill.*

I hugged her round the waist, and she was very shy, so she did not hug me back. She never really did, but it didn't matter. Her little pink smile was enough. Anyhow, she had so many bags that I thought, *If she puts them down, she will never be able to gather them up again.* And she said, 'I didn't know what to get you.' I was so pleased that I had got her a music box, but I did not tell her. It was for Christmas morning. A music box was just the kind of thing she loved, and when you lifted the lid a little circus ringmaster spun round to the music, *Take me out to the ballgame, take me out with the crowd.* She was going to love it. She loved America too. So we went up the hill together. And I carried one of her bags.

The house was so excited and noisy. HE was home. Momma had put all the Christmas food out over the kitchen table, trying to get started for the big day, and the lights on the Christmas tree kept breaking. Baby Cecil cried every time they broke because the light-up Santa heads stopped working and every time they did our twins teased him, 'Santa's dead, Santa's dead,' but then Tom would twist the lights and fix them and would say to Baby Cecil, 'It's okay, Santa's alive again.' I brought Aunty Ida into the kitchen and she said, 'Sorry, am I a bit early?' And HE said, 'I didn't even know you were coming.' But HE did know. She put her bags on the table. 'For God's sake, Ida,' HE said. 'Put them in the hall or somewhere. You can't move in here as it is.' 'Oh, apologies, Edmund. Sorry, Edmund,' she said. And her face got very, very red. And mine did the same sometimes when someone said things like that to me. We were the exact same that way. So I helped her bring her bags into the hall.

Then Momma came downstairs and they said hello, but they didn't kiss because they never did. Because Momma knows Aunty Ida is very shy. 'Will you have a cup of tea, Ida?' Momma said. 'Oh yes, Tess,' she said, and HE said, 'Make it yourself.' Then HE laughed. HE thought lots of things were funny. Then HE was getting a drink because he did not want tea. 'It's too early to drink,' Momma said. 'There's so much to do.' But HE said, 'For God's sake, it's Christmas Eve. If I can't have a drink on Christmas Eve, I might as well give up. Would you agree with me, Ida?' And she said, 'Oh yes, Edmund.' And then HE said, 'Will you have one yourself, Ida?' And she said, 'Oh yes, Edmund.' And Momma looked so crossly at her. I wished Aunty Ida would have had the tea, because later HE got into a mean mood and he said, 'So have you found a fella yet, Ida?' And she went so red and she stayed red for ages. Then HE said, 'No fellas in the office?' And HE thought that was very funny. 'No, Edmund, no,' she said, 'not at the moment.' And HE could hardly stop laughing after he said, 'So we won't book the Gresham yet.' I stayed very quiet and just kept putting the little teaspoons of mincemeat into the pastry that Momma had rolled out. HE gave Aunty Ida more whiskey. 'Oh yes, Edmund, that was it. I've been meaning to tell you. The other day I heard the Mamas and the Papas on the wireless. Now wait till I try to remember. Oh yes, it was the one about the dancing bear. Do you care for that one, Edmund?' she asked. I think she was trying to distract HIM from talking about the Gresham Hotel and trying to make conversation because Momma had gone upstairs to put Baby Cecil down for a sleep and Aunty

Ida didn't like it when the room was quiet and HE was there. It usually made her go bright red. 'Ah, for God's sake. I'll put on some proper music,' HE said. HE went over to the record player and put on a record. Then HE stood with his whiskey in one hand and the Frank Sinatra record cover in the other hand and conducted the song with one finger. Sometimes HE snapped his fingers to the beat. HE stood in front of the paraffin heater and blocked the heat. I saw Aunty Ida give a little shiver. I thought it was not fair because she was the one who had walked all the way up the hill, so she was the one who was cold. I kept quietly filling the pastry with mincemeat. HE turned the record up really loud. It was not a Christmassy song. It was about a man who wanted to fly to the moon. Aunty Ida just smiled at me softly and her small eyes had a kind of web over them. But then HE came over and filled her glass with more whiskey and he said, 'There you are, Georgy Girl.' I was so surprised. That was HIS name for me. Well, sometimes, anyway, ever since Butlin's. When HE drank whiskey especially. HE must have seen my surprised look as I raised my eyes from the mincemeat tarts, because he said, 'Two Georgy Girls.' And HE raised his glass like Uncle Ronnie had done at my cousin's wedding, when he said, 'A toast to the bride.' Aunty Ida looked at me and smiled, but the web on her eyes was even deeper now. It was deeper than the smile. *Nothing could break through that web*, I thought. *It must be because it's Christmas Eve.*

You Shouldn't Drink Vinegar

A long time after Christmas but still before summer came, Momma was finding it hard to cope. That's what everyone was saying. They were saying it when they thought she could not hear. But I heard. I always kept an eye out for Momma. People came to visit almost every day, which was very strange for all of us, because usually only Aunty Ida came. HIS brother Uncle Ronnie and his wife came, even though they did not get on with HIM. And they said, 'You'll have to get her a bit of help.' And they offered to take the little ones to stay with them until our new baby was born. But Momma said no: 'Honestly, I'm grand,' she said. And later I heard her say to HIM, 'They'd come back ruined.' I did not know what she meant by that.

So I tried my best to help Momma with all the little ones. I played with them and put Baby Cecil into his push-chair and I wheeled him up and down our road while the little ones played with all the other children who were out. It was spring now, so the evenings were brighter and we could stay out longer. *A nice quiet house for Momma*, I thought. *She will get better.* Sometimes I played a bit myself too. But I did not like to leave Baby Cecil even for a moment in case the pushchair rolled down the hill or in case he toppled it over with all of his rocking. So if it was a running game like chasing or cops and robbers, I ran while pushing him in front of me. He loved the speed and he held on to the front bar of the pushchair as though he was its driver. He had such a proud look on his face. I was very proud of him because he was only three but he already knew how to join in. And the little ones were good as gold. If they got a scratch or fell or got a nettle sting, they just ran to me and I kissed it better and put a dock leaf on it. So poor Momma had some peace.

Momma lay on the couch with our brother or sister, John Fitzgerald or Jackie, inside her huge, lovely, warm, friendly belly. She stroked her belly gently all the time with so much kindness. All of us put our ear to her tummy, squabbling to be next to listen to the gurgling. We put our hand on her belly very gently to see if we could get Baby to move an elbow or a knee. Momma would say, 'Did you feel it?' Sometimes I did not but I would nod as though I had because Momma always smiled when we felt it. If you sang to Baby, with your mouth really close to Momma's belly, Momma said she would feel Baby move and that it was probably a really musical baby. When Momma lay on the couch like that, I mashed bananas, sprinkled them with sugar and spread them over thick slices of white bread thickly buttered, and we all had that. We had an electric kettle now, so it was easy to make Momma tea. That was her favourite meal, banana with sugar on bread and hot tea. We were so happy, waiting with Momma for John or Jackie. But visitors kept coming almost every day and they sat in our chairs and said hardly anything at all, just staring at us children and nodding and shaking heads with each other. If they were still there when HE got home, he was not pleased, and they soon left after he arrived. Sometimes they gave us money to share between us all, and I walked to the shops with Baby Cecil in his push-chair and got sweets to divide up.

One day Uncle Ronnie's wife said, 'Are you not well?' And Momma said, 'A bit weak maybe.' And Uncle Ronnie's wife just looked at her with a very knowing but sort of mean look and shook her head at Uncle Ronnie. Then she looked at the little ones in a way which I did not like at all. And I thought, *She looks like she wants to eat them*. So I brought them into our back garden for hide-and-seek.

One evening Momma said to HIM, 'I think I'll get Ida to stay for a while and give me a hand.' But HE said, 'She'd be no help at all. She'd sit around and do nothing and you'd be up and down making tea for her!' Momma sighed. She was too tired to argue and she gave in easily. She shut her eyes and lay still and then suddenly she sat up and said to HIM, 'Under no conditions are any of my children ever to stay with your brother Ronnie. Ever. You promise me that.' And HE said, 'OK.' And she said, 'No. I want a promise.' And HE said, 'Fine, I promise.'

So instead of Aunty Ida coming to stay with us and instead of the little ones going to Uncle Ronnie's house, HE brought home a girl who had used to work in his office. One day she just arrived back with HIM in the car and walked into our house. 'Out of the blue,' Momma said later. We all stared at her, and she put her bag into my room because HE said to. Momma was so surprised. She was a lovely girl with a really wide smile, and very large straight white teeth that made me run my tongue over my own crooked ones every time I saw hers.

Her name was Tilly Hall and she was bouncy and busy straight away. She had the kitchen clean in a few minutes, cleaner than I had ever seen it, with every surface shining and clear. Then she said she would pop a chicken in the oven with some nice veg cooked in the French style and she chatted away to Momma and smiled and smiled with her amazing teeth. 'I spent a year in France, you know,' she told Momma, 'and they cook so differently there. Boiled chicken is much more popular than roast, and they cook all the veg in one large pot in the oven. Potatoes too – so it's a one-pot wonder. Though the French put much less emphasis on potatoes. There we are, a one-pot wonder,' and she popped it into the oven: '*Poulet!*'

Tilly was almost eighteen, and being eighteen would make all the difference to her, she said, because there was a boy in France she wanted to go back and marry. *Mariage*, she said, was very different in France because *le divorce* was *pas une problem*. She chatted away to me all the time and told me we had the same birthday month. I listened and watched her carefully. I could hardly take my eyes off her because I had never had a chance to talk to a teenager before. She was very interesting-looking, with red-blondie hair which she said was called strawberry blonde and which she said they love in France. She had huge, staring, green eyes, which they also loved in France, she said. Her clothes were like the teenagers on *Top of the Pops*, which was the only thing she turned the telly on for. She was as relaxed as if she had been born in our kitchen. I began to wonder if we had been living in her house by mistake and now she had come back for it. Even a few minutes after she arrived the little ones had just run off to play and had not stared at her for too long, but whenever she called them they came quickly and happily. Momma used to have to call them thirty times! And so did I when I had their sugary banana ready. She said she was going to teach me two French words every hour. She said I was so clever that I reminded her of herself.

It was nice for the first few days to have her brightness and bounciness about. But like Momma, I got a bit tired of her brightness and her bounciness and would go off to the end of our garden to walk the walls, or to sit and dangle my legs while I read *Flight of the Doves*. Or sometimes I just lay on the grass under our laburnum tree and I thought about what it would be like in America. I didn't really have to help much any more, and when I went to do something for the little ones, or for Baby or for Momma, Tilly would say, 'No, no, *ma petite*, you go play.' And then I got used to running off and playing, after only a week or so. And I liked it.

But it grew strange. The longer she was in our house, the happier HE became and the sadder Momma got. Momma did not come out and lie on the couch any more. She stayed in her bedroom with the curtains closed, and she stopped asking me if the little ones were eating the French food that Tilly cooked. She stopped asking me because the answer was always yes. They always ate Tilly's French food and so did HE, and she said, '*Bon appétit*,' and HE said, '*Délicieux*.' It was strange when Aunty Ida came too, because she would just go straight upstairs to Momma and sit on the bed and chat a little. But they didn't talk much. Mostly they sat in silence, because Momma could barely keep her eyes open now. Aunty Ida hardly came out of the bedroom to see us at all, and sometimes she would just shut the front door quietly behind her and leave. I watched carefully for her to come out from Momma, and if I was on time, I walked to the bottom of the hill with her. Her light brown eyes and round face were even sadder than usual these days. I wanted to say, *Will Momma be all right?* But I did not because I was afraid to hear the answer. And one day when we were halfway down the hill, Aunty Ida said, 'I don't care too much for Tilly.' And it was only then that I realized that I, too, did not care too much for Tilly. And I decided that I did not want to know any more French words. *What is it about Tilly?* I thought and thought. And one night in bed I knew what it was. She was making Momma shrink.

Three weeks after Tilly had arrived, an ambulance backed up into our driveway. We thought that Momma was only getting a lift to the hospital to have John Fitzgerald or Jackie taken out. So I just stood at the gate with Baby Cecil on my hip and waved her off. It all seemed normal. But when I turned back towards our house, I got a terrible feeling of emptiness and our house looked like a big empty shell. And even though the sky had not grown dark, and the wind had not whipped up, and no rain fell in hard steel needles, I thought, *Is the world ending?*

By the time Baby Cecil and I had got inside, Tilly had put on a David Cassidy record with the volume up loud, now that Momma did not need quiet. The door of Momma's room was wide open and a big gush of breeze came through as Baby Cecil and I stood watching Tilly from the door. She had opened all the windows and was changing the sheets on Momma's bed. She waved to me merrily and then came and held out her arms to Baby Cecil to go to her, and he did, without looking back at me at all. And I stood in the doorway while she rushed off to the kitchen with him and I looked at Momma's bed. I breathed in really deeply, searching so hard to reach the air of comfort which always lay just inside Momma's bedroom door. But Momma's smell was already gone.

I went and lay on my bed, and I lay and I lay. I was so heavy that I was scared my body would sink down through the mattress and then down through the foundations of our house and then down and down through the earth until it got to the earth's core. But still I could not get up. I was too heavy. I kept thinking, *Someone will come, someone will come,* and once I opened my eyes really suddenly because I had a very strong feeling that Momma was standing there at the door, which was a little bit ajar, and that when she'd see me open my eyes she'd say, 'Are you all right, my Jeannie Jean?' but she didn't because she wasn't there. And when I opened my eyes and saw no one there – just the door ajar and the doorway empty – it was a very heavy feeling, so I shut my eyes again and I just kept sinking.

Days and days and days passed, but Momma did not come back. Lots of visitors still came, which was really annoying because they sat so long drinking tea and eating Tilly's French pastries and talking to Tilly about France. And when HE came in, he was not pleased to see any of them at all, especially Uncle Ronnie, because he talked so much to Tilly and followed her around the kitchen and tried to speak French to her, which HE could not speak except for the few words she was teaching him. And although Tilly loved talking to anyone, she did seem a bit annoyed with Uncle Ronnie. Sometimes visitors gave us money, which was a good thing, I suppose, but the more money they gave us, the more I was worried about Momma. HE went to see Momma every second day, but Aunty Ida went every day. She went on her lunchtime and she went again in the evening after work. No children were allowed in the ward, HE said. HE said, 'Children carry germs and make noise.' And there was still no news of our momma and our new baby.

The house felt different. It was so clean, and the windows were open all day so that fresh breezes could blow through. Tilly lit incense sticks in the evening to clean the air and create positive vibes, she said. The little ones sat in a bubble bath every night while Tilly sang a French song to them. Mostly she sang '*Père Noël*', a song about Santa, who is called that in France. She sang it to them even though it was not long to summer. She just popped off the light in their rooms and said goodnight and that was the end of them. No story from Momma or from me. And I began to know the words of David Cassidy's songs, and I sang them for my friend Ann in school and she was so impressed. And Tilly got a magazine called *Music Star* and she let me read it and tear out some of the pictures for my wall, as long as they were not of David Cassidy or the Sweet, which was a band where all the men had really, really long hair and wore silver trousers.

HE was in such a good mood all the time now. It was very confusing. HE was like a different man. And in all those weeks Aunty Ida hardly ever came to see us, but when she did come for a quick visit, she explained that this was because she needed to be in the hospital so much with Momma, so I was glad. And I thought, *Will I ask HIM if Aunty Ida eats her dinner with Momma?*, because I was worried that Momma had to eat her dinner by herself. But I didn't. I hardly ever ask the things I want to.

Tilly's French chicken was practically all we ever ate now, but everyone was happy. HE would look at her and say, 'I can never get enough of it.' And they washed up together and afterwards they drank wine and not whiskey, and HE brought home a box of new wine glasses which were really like massive bubbles because she said, 'One should never drink wine out of such small glasses.' HE never put on the telly in the evening any more. Not even for the horse-racing results. They just chatted and smoked. And instead of shouting at us, 'Go to bed,' with a terrible lion's roaring voice, HE said, '*Va faire coucher, petits.*' I was very mixed up. Had our house gone completely French? Even Baby Cecil preferred to be carried by Tilly than to be carried by me, and once he even pulled away from me to find his way into Tilly's arms. That made me very sad.

It got even stranger. One night I got up out of bed to get a glass of water because my throat was aching, my tummy hurt, and I could not stop worrying about Momma and what on earth had happened to our new baby, who by now should have been asleep in the beautiful Moses basket Momma had got ready just on the other side of the very wall I had been staring at for hours that felt like weeks. And Momma should have been there too, on the other side of my bedroom wall. I opened the door and walked downstairs very quietly so as not to waken anybody. There was no light in the sitting room. Instead there was a lit candle on the floor at the side of the couch. I wondered if I should just walk through to the kitchen to get my water. My throat was getter sorer and sorer. But then I heard a rustling sound like clothes moving in deep, dark quiet and a very slight whisper of HIM. Then suddenly out popped Tilly's head over the top of the back of the couch: '*Allo*,' she said brightly, '*va faire coucher, ma petite*.' So I did.

Lying back on my chilled bed, with my throat throbbing and my tummy turning somersaults and screeching like car wheels skidding, I thought to myself, *There's something fishy in this house. The sooner Momma comes home the better.* And I lay there thinking of all the French words Tilly had taught me, and in my mind, one by one, I put them into a box which I labelled 'Things to be forgotten'. *Mariage, maquillage, poulet.*

The next evening, even though my throat was still sore and itchy, I was out playing on our road. It stayed bright until nine o'clock now, and often Tom and I and sometimes even Cissy just stayed out until everyone else had been called in. Sometimes I did not want to go in at all and I stayed out alone and sat on our front wall and dangled my legs, and I was almost invisible as the big branches and leaves and blossoms of the cherry blossom tree leaned down over me. When Momma was home, we always got called in first because she said the chill of the evening is not good for children.

Willie Furlong was the meanest boy on our road. He was always annoying our little ones. Once he even threw stones at our twins. That evening I caught him in cops and robbers and I held him by the jumper. He just kept pulling and pulling really hard, but I kept holding him because he was a cheater. I don't know why I wouldn't give up even after he started kicking me. Usually I would not have cared that much because cheats are cheats and no one likes a cheater, Momma said. I was almost as angry as he was. His hair seemed more jet-black than ever as his face grew hotter and hotter. 'Bitch!' he shouted at me. Suddenly I was not angry and I turned to go in because I thought it was a terrible word to call me and I thought, *This is going the wrong way*. He shouted again, 'Bitch!' And then just as I was about to turn in our gate he shouted, 'Your mother's dying!' And then he said it again in a sing-song way: 'Your mo-ther's dy-ing. Your mo-ther's dy-ing.' So I ran back over to him and I kicked him so hard and then I had to say it, the meanest thing I had ever said: 'Fatty.' And I ran towards our front door, but when I got there, I did not want to go in. I needed to see Momma and tell her what he had said, so I turned and raced down our hill as fast as I could, and I turned the corner and I ran and kept running. I had gone with Momma for her check-ups before to mind Baby Cecil in his pushchair outside, so I knew exactly how to get to the hospital. Once I got out of our roads and past our shops and past the woods and our chipper, I knew that I could get there just by running in a straight line. So that's what I did.

I ran all along the main road, round the bendy part over the train tracks, only stopping once or twice to get my breath. But stopping was worse because the end-of-the-world feeling got stronger and tighter inside my body, so soon I started running again to let it escape. I ran and ran, and all the time I kept thinking, *There's no time to lose, there's no time to lose.* I knew that if I could tell her that she could not leave us because we would not survive, I would not survive without her, then I knew she would not dream of dying. She had just grown tired, I thought, because there were so many of us, but she could keep Tilly after she came home and then she would get used to the French chicken too, and if she did not, well then, Tilly could go. The footpaths grew darker and the street lights came on. I ran on top of my shadow and I ran out of it and on top of it again. Then I had two shadows and then only one again. But I was not afraid. There was nothing in the world apart from this distance between me and Momma, this footpath, these stretches of houses, trees and bridges standing between us. I was practising in my head all the things I would say to Momma so that she would know that she could not die. And I would find a nurse or even a doctor and I would say, 'She cannot die. I cannot live without Momma.'

I turned down Herbert Park Road, which was usually my favourite road in summer with its huge, high umbrella leaves on either side stretching out and meeting in the middle. Now I did not even see the leaves. I just ran. I moved onto the road without even thinking about it because I thought I would move faster there, and there were no cars because it was a Sunday night. Left at the American Embassy, down Northumberland Road, and once I ran over the canal bridge I knew that I was not that far from Holles Street.

I did not stop running until I reached the steps of the hospital. Then I stopped, out of breath and suddenly very unsure, my sandals abruptly locking in the footpath. I had a sharp pain in my side and I held it with both hands. And then as I started up the three steps, I spurred myself on: 'Wait for me, Momma, wait for me.' And I knew that inside she was waiting for me because I had begun to see her face again, especially her red lipstick, and I could feel her goodness close by.

I pushed through the door to a dimly lit lobby, silent but for the quiet sliding of the chains of the lifts as they moved up and down. There appeared to be nobody sitting at the desk, but I went over to it and stood waiting. Quick, annoyed, serious footsteps approached after a few minutes, and a nun, wearing a hat like a nun's, with her hands clasped in front of her, came towards me. 'My goodness,' she said, 'what on earth are you doing here?' I stepped back from the lobby desk startled and feeling that I was in serious trouble, but Momma was more important. 'I have to see my mother.' 'Not at all, not at all,' said the nurse, shaking her head. 'At this time of night. Not at all, out of the question, you foolish girl.' She stepped in behind the desk. 'Now who's with you?' I shook my head. 'No one? Goodness gracious me,' she said. And she made that *tut tut tut* sound with her tongue which made me feel stupid and ashamed. 'Tut, tut, tut,' she said. 'Now, what's mammy's name and address and we'll phone up your daddy and he can come and collect you.' I am always obedient. So I told her and she picked up the telephone and I listened as she dialled each number. The sound each time she dialled a number echoed around the empty lobby. And when she had dialled all the numbers, she stared at me as she waited for an answer. Then she told on me. 'Now sit over there and wait,' she said, pointing to a wooden bench against the wall. And I sat, foolish and ashamed. I sat on my hands and looked at the shining tiles on the floor, as smooth as diamonds from all the thousands of feet that had walked on them.

Then a man came through the doors. I glanced towards him and he glanced towards me at the exact same moment. He had a stethoscope around his neck and he hurried over to the nurse at the desk. I heard them whispering a little, but I did not look up. He was probably saying something like, 'What a stupid, annoying girl. What a bad girl.' But then he was sitting beside me on the bench, his knees turned towards mine, and he was speaking. 'Now, how quiet can you be if I asked you to be really, really quiet?' I did not say anything. 'If I were to guess,' he said, 'I would guess you are a very quiet girl indeed. Would I be right?' I nodded in agreement but still did not look up. 'So then I can allow you to come with me for two minutes and I can depend on you to be very quiet, I think.' I nodded again and he took my hand and I walked beside him. His hand was lovely. Cool and enclosing. It held my hand so softly that if I had wanted to I could easily have taken it back. I cannot describe it. I was afraid, but I took the risk of glancing up at him for a moment and he caught me looking at him and looked back at me. He smiled and nodded at the same time. 'You're fine now,' he said, 'don't worry.' He pulled back the cage doors of the lift and we went in.

Noisily we travelled upwards and I could see more shiny tiled floors as we passed them and once I saw a nurse's shoes and her legs. 'I bet you're the biggest girl in the house. Am I right?' I nodded again. He pulled back the cage door and then, still holding my hand, he bent to me and he said, 'Now, really, really quiet. And I can't show you your mammy up close. All right? Only through the glass window because there are lots of other mammies in there, you see?' I nodded and we walked quickly towards some double doors at the end of the corridor. 'Now look through there,' he said. 'Can you reach?' I stretched up onto my tippy-toes and peered into the dimly lit ward. Four beds on the right, four beds on the left, and at the end of each a little metal cot. In the centre a gigantic statue of Holy Mary with the Baby Jesus in her arms. 'Now,' he said slowly and patiently. 'The second bed on the left – you see? With the little cot and the blue blanket?' I nodded. 'That's your mammy – and that's your baby brother. All's well. Do you see? All's well.'

So there she was. She had waited for me. She was not plugged into a machine. No dark priest sat over her bed praying with his books and his rosary beads. There was no dead baby in her arms. No dark angel hovering over them, saying, 'You're dead, you're dead.' My toes ached, so long did I stay on them peering into the dim room, making out the bump of Momma, so still and quiet under the hospital blankets. Then, turning my head a little, I saw a vase of flowers on the bedside table, and all the cards which we had made her surrounding it. My clenched mouth fell open and a smile slipped across my face. My heart leaped up a thousand steps. 'So now,' said the good doctor, 'all's well. We had better go before we are in trouble.' So I came down from my peering spot, my toes cracking a bit from the strain of standing like a ballerina.

He took my hand and we travelled together in the cage lift back to the lobby and he held my hand as he delivered me back to my waiting spot on the wooden bench. He bent to me. 'Now,' he said, 'will you do something for me?' I nodded. 'Will you stop worrying?' And when he said that, he put his hand on my cheek. And except for Aunty Ida, I have never felt anything as light as the lightness of that touch. Not ever. Not in my whole life.

After about twenty minutes, Tilly came through the doors. She went to the desk before she saw me. She spoke to the nurse, who turned to me as she tut-tut-tutted in my direction. We took the bus home and Tilly was very kind and said we could sit upstairs, but I said, 'No, thank you.' I was getting surer and surer that it was Tilly's fault that Momma was shrinking. It had started the day she came, when Momma first went to lie in her own room instead of on the couch with all of us running around her. Before Tilly, I used to say every day, 'Would you like to lie in bed, Momma – it would be quieter?' But she would always say, 'No, sweetheart, I like the sounds of you all.' But after Tilly came, she always stayed in her room and that is when I first noticed the shrinking.

Tilly chatted away and pointed to things out the window, like her old school and the house where an old boyfriend lived and the park where she always met up with her friend Yvonne, who was half French. When the bus conductor came round, I did not have to pay much attention to her any more but could just stare out the window because he chatted away to her for the rest of the journey. And of course she told him that she had lived in France and was going back for *le mariage*. And he teased her about that and asked her if her hair colour was natural. Then she gave him a few pulls of her cigarette. He told her she looked like Twiggy. He took a transistor out of his pocket and put on some music and held it to her ear so that she could hear his favourite song, which I thought was a terrible song. And anyhow his radio was all crackly.

When we jumped off the bus at the stop near our shops he shouted after her, 'Hope you ride my bus again.' And she tossed her strawberry-blonde hair in the air and said, '*Bonne chance*.' The bus conductor threw me a full roll of bus tickets, but I did not catch it. I did not even try. Tilly went and picked it up for me. She put her arm around my shoulders and I wanted to push it away but I would never do anything like that, though her arm felt like a ton of bricks sitting on me. '*Des frites?*' she said as we were coming up to Forte's, our chipper. I did not answer yes or no, but she went in and got me a bag of chips and a tin of TK lemonade. When I held the chips in my hand and smelled the vinegar, I forgot about everything for a moment. She held my lemonade while I ate them. I suppose Tilly was kind. I offered her a chip but she said, 'No, no. My

74

body's a temple.' I had no idea what she meant, but later I would wonder what mine was. The bottom of the brown paper chip bag was soaked with vinegar, and although I wouldn't usually, I held it up to my mouth and I sucked and sucked all of the vinegar out of the paper and Tilly said, 'One should not drink vinegar. Look at your lips – they are as white as snow.' And at that moment she stopped and took her lipstick case from her pocket and held its little mirror to her lips and painted dark red lipstick on them until they sat on her pretty face like a rose. Then she held the little mirror up for me to see my own lips: 'You see,' she said, 'white as snow. One should not drink vinegar. *Jamais, ma petite.*'

HE opened the front door for us, smiling at Tilly, and he did not look at me at all. 'There you are,' HE said. I walked towards the stairs to go up to bed and I heard HIM say, 'Will we finish that wine before you go up?' But Tilly said, 'It's straight to bed for me. I'm worn out after all that.' So that was that, I thought. Until HE arrived in my room when I was about to put on my nightie. I turned round from where I stood at the bed. 'Where the hell did you think you were going?' HE said it both like a whisper and like a shout, as though he were holding back a terrible roaring lion voice coiled up in his throat. I thought, *He's angry because the wine is wasted*. And then something terrible happened. I said what I wanted to say, and I hardly ever say the things I want to say, but I said what I wanted to say this time. It was coming and I could not stop, I could not hold back: 'You should have gone in to see Momma.' The lion snapped. He sprang. He pulled back his big paw, right back behind his mane, all the birds fled from their hiding place in the trees with a terrible swooping sound, and the lion lashed out his big paw with its long, sharp, dirty nails and whacked my face. I heard the smack, the slap, the bite, the sting, the gunshot, the crack of the whip, the lash of the belt. All cutting into my cheek. And I fell back. Right back down onto my own bed I fell. And before I had time to stop those cartoon stars from spinning around my head, the lion had stalked out of my room. Mine and Cissy's. And I lay on my bed just as I had landed. I did not get up. I did not move. Cissy stirred. I did not move. Dawn came. I did not move. I did not get up. I thought and I thought. And I remembered on the telly how I had seen a film about American ranchers and I thought of the poor calves being held as the brand was placed on their hides and held until it had burned into them so that they would have the mark. So that everyone would know who owned them until the day they died, Tom said. My face burned and burned until the light started to come through the edges of the curtains and I knew it must be very red but I did not go to look in the mirror. I did not need to because branding is forever. That's why they branded the calves, Tom said.

Almost Eleven

Little Sparrows

Momma had come back to us thin. Her whole body felt so different, so delicate and light, like it might break if you hugged her too hard. But she had not changed. She kissed the little ones every time they passed her, and she pulled me into her for a kiss every time I went in or out of the room she was in. Even Tilly's constant talking and listing of French words, and of the differences between the French and the Irish personalities, did not seem to make her need to lie down. She seemed happier to chat to Tilly than before she had left us. And she would say to Tilly, in a tone quite strong for Momma, 'No, leave that, Tilly. I will do that.' Except of course in the evening when HE came home and Momma would say, 'Are you not going out to see your friends, Tilly? Go on, I'll manage.' And Tilly would say, 'Oh, it's so far to the bus stop.' And then HE would always say, 'I'll drop her to the bus.' And off they'd go.

After HE dropped Tilly to the bus stop, maybe he would call to a man he worked with, or go to collect something he had forgotten in his office, and then he might wait there to pick Tilly up; or he might go and clean the car or something. HE was usually gone for hours. Those were nice hours with just me and Momma, and Tom and Cissy, and the little ones and our new baby, John Fitzgerald Kennedy. How sweet the house felt. I would hold Baby John F. and rock him gently while Momma got to her feet and said, 'Now would you like chips or buns?' And she would make them there and then from scratch as we all sat watching *Bonanza* or *The Virginian* or *Lost in Space* or the *Pink Panther* cartoon. We could watch whatever we liked when HE was out. We laughed and laughed and stayed up late with Momma and she was so glad to be home. She would say to me, 'I can hardly take my eyes off you.' And I would say to her, 'I can hardly take my eyes off you.' And then I would kiss Baby John F.'s sweet-smelling hair and say, 'And you, my little one, I can hardly take my eyes off you.'

Tilly sometimes went out on Friday and Saturday afternoons to meet her friends in the bowling alley in Stillorgan, or into town, to get something with her Green Shield Stamps or just to sit on the grass in Stephen's Green or walk round the Dandelion Market where she bought her incense sticks. Later, Tilly would call from the phone box near the bus stop and HE would go and pick her up, though Momma would always say, 'But the walk is good for her. And it's not raining.' But HE would always go anyhow. HE would drop everything to pick Tilly up, even the horse-racing news. I wanted to say, *That's not fair. You make Aunty Ida walk. She has to walk from the bus and she is older and heavier and she has so many bags. That's not fair.* But of course I never did. I hardly ever say the things I want to say.

So this one afternoon in May, just before tea, when the

laburnum lanterns were shining over us and snowing gently down on us whenever the breeze kicked up a little, was a Friday. How could the world be more brightly lit than today? I thought. Momma was out of bed. Before I had come out to play she had been watering the plants in the kitchen. They had all dried up when she was in hospital having Baby John F. Tilly had forgotten about them and so had I. No shame to Tilly, though, for she was not Momma's girl.

The long evening lay in front of us. I knew we would be out playing for ages. Though it was chilly in the breeze, it was our first day to wear summer clothes and I felt so light, like I could run for hours. Momma came to the gate from time to time with Baby John F. in the pram and the little ones hanging on to it, for since Momma had come home they did not like to let her out of their sight. Though I was big, I felt the same and whenever Momma came to the gate I waved to her. She would wave back and blow me a kiss and I kept running and showing Momma how fast I could run now. Some of the neighbour women came out and stood beside Momma and leaned into the pram to see Baby John. HE had just got home from the office and was inside somewhere. HE, too, was in a good mood and had been whistling earlier. HE had the telly all to himself and the house was quiet because we were all outside. Tilly had gone into town.

Then Momma called us in for tea. 'Come in,' she said, 'come on. It's nearly half past five.' She had just said that when – BOOM. And we all stood totally and completely still. We had been chasing after the other team, who were the robbers. After the BOOM, our feet did not move from that spot where we had stopped, and I felt my toes pushed to the end of my sandals. Cissy suddenly burst out crying. And then before anyone had a chance to speak, and just as Mrs O'Sullivan came out her front door, there it was again, BOOM! And the adults asked each other, 'What in God's name was that?' and Mrs Devereux, who had been chatting to Momma and Mrs Furlong, said, 'Holy Jesus,' and reached out and held Mrs Furlong's hand, which was very unusual because Mrs Furlong was a bigot and Mrs Devereux was a Protestant, which was not her fault, Momma said. And they looked from one to the other because no one knew. And then Mrs O'Malley came to her gate and called and beckoned to her children to go inside. And then everyone else started going in. So after such a perfect afternoon, we all suddenly, on that laburnum-lit day, found ourselves inside, in our own houses with the doors shut, the sunlight left behind us.

HE had the radio on. The first thing HE said when we entered the sitting room was: 'Shhh.' And the second thing HE said was: 'Get out, out, out.' And HE got up from his armchair and he pushed us all out the door. Even Momma, who was as small and as thin as a little sparrow since her sickness that she got from the hospital when she was having Baby John F. We all stood with Momma in a little clump outside the door, looking up at her with Cissy still crying. 'Go into the good room,' Momma said, and she turned round and pushed open the door and went back in to HIM. 'And don't go outside at all,' she said as she shut the door behind her.

So we all walked into the good room in silence, except

for the sound of Cissy's crying, into the room where we were not usually allowed, and we sat in two rows on the edges of the good couches like people in a doctor's waiting room. And I made the little ones take off their sandals because when they sat on the couches their feet touched the edges of the cushions and I was worried about the good furniture. We sat quietly and the only sound was of Baby John F. sucking his soother. I was worried that there might be another BOOM. Instead there came the sound of HIS lion's voice roaring at poor Momma. Then the sound of the front door slamming. Then the sound of the car crunching the gravel of our driveway and gathering speed with a roar of the engine as HE pulled out and sped up the road. I heard Momma go to the front door and open it. Then she closed it. And I heard her sobbing. I should have gone straight to Momma, but I thought, *I better stay with Cissy because she looks so frightened*, and now her crying had become a sobbing, and Aunty Ida always said, 'Don't sob. It can affect the heart.'

'Don't sob, Cissy,' I said, 'it can affect your heart. Take a deep breath, Cissy. It's only an argument. And the BOOM was just . . . the thunder . . . far-away thunder and it's gone now.' 'Thunder?' Cissy said. 'Yes. I'll go ask Momma if the thunder is finished, but you have to stay here and play I Spy with the little ones when I'm gone. And don't let them near Daddy's records. All right?' She nodded, sobbing a little less now, and she began to lay out the rules of I Spy to the little ones, who were so good and had put their sandals in a neat row at the door, ready to leave the good room, and Cecil was lying upside down with his blond hair sweeping the carpet and Tom holding on tightly to him.

I went to Momma, who was watching the six o'clock news now, and I could hardly believe what I saw. At first I thought it must be Belfast, but then I saw Guineys' shop blown to smithereens and cars blown into pieces and glass everywhere and I knew that what Aunty Ida had always worried about was happening and that the war had come down from the North. Momma and I just stared at the telly, hardly able to believe it, and then she said in a very shaky voice, 'He's gone into town to find Tilly. And I asked him not to.' I rubbed Momma's arm up and down and up and down. The phone rang then, and I followed Momma out into the hall and listened as she picked it up, and I stood beside her and kept rubbing her arm because she was shaking and sobbing, and sobbing can affect the heart. I could hear a woman's voice on the other end and then Momma suddenly got really cross and said, 'Well, if you don't even know where your own daughter is, I don't know what to say to you. She should be living with you, in her own home, not here. You're a disgraceful mother.' And Momma slammed the receiver down.

About two hours later, after I had got Cecil to sleep for the night and the little ones had gone to bed, there was a knock on our front door. Momma would not let me open it. She said, 'No, not today. I will do it.' I stood behind her and Momma opened the door to find two people we had never seen before, standing in our porch. Momma just stared at them. The woman said, 'Is Matilda here?' And Momma said,

'So you're her mother. No, she's not here. She's still in town.' 'Well, we'll come in and wait.' So it seemed poor Momma had no choice and she stood back and let the man and the woman come in.

She opened the good-room door and they went in there. For a while we all stood just looking at each other and no one said anything. 'Will you sit down,' Momma said after ages, and so they sat on the edge of a couch. But Momma did not sit down. She stood staring at them, and then after a while she turned her back and stood staring out the window, bouncing Baby John F. about in her arms even though he was already fast asleep. Cissy stayed for a while, but then she got bored and ran off. The man's head was bent low all the time and he never really made eye contact with any of us. Tilly's momma was mean-looking with squinting eyes and a ter-rible brown coat and a hard leather black bag which she kept on her lap the whole time, and very fat ankles spilling out over her black pointy shoes.

We sat and we sat in the quiet, except for the few times when Tilly's father cleared his throat in such a way that I thought he might be about to say something. But he never said a word. I did not want to leave Momma alone with them, so I stayed sitting there, even though I was missing the end of *The Virginian*.

Then I heard the sound of tyres on the gravel on our driveway and Momma passed Baby John F. to me and rushed out to open the front door. And there HE was, climbing out of the car, and Tilly climbing out of the passenger seat and slipping past our hydrangea bush. Tilly's parents stood up and just walked right out of the house, straight past HIM, straight past Tilly, and straight out our driveway.

On the Shelf

It was funny how Aunty Ida and I fell in love at the exact same time. And both of us for the first time too. She did not say, 'I have fallen in love,' and I did not say, 'I have fallen in love,' but when I thought about it and when I looked at her carefully and saw that the webs were gone from her eyes and instead they were twinkling, and when I listened to her chat with Momma, I knew that it was true. To Momma she said things like: 'Do you think he likes me?' But she said it in a whisper. And she only said it in the evening after she had had a whiskey or two. Momma said, 'I am sure he likes you. You have a lovely manner.' But that is as far as she went. Aunty Ida said, 'Is he a bit like Spencer Tracy, do you think?' And Momma said, 'Well, he sounds a lot shorter and he's bald, but I suppose a bit on account of the pipe and the trilby. Does he ever take it off?' And Aunty Ida said, 'No, not that I know of.' Then one evening, after quite a lot of whiskey, she asked Momma, 'Did you ever think I might marry?' And Momma, who was ever kind, said, 'You never know what lies ahead.'

Mine wore a hat too, a baseball cap. I saw him first at Mass, standing at the back with his father. I thought he must be American. I nudged Tom and I said, 'Is he in your school?' And Tom looked at him and shrugged his shoulders. After Mass I caught a glimpse of his back as he climbed into the back of his enormous car with his father and his brothers. 'What are you gawking at?' Tom asked. I said, 'Nothing,' and Tom pulled my arm to get me to catch up with my own family.

I never saw the boy again at Mass and for a while I wondered if his family had gone back to America. This gave me a double feeling: I would be glad to think about him there, in his American school with his American clothes and his baseball jacket, and I could even imagine myself there with him. And with no school bag, because Americans did not have them. Instead they carried their books and did not have as many as we had, and if a boy liked a girl he carried hers for her. That was the first sign of love from an American boy. But the other feeling was like a big, deep, dark hole inside me. I had almost given up hope completely when one day I was sitting on our wall, watching the boys playing football, when he appeared around the bend past which Momma did not allow us to go until after our twelfth birthday. I couldn't believe it! He called out to Tom: 'Can I play?' and Tom said, 'Sure, we're short one anyhow.' And then Tom said, 'Yeah, but Stephen, you have to take off your baseball cap. This is soccer.' And the boy just grinned and threw it on top of the grass verge, where it landed right beneath my feet. 'Sorry,' he shouted, but I did not look up. I pretended not to even notice the cap, but when they were all in the middle of their match, I hopped down and picked it up and put it on the wall beside me so that it wouldn't get stood on. Then I ran in because all of a sudden I had turned the brightest red of my whole life.

Aunty Ida got lucky too because she found out that the man she liked lived in the area. She had seen his dark green Morris Minor van parked outside Keveney's shop and had watched him come out with his newspaper and cat food. And that is when our long walks began. She would come a few times in the week, as she always did, and she would say, 'Sorry I'm a bit late,' or 'Sorry I'm a bit early,' when she was neither. After a very quick glass of water, no tea at all, and a hasty and incomplete distribution of comics and other things that she always knew we were dying for, she would say to Momma, 'I'll bring them for a walk, and you can get on with having a rest.' This delighted Momma, who really wanted Baby John F. to get some fresh air. So I strapped Baby John F. into his pushchair, put the walking reins on Cecil and waited for Aunty Ida. She stood in front of the hall mirror, delicately applying a scented powder puff to her round, sad face, which was a little less sad these days. And I watched her as she applied pink lipstick to her wide, thin lips, which were not like Momma's at all. And I wanted to say, *Aunty Ida, get Momma's red lipstick. It is much prettier.* But that might have made her give up hope, so I said nothing at all until the moment she looked down and pressed her lips together and said, 'Now, we're ready.'

One day before we left for our walk, Momma said, 'Don't walk so far, Ida.' And Aunty Ida and I looked at each other knowingly because today we knew exactly how far we had to go. And it was not far. Aunty Ida had got to the bottom of where he lived. When we got to the road his house was on, we walked up one side, crossed over and then walked up the other side. Then we did that all over again, and again. And then it happened. We were just passing the end of his driveway when the front door opened and he came out. He was about to climb into his green van when he glanced in our direction. Aunty Ida had stopped and was leaning into the pram as though she were fixing Baby John F.'s blankets. When she was getting up, they caught each other's eye and he nodded to her and continued to get into his van. But she called out in a voice I had never heard her use before, so precise and polite and so posh and so light and airy: 'Hello, hello.' He turned towards us. Aunty Ida called, 'Good afternoon, are you quite well? Did you see a little cat at all?' *Are you quite well* – that was not a good thing for her to say, but I knew she had got it off *My Fair Lady*. He looked blankly at her. 'I see lots of cats,' he said. I thought he sounded a bit grumpy and I think she did too, but then she recovered and pointed to us and said, 'Well, this is a precious little cat belonging to these little children – my sister's children.' I tried to put on a sad expression, as though it were my cat missing. 'A marmalade type of colour,' said Aunty Ida, and I nodded in agreement. The man shook his head and started climbing into the van. 'Can you move from the gate? I need to reverse,' he said, and now I was sure that he was cross with Aunty Ida. So we backed up to the pillar at the gate and we peeped round it as the van started to reverse. And just then a short, round woman came out of the house, slammed the front door behind her and climbed clumsily into the van. The van reversed past us. We began to walk towards home. We did not speak until we were almost there, until we were turning the corner to face our steep hill, which seemed especially steep today. Aunty Ida said, 'I think that might have been his sister.' And I said, 'She looked the image of him.'

You've a Thread Hanging from Your Skirt

Momma knew that Baby John F. would have to be our ever-lasting baby. She was a bit sad, because she knew she would not have eleven babies like the woman who was voted Housewife of the Year, whose photograph was on the cover of *Spotlight* magazine and who was even on *The Late Late Show*. Looking at the cover of *Spotlight*, at the woman with her eleven spotlessly clean, smiling children, Momma said she was a wonder and HE laughed over her shoulder and said, 'She looks like a horse.' Momma read out loud to HIM all about the housewife of the year, but he was not listening. So I listened instead:

'"After an interview and cooking a four-course meal for eight people, Margaret Hughes from Killarney in County Kerry was announced the winner. Her prizes include a cheque for £500 and a luxury oven. The mother of eleven says she enjoys being a keen member of her local knitting circle as well as a number of other hobbies. She volunteers annually in the Rose of Tralee festival."'

'Well, that's that,' said Momma. 'I don't even play bridge.'

I don't think Momma had ever got over not even being a runner-up in the Mother and Child competition at Butlin's.

This September evening Baby John F. had fallen asleep in

my arms while we had all been watching *Top of the Pops*, because that was what Tilly wanted to watch and HE said that she was our guest so should be allowed to see at least that one programme every week and after that he and Tom would watch the football. HE did not mind missing the first half. Even Momma wanted to see *Top of the Pops* that night because Joe Dolan was going to be on and Momma had been to dances before she got married where his band had played. She said that if Joe Dolan had been born in America, he would have been another Elvis, but HE said, 'Rubbish.' It was a boring, boring programme and I did not like Joe Dolan and I did not like Jimmy Savile with his gold jewellery and how he kept saying, 'Boys and girls, boys and girls.' Uncle Ronnie and his wife had driven over too because they did not have BBC and Aunty Gertie liked Joe Dolan. The room was smoky and sour with the sickly-sweet smell of Mikado biscuits and shop-bought apple tart and custard that had spilled somewhere, and I sat completely squashed up between Tilly and Uncle Ronnie. So I was relieved when Momma asked me to put Baby John F. down in his cot. I was very good at that. Momma said I had the magic touch with babies. I knew just how to put him down really gently and how to slide my hands from underneath his head while humming to him. Even if he did waken a little, I knew just how to get him back to sleep again by stroking his soft, blond, feathery hair and singing the song he liked best, 'Sleepy Little Engine'. Though it is a mistake to sing about trains to a baby boy because they love them so much that they just get livelier and more excited instead of sleepier, this song is about a slow train with a sleepy-sounding whistle. Whenever Tilly sang to Baby John F., he would open his eyes wide straight away because she sang too loud and too fast and she always sang the Casey Jones song, but I did not tell Tilly the trick of this lovely lullaby because I was Baby John F.'s favourite. It was a bit mean of me, I know, but he was very important to me and I really wanted to stay his favourite.

Just as I was pulling up the blankets on him, he stirred a little, so I began to stroke his lovely hair and to sing very softly in the darkened room: '*Slowly through the valley, Baby's head goes down, gently rings the ...*' My hand jumped slightly on poor Baby John F.'s head when I felt something hard pressing into my back, pushing me into the bars of the cot. *Don't waken Baby. Keep singing.* In that dark, sombre room on that late September evening, I felt the presence of the black demon bird who had stood on the black rock, gaping out to the Irish Sea, which I had foolishly mistaken for the Atlantic. Baby John F. must not see the demon bird. Babies can die of fright at such things. It can affect the heart. So I tried to steady my hand on his soft little feathery head. 'Isn't he lovely,' whispered a voice, the voice of Uncle Ronnie. And then his hand came under my skirt, my school-uniform skirt, and it crept up higher and higher. It was heavy, and hot, and sweaty, and sneaky, moving fast up my leg onto my thigh and into my knickers and then he pushed inside me. It hurt so much and he kept pressing me against the bars of the cot and his breathing was sour and fast and heavy. My hand just kept stroking Baby John F.'s head. But I had stopped singing. I had become a blank.

And then the hand slid quickly and sneakily and sweatily

down my thigh, to my knee and out from under my skirt. I felt a little pull on the hem of my skirt. 'You've a thread hanging from your skirt,' he said. 'There, that just took a jiffy.' So that was it. It was not the end of the world at all. It was just a thread hanging from my skirt.

I stood over Baby John F. and I did not stop stroking his head. The heavy, fast, sour breathing had stopped. I stood very, very still apart from the slight movement of my hand on Baby John F.'s hair. My fingers began to ache and tremble from so much stroking, and I think even he was tired of my hand because he turned his poor head away a little once or twice and gave a sweet little baby giving-out moan.

And then I heard the front door close and Uncle Ronnie and Aunty Gertie saying goodnight to Momma. 'Goodnight,' said Uncle Ronnie. 'Goodnight,' said Momma. The door behind me opened very gently then, and I began to sing again softly, '*Gently rings the church bell . . .*'

And Momma whispered, 'Not asleep yet!' and she pulled the door gently behind her and went away. '*Shepherd on the hillside gives a friendly wave . . .*' I kept singing until my singing became just mumbling and then a humming with no notes. I stood there, leaning over Baby; the whole room closed in around me and I was in a shoebox, dark with no air holes; tussles of tissue paper enclosed me, pressing against me and making my mouth drier and drier. And I did not try to move because there was no space around me, only cardboard walls and a terrible stillness and a choking quietness and no air for me at all. And I wondered how I had become so small that I could fit into this terrible airless cardboard shoebox.

How am I in this shoebox? How can I move? How will I ever get out of this box? It is like a jail. And my head spun round and round; and even though I had stopped singing and was just humming a kind of nothingness, the song wouldn't get out of my head. It went on and on and on . . . And I can't remember if I cried. Do you need air to cry?

Dying

I lay down, twisted and turned, sat up for a while, and then lay back down and then sat up again. I tried to read my book, but my hands were so cold outside the covers that I couldn't follow the story. Then my pyjamas grew too hot, and then they turned as cold as snakeskin and I felt a big heavy stone stuck in my throat. I was dying. All the singing and all the humming had given me throat disease, like Madeleine Flynn's grandad who had died of it and Madeleine said he couldn't even swallow jelly in the end. The thought made me leap out of bed. I stared at Cissy, who kept turning and smacking her lips and giving little Cissy sleep sighs. I went and peeped through the crack in Cecil's bedroom door, but he was fast asleep and completely still. And his little chubby arm was sticking out through the cot bars and that wasn't surprising because Momma was always saying, 'He'll be ready for a big-boy bed soon.' I wished I could go and tuck his arm in because I knew that would waken him and then I could bring him in beside me.

I could hardly swallow now. I wished I could scream out

to try and get the lump to budge, but I had to be as quiet as I could because I didn't want to waken everyone. Then by mistake I wished a wicked thing, the most wicked thing I ever wished in my whole life: I wished that HE was dead in a car crash, because if he was dead I could have just gone into Momma and got in beside her. And I knew what I wished was a terrible, terrible, evil sin. I could hardly believe that I had wished it. And when I got back into bed, I couldn't stop imagining the car crash and I kept thinking, *Oh no, poor Daddy, poor Daddy*. I crushed my hands together and prayed really, really hard to cancel out my wish.

Then I crushed them together again and prayed for day, but then, when it started to get bright, it was a terrible brightness that pushed against my eyes like two fat thumbs. I got dressed and hid my pyjamas under the bed because they were so sweaty that I thought Tilly might think I had wet the bed. I sat and stared at Cissy. Each time she moved, I got my hopes up and thought she might be wakening, and I thought, *At last it is morning and I will hear Cissy's chatter*. But each time she stirred it turned out to be just a false alarm.

I don't know what happened then, because next thing Cissy was the one looking down at me and shaking me by the shoulder and asking me if I had slept in my school uniform all night – and with my shoes on. I got such a fright because I couldn't even recognize Cissy's eyes. It was really strange. Then I asked her, 'Is it morning?'

Momma and Tom and Cissy and the little ones were all gathered around the table, some sitting, some standing over their
bowls of cornflakes. HE stood away from the table in the
corner because he was wearing his suit and he did not like to
be near the little ones when he wore his suit because they
were milky and sticky, he said, and he could not be expected
to go to the office milky and sticky. Momma went back and
forth, filling HIS coffee cup from the stainless-steel jug of
Nescafé which she made for him every morning because that
was how he liked his coffee made. HE did not even have
toast in the mornings, only cigarettes and coffee, and
Momma would say, 'You'll get an ulcer.' And HE would say,
'Don't be ridiculous.' When Tilly had made croques monsieur for HIM those many mornings when Momma was in
hospital, he had always eaten them and had always said,
'*Merci, délicieux.*' But now Tilly had lie-ins because Momma
liked to get us out herself in the mornings.

I was not hungry. The lump in my throat was smaller now
but it had not gone. So I just stood for a few minutes and had
a little bit of toast with jam and stuck the crusts in my skirt
pocket so that Momma would not keep saying, 'Eat something, eat something, eat something.' I was not in the mood
for voices this morning, not even Momma's. She went back
and forth to HIM with coffee and she cleaned his ashtray and
brought it back over to him wiped clean, and once she
dropped it when it was nearly full and his left shoe, which he

had only just polished, got sprinkled with dirty silvery ash. HE tutted at her and said, 'Housewife of the year, my neck.' But HE was only joking. Momma said, 'Get a cloth and wipe Daddy's shoe.' So I did. I knelt down on the floor, and HE held his left shoe out for me to wipe it. I could smell the shoe polish on HIS long brown shoes with the pointy toes.

'I need to be in early,' I said to nobody at all, and I turned to leave. I did not need to be early, but I hated being late because if I were late my friend Ann would already be playing with other girls and it was hard to join in if the game had already started and I would just have to watch and hope she noticed me. If she didn't, I had to sit on the bench in the bicycle shed and pretend to read my library book.

Momma said, 'Be careful on the bike.' She said that every morning: *Be careful, be careful, be careful*. I turned to leave, and this was the only morning when I did not stop to kiss all the little ones. I did not even kiss Baby John F. But no one seemed to notice. Momma called after me, 'Wait, come back,' and her voice grated like a big monstrous rusty wheel making a terrible sound inside my head. I looked at her enquiringly and I knew my face was cross, all its parts crossing into the wrong place.

'There's two pounds under the fruit bowl for you. Uncle Ronnie left it for you because he said you're always helping me.'

'News bulletin,' HE said. 'The greatest miser in the country parts with two pounds.'

I walked back out into the hall. 'I don't need it,' I called back.

'I'll have it,' Tom said.

'Tom, put it back,' said Momma. 'That's your sister's.' I was halfway up the hall when I turned round and went back. I pulled the money out from the fruit bowl and gave it to Tom. 'Here, buy your Tottenham jersey,' I said.

'Ah,' said Momma, 'Jean is the kindest girl.'

What Is It About Tom?

After that, I had a good idea. *No one troubles Tom*, I thought. *Tom does fine. He gets on with what he needs to do, with what he wants to do.* I had been observing him for weeks, without him even noticing. And so I thought, *How can I become like Tom?* Maybe if I could think like Tom, and talk like Tom, and walk around the house the way Tom did, and sit at the table in the same way that Tom did, then I might be left alone.

What was it about Tom? I began with his clothes and I thought, *I will dress like Tom.* So I asked Momma to buy me some trousers. And then I looked at Tom's body and I thought, *It is different from mine. It is straighter and harder and leaner. I should be more like that. It is a better way to be. People leave Tom alone. If he makes a joke everyone laughs, if he has homework to do everyone is quiet, if the football results disappoint him, he gets a shilling.* And that is how I became a tomboy, while trying to fake a boy's body. I wondered why I had not thought of it before.

Momma said, 'You cannot cut your hair, that's going too far, and it took so long to grow it.' So I tied it back behind my head and doubled the ponytail so that from the front it looked short, like a boy's, though not as short as Tom's of course. And I started to follow Tom everywhere: in the house, in the garden, playing on the road. I would just sit on the wall and watch him play with the boys because of course Tom would not let me play, even though I had gone to so much trouble to look like him.

Then one day Stephen with the baseball cap – whose surname was McCourt but who we all called Stephen Squirrel because his house had squirrels on the gate – called to me as I sat on the wall watching their game of Bulldog's Charge: 'Come on, you can play.' That was the first time he had asked me to play and it was the second time that I fell in love with him. And I thought, *Even the boys think I am a boy now*, and Tom only scowled for a few minutes and then I was in the middle of the boys' game. I hoped that the black demon bird, lurking somewhere high up in the great copper-beech tree at the top of our road, would look down and say to himself, 'Leave it now. She's in with Tom.'

Caroline came and leaned against the wall where I had been sitting. And from the corner of my eye I could see her trying to heave herself up onto the wall and how her roller skates kept making her feet slide away from it, and how that, combined with how short for her age she was and how fat she was, was almost funny in that way which makes you think maybe you are going to cry by mistake instead of laugh. I should have run over to help her, but I had to keep in with Tom. When I looked the next time, she had succeeded and was tapping her skate heels against the wall and watching the game with a wide smile on her face and her big front teeth protruding over her lower lip like they always did. I could tell she was trying to look as friendly as she could. I felt very guilty and sad. 'Can I play?' she called out to Stephen Squirrel. 'No,' said Tom, 'no girls.' 'Yeah, that's right, sorry,' said Stephen. Caroline said, 'Okay,' and she kept smiling but I knew her face so well and I saw the cracks of sadness and disappointment. I knew I had betrayed her, but I had to find some way to keep this terrible trouble at bay, to find a new place for myself, and it seemed that the best way was to keep in with Tom.

I continued to follow Tom, day and night. I got his old clothes from the suitcase on the top shelf of our hot press and they became the clothes I wore every day. Tom, of course, did not like me following him about and was impatient and told me to go away and leave him alone, so I began to pay him. I gave him my pocket money every week. On the nights when Uncle Ronnie visited, I begged to sleep on his bedroom floor until Ronnie and Aunty Gertie had gone, and Tom added extra charges for this.

Well, there's something quite funny about a girl in boy's clothes. Stephen Squirrel thought it was fine and let me play and was really very nice to me. He even offered to call me John instead of Jean if I would prefer that, and I said that I would think about it. But there's something quite funny about a girl in a boy's clothes. HE said, 'She looks ridiculous. What's going on? I don't want any women's libbers here.' Momma said, 'It's just a phase, a flash in the pan.'

One day when me and Tom and Stephen Squirrel and

some other boys from Tom's gang were walking back from the shops, after I had given Tom two shillings to let me go with them, a group of girls were sitting on the grass verge in the sun, making daisy chains. They watched as we passed and then they giggled and one said, 'You, with the ponytail.' I turned round. 'Are you a boy or a girl?' It was a genuine question. And when she asked it, all the boys and Tom and Stephen stopped and looked at me to see what I would answer. 'A boy,' I said, and we all turned round and continued towards our road. Tom came up behind me and pulled my hair out from under my jumper and shouted, 'A girl,' and he laughed, and so did the other boys, and the girls laughed too.

Uncle Ronnie and Aunty Gertie came to our house to watch the Irish team playing football, because the reception on their telly was awful. Tom and I stayed up late to see if Ireland might qualify for the World Cup or something important like that. I sat next to Tom for the whole evening and Momma sat on my other side. I sat still and kept my eyes on the telly the whole time. I did not move an inch. When it was over, HE said, 'That's it. Bed.' I went to follow Tom to his room. I had just laid down on Tom's floor and pulled my blankets round me when HE came in. 'Out,' HE said. 'You're getting too old for this.' Well, that was just what the black demon bird was waiting to hear. I wrapped my pillow in my blanket, and Tom said, 'Yeah, I'm sick of her, Dad.'

Which Is Worse?

Momma had to go back into hospital for two nights in October. She climbed thinly into the car and then I followed the car, blowing her kisses, as HE backed it out of our driveway and I ran after it all the way to the bottom of our hill. I looked at my watch and said to myself, 'I will count the hours from now.' It was half past two. And as I turned back to walk up our hill, I felt heavy and weary inside and outside, as though all of my body and even my heart was dripping down the pavement to the bottom of our hill.

For a while Tilly had gone off France and talked about London instead. How she would go next year when she would be nineteen and get herself a modelling job – they were wild for strawberry blondes, she said – and she would have a Mini car and a central London flat in no time. Twiggy had a Mini, she said. But that evening, with Momma gone, she was back at her French cooking and mixing French words into her speech. And HE followed suit and suddenly we were back with *merci* and *délicieux* and *va faire coucher, mes enfants*. It was as though they were reliving the time when Momma had been for so long away from us.

So we all sat around a piping-hot casserole dish of Tilly's French chicken, a one-pot wonder, and they drank wine and we had a bottle of raspberry TK to share which made Tom burp, and HE and Tilly laughed so much. 'You must say, *Excusez-moi*,' Tilly said. And then just at that moment, as I was joining in their laughter at Tom's burps, a strange thing happened inside my mind. I saw a picture of myself knocking all the food off the table, spilling all their wine. It was a strange, out-of-control feeling. So when HE said, '*Va faire coucher, mes enfants,*' those words which I usually hated were the most welcome words of the day.

The next morning I was sitting on our back-garden wall, just swinging my legs and missing Momma and wondering if she was right at the same moment missing Baby John F., when I heard a strange hissing sound. It was coming from near the house. I hopped down and moved closer to the house, taking cover behind the great fat trunk of our biggest laburnum tree. There by the back garden door were HE and Tilly, both smoking furiously. Her arms were folded tightly, and HE was hopping from one foot to the other. Though they were whispering, it was really angry, like two snakes spitting at each other. HE kept saying, 'You can't go,' and she kept saying, '*Ooh la la,*' sounding crosser than I had ever heard her.

I crept back and sat on the wall, keeping an eye on them through the branches of the laburnum. And then Tilly went inside, and HE flicked his cigarette butt onto the patio and then suddenly stormed across the garden and out our side gate. I heard HIS car revving up and zooming off and he was gone.

I jumped down off the wall and ran into the house, think-ing to myself, *What is going on? Where is Tilly going?* HE never usually got that angry when she was going out. And then I realized: Tilly must be going away, and where else could she be going but to France at last for *le mariage*. At first I was sort of pleased that Tilly would be going away, but I soon realized that now HE would be angry all the time. I couldn't work out which was worse: our house with Tilly or our house without Tilly.

Tilly Leaves for London

I was wrong about *le mariage*. The next week, after Momma came home from hospital, Tilly took the mailboat to London. She got up very early that Monday morning and HE drove her to Dun Laoghaire, and when he came back he slammed the sitting-room door behind him and put on his records louder than he ever had before, so that you could hear his music in every room of the house.

HE stayed in a bad mood for days and days. HE said the house fell into chaos with Tilly gone, and he could not stand it, he said, because after a hard day's work he needed order-liness, made beds and a meal on the table. Momma grew upset and flustered trying to get everything done, and I couldn't help thinking that all her dreams of being on the cover of *Spotlight* magazine and winning the luxury oven would never come to anything.

One evening when HE came in, he tore his tie from his neck and flung his suit jacket across a chair. 'That's enough,' HE said, 'I'll get another girl. I know someone in the office.' 'No,' said Momma, 'that's quite all right. Mrs Burke only needs her woman two days now, so I can take her for the other three.' But HE insisted: 'No, I'll get a live-in. Much better for you.' 'No, no,' said Momma, who sometimes could be strong, 'that's quite all right.' So HE poured a whiskey for himself and turned on the telly. 'What's all this women's lib all of a sudden? I thought you were against it. Next thing you'll be picking my car.'

HE sulked and stalked about the house and banged doors and shouted at the little ones, but I stayed away from him. At night I would hear them argue through the bedroom wall and poor Momma would end up crying and I'd hear HIM go downstairs. And anytime HE came home to find that Mrs Pyke was still there helping Momma, he would pick up his keys and walk straight back out the door again.

And then, HE won. Mrs Pyke left and for days and days Momma had no help and Baby John F. cried so much, just stood in his cot, gripping the bars with frustration and anger, his little face blown up and red, while Momma tried to get us out to school and we wore dirty clothes and no jug of coffee was made for HIM. One evening at about half past ten, she was washing the dishes in the sink and I was drying up for her when HE got up from the telly and stood behind us and said to me, in quite a kind voice, 'You go to bed. You've to be up for school.' I was so surprised. I got a lovely warm feeling inside me and I wanted to say, *Thank you, Daddy.* But I said nothing and as I was drying my hands to leave, HE put his arm round Momma's sparrow waist and led her from the sink. 'Come on, love,' HE said. 'You'll wind up in John of God's. I'll sort something out. You're working on your poor nerves.'

So the very next day Tilly's friend Annamarie arrived

home from the office with HIM and you are not going to believe this, because I could hardly believe it, and Momma's face was so white from shock that her red lipstick seemed on fire – Annamarie was half French! Then, one morning, Annamarie was gone. Completely gone. And a few days after that Tilly came back.

How I Became Unboyed

Although I was content enough to wear Tom's clothes, and to play with the boys on the road instead of Caroline, and although I did not mind the girls teasing me – in fact I welcomed it because it brought me closer to Stephen Squirrel – it was my sister Cissy who showed me where my duty lay and where my heart belonged. For she said to me one day as she watched me knot my hair into a double ponytail and tuck it into my jumper, 'Do I not have a sister now?' And her gentle little voice sounded so forlorn and so lonely, and I thought, *I am her only sister. She has no other. She is my only sister. I have no other.* So I said, 'I will always be your sister.' But I wished I could explain to her how much easier it was to be among the boys, how if I sat beside Tom on the couch and lay on his floor at night, I seemed to disappear behind him. I wanted to say, *Cissy, I will cut your hair and you can wear boys' clothes because I am afraid that some day the black demon bird will creep up behind you.* But I could not say that, of course. I could not frighten Cissy. All I could do was keep a watch out for her.

I put Tom's clothes back into the suitcase in which I had

found them, and I put on the red and white checked dress that Aunty Ida had bought for me, and my nice light beige cardigan with the daisies on the cuffs, and my white knee socks with the lace trim which I had worn for my confirm-ation, and I went downstairs and I opened the kitchen door. Momma's head turned to me at the same moment as Aunty Ida's. 'Oh!' they said together. And Aunty Ida smiled so sweetly at me, and she said, 'Isn't she lovely, Mammy. Some day you'll have a lovely husband – just like your own daddy.'

The Trouble with Filth

Although I had seen Momma tearful, and although I had heard her speak with a trembling, shaky voice, I had never really seen her cry. Then out of the blue one day, Momma started crying and she cried and she cried and she cried. HE had gone to drive Tilly to the bus stop and said that he would not be long. Me and Tom and the little ones were all just lined up in front of the telly watching the *Pink Panther* car-toon and Baby John F. was asleep in his pram in the corner. It did not seem that anything was wrong. But then the ads came on and during the ad for Nimble Bread, just after the girl runs off with the man's hat for fun and the man says, 'Nimble, for girls at their best in bikinis,' I heard a kind of snivelling sound coming from the kitchen. I turned to look, and although Momma was standing at the sink with her back to us, I got a feeling she was crying. So I got up and went over, pretending to need a glass of water, and as I reached across Momma to the cold tap, I glanced up at her for a second and there were tears streaming out of her eyes and falling into the sink. I rubbed Momma's back a little and she looked round at me and she said, 'Oh sweetheart, why the worried face? I told you not to frown. You'll get lines.' And when she said that she had a smile across her mouth, a broad happy smile, but the tears kept pouring and pouring out of her eyes which were so light brown now from the streams of water lying in them. 'Go on,' she said, 'I'd like you to sit and watch your programme. Go on. I'm going to make a few buns and you can ice them.'

She began weighing out ingredients and beating the eggs into the butter with the wooden spoon. Then she folded in the flour carefully and patiently and, seeing me watching her, she smiled and said, 'Now we don't want lumpy buns, do we?' And I tried to smile back at her, and even as she smiled again so broadly at me, the tears flowed and flowed and flowed and some of them plopped into our bun mixture. 'Oh my goodness,' said Momma, wiping her face with the tea towel, 'we don't want salty buns either, do we? No, no, no, no salty buns.' Then she cracked so many eggs at the side of the bowl that she had to go to the fridge and get more and crack them too. She must have cracked at least a dozen, and I thought, *The whole world is broken*. Baby John F. woke and she said, 'Now bring him to his cot, Jeannie, there's the best girl. The best girl.'

When I came back to the kitchen later, Tom and Cissy and the little ones had all gone to bed. Momma was standing on a chair now, emptying the presses and putting everything out on the counters, wiping the surfaces of the shelves and the doors and the door handles. 'Put the kettle on there, my love,' she said in a cheerful voice. 'We'll have a bun and a cup of tea. Just us girls. Just us two.' So I put the kettle on and we had tea, and although I sat at the table for mine, she drank her tea standing on the chair as she wiped the presses. 'It's good to keep things clean,' she said, 'really, really clean. Things can hardly be clean enough when you have a young family. I should have done this years ago, my love. I just couldn't see it. I feel great now. So livened up. Sitting around is very bad for you, my sweetheart. Remember that. I was just sitting there and all this filth was building up around me. Isn't that shocking – how it can build up! My God, the foolishness of it. Look at the dirt in the water in the basin! The filth! Here, look, you take this little cloth and wipe over all the jars – they're all sticky. Good girl. You're the best girl, Jeannie, do you know that? I'd be so lost without you. Now. Good girl. That's it.' I wanted to say, *You're crying, Momma, you're crying. You have to stop. Your body will run out of water. You're only human.* But it was just not possible to say that. 'Now,' she said, climbing down off the chair, 'that one's done.' And then she pulled the chair along to the next section of presses, and she pulled it so fast that it made a screaming sound along the tiles. 'Nearly finished,' she kept saying. 'Now how would you say that in French? Hmmm? What do you think, Jeannie? How would you say that in French?' And then I started to cry. It just came with no warning, and after all my efforts to remain calm, not to cry, to bite my lip, I burst into tears like one of the little ones when they fell over in a game of chasing, when they first noticed their knee was split open and the blood gushed. As if to say, *Stop the game.*

She climbed down from the chair and with her rubber gloves still on she pulled me close to her and held me so tightly. She kissed the top of my head over and over. 'Now, now, Jeannie. What are the tears for? You think I am crying, is that it? Is that it? I don't know where all of these tears are coming from because I am not actually crying. Sure look at me.' And she held me away from her and beamed the broadest smile I have ever seen on her face and her eyes glistened in the way that Baby John F.'s eyes glistened when you gave him something sweet to eat. 'You see that,' she said. 'It's the relief of getting things done. That's all. This filth has been on my mind for ages. Gnawing away at the back of my mind like a filthy little demon.' I nodded as though I understood completely. 'Do you understand now?' she asked, still holding me at arm's length from her. I nodded again as convincingly as I could and tried to wipe my tears. But now I was like Momma and they just wouldn't stop. 'So now,' she said, 'will we get on? Come on, you keep wiping those sticky jars. Sure Daddy hates sticky jars, isn't that right? We'll have it lovely for him and Tilly when they come in and she will say – *ooh la la* – or something – *ooh la la*. Or what will she say, Jeannie? What do you think she will say?'

And she climbed back up onto the chair and began to take all the cereal boxes and bags of flour and sugar out of the cupboard and put them onto the counter. 'Just keep going, my love. That's the key – just keep going.'

By the time HE got back with Tilly, the kitchen was

sparkling but Momma had not yet had a chance to put the jars and boxes and packets back into the presses. 'Now, they'll take a while to dry,' she had said before they came in, 'and we don't want the packets and boxes wet now, do we, my love?' When HE came into the kitchen, the long hand of the clock had just clicked onto the 3, making it 1.15 a.m. Way past midnight and the latest I had ever been up. 'What are you doing up?' HE said, very crossly indeed. But then HE saw the bags and packets and boxes all over the counters and the table, and Momma, still up high, was standing on the countertop now instead of on the chair and she was reaching along the tops of the highest presses. 'Ugh,' she said, 'covered in sticky fat – from frying I would say. Do you see that, Edmund? The filth of it. The filth.' And then HE looked very, very startled indeed. 'Get down,' HE said, but she ignored him. 'This filth cannot be allowed to take over the house,' and she dug deeper into the wood with her tiny sparrow bones jutting out of her elbow. 'Get down,' HE said, and he walked over to her, grabbed her arm and started to pull her down towards him. Well, she could not stop laughing. And HE turned to me: 'You go to bed. Out now.' I began towards the door, but I stopped when I reached it because I did not like him pulling Momma's poor sparrow arm like that. And HE pulled her hard and she jerked towards him, but she pulled away with all her strength, and she stuck her foot into the basin of water and suddenly she gave a great kick and the whole basin of water, which was grimy and cold, spilled all over his trousers and his shoes. And HE was still wearing his office clothes! But even then, she could not stop laughing.

And then, very roughly indeed, HE grabbed both her arms and he pulled her down off the counter and she landed on one knee on the floor. She was laughing more than ever now, and all her tears were mixed in a mess around her hair and her face. And then she began scraping at a piece of dirt on the tiles with her nail. 'Filthy, filthy, filthy.' HE stepped away from her and looked at her with disgust. 'Jesus Christ,' HE said, 'Jesus Christ, what's wrong with you?' And I wanted to help Momma now and get HIM to stop staring at her with such a nasty look, so I said, 'It's the filth.' 'Get out!' HE roared, but at least I had distracted him and got his fiery eyes off Momma. So I slipped through the door quietly but I went back straight away and stood really still, peeping round the door, because I was afraid of what HE might do. Momma just could not stop laughing and the tears still rolled and rolled, and I knew that by now her body must be almost completely out of water. HE put his arm around her waist and sort of pulled her across the kitchen, with her bare feet sliding on the floor. And she was flapping against HIM like a rag doll. She said, 'Are they your keys on the counter?' She picked them up and she held them close to HIS face and she said, 'I told you not to leave your keys on the counter. Cecil takes them and then you are like a bull looking everywhere for them.' HE pulled them out of her hand, very roughly indeed, and put them back on the counter. She leaned back and picked them up again, and she hit HIM with the keys. She hit HIM hard on his cheekbone with the keys. And HIS arms dropped away from her and then she hit him again, really, really hard. 'Stop it, stop it,' HE shouted, and he pulled the keys from her hand and he flung them across the room. Then HE held both of her wrists in one of his hands and he began to drag her again, rougher than before. I ran in: 'Leave her alone, please, please, leave her alone.' And HE reached out with his arm and swept me aside as though I were as light as a balloon. And Momma said, 'Oh no, no, Jeannie. It's just a game. It's Daddy's favourite game, *le plus préféré dans tout le monde.*'

HE half carried, half dragged her into their bedroom. The bedroom door shut and I went and lay on my bed. For a while all I heard was the prickly, crackling, fizzy sort of silence bouncing around inside my ears, and then that ring-ing bell that I sometimes heard. I jumped out of my skin when Cissy smacked her lips together and then turned in her bed to settle again. And then I heard their bedroom door open and HIS steps on the stairs. I waited until HE was at the bottom and then, with my heart thrashing, I crept quickly to the door into Momma's room and stood watching her. She lay on the bed, on her back, very still in her white slip, and through the dim lamplight her red lipstick shone. I couldn't tell if she was breathing. I crept across the floor, my toes picking out obstacles that might have made a sound, and I stood over Momma. Her eyes were open and staring at the ceiling. After a few moments her gaze turned towards me, but just for a moment, and she put her hand on her beautiful rose mouth and blew me a kiss. And it was only then that I noticed how raw and red her hands were from hours of scrubbing out the filth. Footsteps then on the first three steps of our stairs, the second step squeaking a little as it only did under HIS foot and no one else's.

I crept back to my bed and lay there, still and stealthy, listening until the ceiling turned grey and then white; and then the crows began their day. Caw, caw, caw. A terrible sound. Caw, caw, caw.

A Dangerous Lunatic

So it was morning. But still that part of morning where the night hangs on and the crows were the only ones parading their brutal song. My stomach was turning and a bitter taste clung to my tongue, like the taste that I found so hard to get rid of after I had had the chickenpox. I lay still. And then, at last, movement. A sound other than the caw, caw, caw. A quiet clicking as Tilly's hand pulled her bedroom door shut and her massive blue-stone ring tapped on the door handle as it always did. Steps on the stairs, going down. The front door. Open. Quiet again. Shoes on the gravel. I pulled the curtain back, but not so much that HE might see should he unexpectedly glance up, and not so much that the light might waken Cissy. HE walked with Tilly as far as the gate, and then she walked away, down towards the bus stop. HE stood and watched her for a while. Then HE walked up and down our driveway for a long time, smoking.

I got back into bed and I wondered what was going on. Tilly always went out on a Saturday because it was her day off, but never this early. It was barely bright. I thought, *Now HE will be in a terrible mood all day*. I would not go downstairs alone. I would wait for Cissy to waken. I closed my burning eyes but I couldn't get to sleep. I wanted to go back in to Momma to check on her, but it was too risky. I tried really hard to think of other things. At last I was able to imagine the smell of the leather seats in Caroline's father's car, and then the sand in Silver Strand was warm beneath my bare feet.

When I woke, Baby John F. was sitting on my tummy, sucking his soother rhythmically. So the world had not ended. I rocked him a little and made the sound of a car engine and he said, 'Beep, beep.' Then I bounced him up and down and sang until the sound of an unknown man's voice came through the wall. And then I remembered what had happened the night before.

Baby John F. and I got up and stood in the doorway to our parents' bedroom. HE was standing by the window, his arms folded, watching as the doctor examined Momma. The doctor wore a brown suit, and from the back his hair was black and curly with some silver threads running in and out of the tight curls. The room was silent, except for when the doctor said, 'Breathe in . . . and out,' and, 'Well now.' And I heard Momma's breathing, in and out, and Baby John F. must have been listening carefully too as after a few minutes he seemed to be sucking on his soother to the same rhythm.

'Well now,' said the doctor again as he stood up, and then he noticed me and Baby John F. standing in the doorway: 'Well now, you must be number two and number six.' And HE said, in such a nice, friendly voice, 'No, number two and number seven, Dr Boyce.' And I noticed for the first time that HE had a bandage taped across his cheekbone from the keys the night before. 'Go down now and have some cornflakes,' and again the nice, friendly voice. I glanced across at Momma, so still and quiet in the bed and still wearing only her white nylon slip. She seemed in a sort of sleeping state, but not asleep. Reluctantly, and with a heaviness in my body that reminded me of the heavy aura which surrounded Aunty Ida when she was at the bottom of our hill, I turned my back to Momma's small figure in the bed. I left her.

I shook cornflakes into bowls from the box which still lay on the counter from the night before with the other packets and bags and jars that Momma had not returned to the presses. I looked at the clock. It was almost ten. Then I looked at the tiles on the floor, trying to identify the spot where her knee had landed so hard, to see if there was a bloodstain. But there was nothing to be seen. I was glad that she had not bled, but disappointed that I could not shout upstairs, 'Look, Momma bled and you didn't give her a plaster.' But of course, I would not have said that. Because I hardly ever say the things I want to say.

Baby John F. sat in his highchair and the little ones began to come down one by one, so I poured their cornflakes or their Rice Krispies, or made whatever they wanted, toast and jam, toast and honey, toast with butter and sugar. It didn't matter. Whatever they wanted. Then HE slipped in and glanced at us and went back out, shutting the kitchen door. I hurried to it, pressing my ear against it to try to hear what HE was saying to the doctor in the hall, but I could catch only a few words. HE said, 'Is it a nervous breakdown, Doctor?' But after that I couldn't hear much because the two of them were almost whispering. The only other words

I caught were 'unable to cope' and 'dangerous' and 'risk' and 'women'. And the last thing I heard the doctor say was: 'She seems like a nice girl.'

I had decided that once the doctor had gone I would bring tea and toast and honey and sliced banana with sugar up to Momma for her breakfast. And I had decided to check her knee because the doctor may not even have bothered. And I had decided that I would stroke her forehead with my cool hand, just as she had stroked mine when I had been so hot with chickenpox. But I knew that Momma did not have chickenpox. She didn't have a single spot. While I was cutting Baby John F.'s honey toast into little triangles, HE came in and he began to make coffee. I watched him for a moment and then stealthily, slyly, I slipped out the door. At the landing I saw that her door was wide open. I thought HE would have shut it, to keep the noise down. But it was wide open. And the bed, where I had only seconds earlier imagined Momma in her white nylon slip with her hair spread on the white pillowcase, and her eyes closed peacefully, her chest rising slowly, evenly – inhale, exhale – was empty. And I knew. I knew that the doctor had taken her away, because her smell was already gone.

Almost Twelve

Too Early for Blackberries

With Momma gone, the visitors started again, and they came, and they sat, and they sat. The women with their handbags on their laps, clutching them, and their husbands, leaning back in the armchairs with their legs crossed, jingling their car keys in their pockets. When Baby John F. toddled over to them, they would take their car keys out and jingle them for him and then he would reach out and take them and they would say, 'Here. Come back here with those keys,' and they would pull them from his little fist and he would burst out crying and I would have to distract him. If the racing or the news was on the telly, they watched that. Otherwise, they just sat and sat, and checked their watches. Tilly buzzed about and made them tea and told them about French cooking and her soon-to-be *mariage* and how she hoped that Mrs Kennedy would not be in hospital too long because she had no intention of delaying her *mariage* forever. And the women – aunts and cousins and great-aunts and cousins of cousins – clutched their handbags and listened to Tilly and stared at her and nodded to each other. And Aunty Gertie always looked at the others and raised her eyebrows as she said, 'Is that so?' whenever she did not believe Tilly.

And they stared at us children and said things like: 'Isn't he lovely?' and 'God help them' and 'Sure your mammy will be home soon.' And sometimes they brought an apple tart, or an Oxford lunch, most of which they ate themselves, or sweets for us, or sometimes they gave us a shilling or two, and once Aunty Gertie brought a huge dish of shepherd's pie which HE emptied straight into the bin before she was even out the driveway.

One Saturday morning in July, thirty-six days after Momma had been taken away, and two days before my birthday, Uncle Ronnie and Aunty Gertie reversed their Ford Cortina slowly and almost silently up the gravel of our driveway. The feeling in my stomach was the same as if I had just seen a wagonful of snakes reverse towards our front door. Tilly made them tea after ten minutes of trying to persuade them to have coffee, which was more French at this time of the morning, she said, while HE went into the back garden and cut the grass. I brought Baby John F. out to the garden and began to make him a grass house, but Uncle Ronnie soon came out too. 'We were going to bring her up the mountains for a drive for her birthday,' he called to HIM. 'Fine,' HE said. I dropped the armful of grass I had gathered and stood staring at HIM. I wanted to say, *NO!* but my voice was gone. I had had no voice since Momma had been taken away. The day she left, I lay down on my bed for a long time and when I got up, I discovered that I had swallowed my own voice, which may sound impossible, but it is not. I could feel a lump in my throat and any time I tried to speak I felt my words all caught up on that lump, like the way a jackdaw's singing is caught in a throat that just can't sing. I did not go out to play any more. I did not speak in school. I did not play with anyone in the yard since Momma had gone. Of course I had kept some voice for Baby John F. and of course I had kept some voice for Cissy and the little ones. But not much. Just a small, small voice, a few words from a dry, tingling mouth. 'Get ready,' HE said to me, and I knew that he could not wait for Uncle Ronnie to leave.

In the kitchen, Tilly was reading her *Music Star* magazine and Tom was sitting in the corner concentrating on his new model Mercedes kit. Aunty Gertie had followed Ronnie out and was walking around, sniffing at all our roses. 'I don't want to go, Tilly.' 'Oh, just go,' said Tilly. 'You won't be long. They want to be nice to you. They'll give you money. He always gives you money, doesn't he? Go on.' 'But I don't want money.' 'So give it to me,' she said, 'I'm saving desperately for a stereo record player.' 'Please, please let me stay.' 'It's not my decision, Jeanne-Marie,' she said. And quietly I asked, 'Can Tom come?' But Tom heard me. 'I'm not coming!' he said. 'You must be joking.' Tom always knew the right things to say.

As Uncle Ronnie drove down our hill, I looked through the window of the car. Tom had come out and was playing kerb ball with Stephen Squirrel, and as we passed, Stephen noticed me and gave me a little wave and I waved back until our road disappeared behind us.

Their car smelled like stew or cabbage or some rotten stale food, and Aunty Gertie's boots sat on the back seat beside me and I thought we must be going for a walk together, though I had not brought my own wellington boots. They did not speak to me at all, but then they hardly spoke to each other either. Sometimes she said, 'You missed the turn.' And he said, 'Is that so? Would you like to drive? Oh, I forgot, of course, you can't drive.'

I began to drift away with the rhythm of the car and the stale sleepy air, and tried to distract myself. I would not be out for long, I kept saying to myself; I would be home with Baby John F. to finish the grass house soon. And then I thought about how I might even extend the grass house to include a room for Cecil. But then I started to worry that HE might pick up all the grass and dump it at the back of the garden and there would be no grass house in the end. The smell got worse. On and on we went, further and further away, steeper and steeper the climb, louder and louder the engine, past gigantic trees sticking up out of yellow, rocky hillsides. The bends began to make me sick.

'I want to show you this lovely little wooden church,' Uncle Ronnie said to Aunty Gertie, and then he almost missed the turn and had to jam on the brakes. 'Ah now,' he said. 'It looks like Mass is about to start.' 'Lovely,' she said, 'we'll go in.' 'Well, you go in, love,' he said. 'I want to take Jean to pick some blackberries. That was what we promised her.' So she climbed out of the car and banged the door, and then she opened it again and said, 'As you well know, it's too early for blackberries.' She slammed the door, pulled her hard, square, black leather bag up onto her elbow and joined the crowd heading into Mass. I watched her until her wide brown coat disappeared into the dark portico that was shaped like a giant keyhole. So there I was. Reversing the car out the churchyard gate, he said, 'Well now, I don't think it is too early,' and he winked at me in the rear-view mirror.

Past the junction, past the small sweet shop with the cat outside indistinct in colour, past the Wall's Ice Cream sign tilting slightly in the breezy day, past the tall summer trees blowing light and darkness into the car, past the juggernaut that swept by like a speeding dragon blowing smoke and grit and a great *WHOOSH* through Uncle Ronnie's partly opened window, past heather and tall sombre trees with twisted faces in their bark, until he said, 'Climb into the front. Come on, I'll slow down. Come on.' I sat on my hands, my head dipped low because I did not wish to be looked at any longer by the centuries-old twisted faces in the giant trees, so cross with us for parading beneath them in the metal wagon with all of their dark, ancient knowledge. I sat on my hands and I bowed my head. 'Climb in, you'll see out better. Come on, I'm lonely up here all by myself.' Momma said poor Aunty Gertie and Uncle Ronnie had no children. They would have liked some children, but Aunty Gertie couldn't ever since – for some reason – some surgery, some problem. *Don't tell me, don't tell me, I don't want to know*. 'Come on, I'm lonely up here. Climb in before the next bend.' *Poor Ronnie has no children and now you are making him lonely. You have to do what you're told when you're told to do it or something bad might happen – bad things happen when you do bad things – so hop in front there or he will keep saying it: Come on, I'm lonely up here, come on, I'm lonely up here, come on, I'm lonely up here all by myself up here with no children to love me and my wife fat and mean with feet like yellow* sponges spreading out over her fat shoes come on don't delay hear my voice is getting impatient now do you hear that look how fast I am driving now I might crash into the side of those rocks that already look like they will slide down and bash into the car and if I keep gathering speed you won't go home in one piece to Baby John F., and Momma has already gone and what will Baby John F. do then, who knows what song is Baby John F.'s favourite song you know only you know. This is embarrassing get it over with – climb over – Mass will be over soon and Aunty Gertie's sponge feet will walk towards the car and she will climb in so heavily with such a thud and bring the bad odour she always carries – and now I am on the front passenger seat and I sit on my hands and I dip my head low – dip it low in shame dip it low keep it down because if the centuries-old faces embedded in the bark of the sombre summer trees see this they will be so sickened – they have never seen anything as disgusting after hundreds of years of people in their boots and on their donkeys and in their carts and jammed into their metal wagons passing beneath them – you may pass through but you disgust us – why does he take your hand like that why does he pull it to him like that – your arm is not long enough he has to pull you over a little on the seat close to him there we are it is long enough now – now he is driving much slower now he has stopped under the great sombre summer trees – look down don't look up if they catch sight of your face if you catch sight of their faces it will be seized from your body and slapped into the tree bark for centuries and centuries and when they come to look for you they will whizz past in the car and they will not even notice how your face was stolen on this very very day by the giants of the trees – there is a smell now I don't do anything he only needs my hand here cut it off you can have it I can smell something bad like a *dirty toilet and look how much he is relaxed now and his head is leaning back on the seat and he is sighing a bit like a happy man after a big gulp of whiskey on Christmas Eve. There look he has given you your hand back you can have it he doesn't need it — it is for you — here is your hand and here is your face on the tree bark twisted with the others twisted for centuries like theirs BUT yours is new to the forest you are the new girl in the forest some people say this will pass, that will pass, all things pass, this is a flash in the pan, give it time, but I only have today there is only today for me — would you like an ice cream — why do you fuss so much you got your hand back didn't you?*

The Hollow Brick Road

Two days after I became twelve, forty days after Momma was taken, I was sitting on our front garden wall, beneath the cherry blossom tree. I always liked the feeling of sitting on that wall, and I liked it now as I sat and hoped that someone might come out to play soon — Caroline, or Stephen, or even Helen would be fine. For now, I had nothing to do but wait. But I liked the feeling of sitting there, glancing sometimes down the hill, half expecting Aunty Ida to appear at the bottom, imagining her aura lightening and lifting as I jumped down from the wall and ran to greet her. And these days I always greeted her with the same words: 'Did you see Momma? Is she getting better?' And she would always say, 'She is indeed. Because she is thinking of you. Now,' she would say, 'that's the message from your mammy.' Then I would take one of her bags and carry it up the hill for her and I would say, 'Do you know when she's coming home?' and I always asked that at the exact moment when her hand passed the bag into my hand. And she would say, 'Soon. Oh, very soon now,' and she would pat me lightly on the head. You have never felt anything as light as the lightness of her touch. But her visits were very short now, because when she said, 'Sorry I'm a bit late,' or 'Sorry I'm a bit early,' HE would always say, 'We weren't even expecting you, were we, Tilly?'

But this day, I knew that she would not come. I watched Mr Whyte reverse his Ford Escort out their driveway, slow as a snail through their swallow gates, and when he was through, I could see Caroline sitting in the front seat. I watched them drive away down our hill, and I wondered where they were going. I wondered if they were going to Silver Strand without me. Things had not been the same with me and Caroline since I had spent my spell as a boy and left her with only Helen to play with. Maybe now she liked Helen more than me, and if she did it was my own fault.

It began to drizzle a little, but I could only see its mistiness and could not feel its wetness because of the cherry blossom tree and its full summer leaves. There was nothing to do. Tilly was inside and HE was inside. They were both in good moods. HE had been whistling earlier. Baby John F. was napping; the little ones were lined up on the couch in front of the telly. Cissy had reluctantly and tearfully gone to a birthday party and I had dropped her at the door and pushed her towards the mother and then I had left, feeling like I had betrayed her. Why do adults think children like birthday parties? Why do they force them to go? Tom had gone off to play football. He had become so good that HE thought he might play for the first team, and maybe even for Ireland.

I tapped my heels against the wall and glanced up at the sound of a car engine as it approached from the bend. Stephen's parents' car crawled past. Stephen sat in the front seat looking at something on his lap, so I didn't even bother to wave. His mother was driving. They too were going out. They rolled off down our road. Mrs McCourt always drove so slowly. They crept around the corner in their big American car, wide as a barge. Everything became silent again, warm and moist like our road was being soaked up by a giant yellow sponge and I was the only one seeing it. I tapped my heels against our chalky red-brick wall, but because of the warmth and the moisture the wall stayed silent and did not tap back to me in an echo like it usually did. The hollowness of the day, its emptiness, seemed to have burrowed into my chest.

The O'Sullivans' dog came out of his garden and shuffled and sniffed along their garden wall and I called to him: 'Here, boy. Here, boy.' He looked at me and then back to the grass verge he had been digging into. 'Here, boy. Here, boy.' He looked over at me again, but I could see that he wasn't interested. Then he lifted his leg, gave me a last glance and went in. The road was silent and still again, and I thought, *Something has changed on our road and it is a terrible change, a change for the worse.* I hoped that I was wrong and that this was just one of the bad feelings I sometimes got when I couldn't imagine Momma's face properly. I bowed my head and looked down at our grass verge with the drizzle-speckled spider-webs. My head felt better bending down, and I suddenly realized how heavy it had become. I glanced from my sandals to my thighs to discover that I was sitting on my hands. I pulled my hands out and set them on my lap instead. That felt just as wrong, so I tried dangling them at my sides, but that felt too strange and unnatural, like I had a rag doll's arms. So I tapped the wall one hand at a time and I sped up when I felt this working quite well, until I was going very hard and very fast. Until my hands were stinging and smarting, stinging and smarting. There, that felt better. Less hollow.

Giving In to French Cuisine

I had counted the days, the hours, the minutes. I had counted the cracks in my ceiling, the bricks in our garden wall, the tiles on the wall beside our bath on Saturday nights when I would lie in it until the water got cold. I had counted the tiles around the toilet when I would sit there for ages trying to relieve my tummy pains, the panes of glass in my class-room windows, the number of lockers on our sixth-class corridor. And I had done nothing else but wait and count, count and wait. I had not played, nor learned, nor read, nor sang, nor spoken very much. For bringing her back would take all my strength, all my concentrated waiting and will-ing. It was a bit like the way you focus on the sound of an aeroplane engine to stop it stopping. I knew that I would not for a moment or a day or a night forget about her, because it seemed to me that everyone else had done just that. They had forgotten about her, except for Tom perhaps. We never spoke about it, but we looked at each other a certain way, and at those times, for once, Tom and I had something in common.

We had not expected her homecoming and so had not prepared. No *Welcome Home* signs decorated with the new packet of markers I had set aside and hidden from the little ones so they would not be used up, so that the colours would be vivid; no cake with *Welcome Home Momma (Never Go Away Again)* written on it. The cake and signs I had been planning for the one hundred and thirty-one days we had been without her. She just arrived, apparently in a taxi, though I did not see it. She was all at once standing in our kitchen on a grey mid-September afternoon when I was doing my homework and the little ones were playing about while Tilly crushed and chopped garlic, the smell of which we were all used to by now. When I raised my head from long division to see who had entered the room, I mistook her at first for a visitor, a cousin or a cousin of an aunt, the sort of person who in those days could just turn up. But it was Momma. But it was also not her. Her sparrow body, her poor sparrow arms and legs and elbows, had been wrapped in layers and layers of pink glowing flesh. Her pretty small face was encased in a much larger pale moon face, and her rose mouth, although still red, seemed to have shrunk to the size of a tiny flower. The clothes were unfamiliar: wide black pants with a wide unfastened black top hanging loosely and a black and white poncho over it all. Her hair was shorter and someone had curled it, tight waves rather than her true sleek, straight brown hair cut to her shoulder. It was Momma and yet it was not Momma.

The little ones looked at her now and the room grew quiet. She looked at Baby John F. sitting on the floor with his cars and lorries, and got down on her hunkers, stretching her arms out to him. He looked afraid and glanced to Tilly for reassurance, then back at Momma with his fingers in his mouth now, because he was concerned, and that is what he did when he was concerned. Then Momma got up and said, 'Maybe in a little while,' and it was when I heard her voice that I knew it was okay, that she was really home. I walked to her so shyly and put my arms around her waist, which felt so unfamiliar to my arms because no bones stuck out any more. She hugged me tightly and kissed the top of my head many, many times, and then Tom and Cissy came over and joined in, but the little ones just stared. I turned to them: 'It's Momma home.' Baby John F. ran to Tilly, who picked him up and carried him to Momma. 'C'est Maman,' she said, and he turned his head into Tilly's shoulder shyly.

Over the first few days of Momma's return I noticed how slowly she spoke now, and that words were difficult for her to find. Lots of things became 'the thingy', or 'the whatcha-macallit thingy', and when that happened she seemed very frustrated and upset. She did not get up early in the mornings and see us out to school, though I always went into the bed-room and kissed her before I left, even if she was sleeping; and Baby John F.'s cot remained in Tilly's room. On Saturday and Sunday mornings, she did not get up until twelve or even later and HE took her a tray of breakfast and sometimes she would shout down the stairs for a top-up of tea or more toast. HE was always cheerful when Momma stayed in bed. HE loved Tilly's croques monsieur for breakfast. Momma grew to love Tilly's pancakes covered in *sucre et citron*. She seemed to have given in to the French cuisine. I sat with Momma as much as I could, but she dozed a lot and wanted the radio on quietly all the time, for background, she said.

When she sat with us in the evening, she seemed to have a new habit of staring at Tilly, even if the telly was on. In the daytime, too, she sat in the big armchair in our kitchen and stared and stared at Tilly as Tilly moved about doing this and that. I do not think Tilly liked it, because she did not jabber on in half-French, half-English when Momma was there in that chair. I sat on the arm of Momma's chair as much as I could, and I stroked her hair and I brushed it. Sometimes I brushed it for ages because secretly I was trying to get it back to normal. Sometimes I put red lipstick on her and I showed her my copybooks. Tom sat on the arm of the chair for a little while each day and gave her his football news and she loved that. Cissy sat on her lap sucking her fingers and twirling a little bit of Momma's hair in her hand before she went to bed, and Momma would pat Cissy's leg gently. But the little ones, it seemed to me, had gone over to Tilly.

So Momma sat, or dozed, and she ate and she ate; she ate everything that Tilly cooked. Then one evening while I was reading the fairy tale of Hansel and Gretel to the little ones, I suddenly realized exactly what was going on. HE and Tilly were fattening Momma up.

I began to worry that Momma would just grow and grow and never stop, and I was frightened that one day her puffing would stop altogether, and she would stop breathing. After Halloween, one Saturday afternoon Momma and I went into town and we had cream cakes in Bewley's and walked round together hand in hand until my feet hurt and burned, but I did not mind. Momma puffed a bit because it was not so easy for her to walk far any more. She said not to worry though, it was just her special pink tablets, the ones HE put on the tray for her every morning. She bought me two books in Greene's Bookshop – one was called *I Am David,* and one was called *Go Tell It on the Mountain* – and a new wooden pencil case with a sliding ruler as a top. Then we went to Switzer's, where Momma tried on lots and lots of clothes. She turned this way and that way in front of the long mirrors in the dressing room, and I sat on the floor watching her, and got up and down to pass her things in different sizes, and then put things back on the hangers for her. She tried to find something that made her look the way she wanted to look in the mirror, but her reflection just seemed to make her grimace. She pulled skirts and trousers over her fattened legs and thighs, and if she could pull it no higher than the top of her thighs she would say, 'No, no good.' And her breathing was heavy and tired. It was the saddest sound I have ever heard.

PART TWO

Whirligig

(1976–1980)

Twelve

Goodbye, Laburnum Lanterns

Adults forget that children can hear. I was a great listener, creeping about quietly, keeping an eye on Momma, listening like a safecracker. I had become so good at listening that I could hear not just with my ears, but with my eyes, and I could even hear with my feet, which felt the vibrations at night as HE scuttled into Tilly's room. I heard comings and goings and I even heard moods. I could hear Momma's sadness just by focusing hard on the wall that stood between me and her at night.

One night, it was not difficult to hear at all, because there was much annoyance and shouting and pleading and crying. I got up and stood outside their bedroom, my ear to the door for better listening power. I needed to be ready to burst into their room if HE tried dragging Momma along again with her poor toes bent like a ballerina's scraping on the carpet, and I also needed to be ready to scramble away if I heard his feet begin across the bedroom carpet towards the door where I was crouched and listening. Momma was speaking in her shaky voice, and every time she said something HE just got louder and louder. I couldn't believe my ears – we were moving house. Momma hadn't even known, because she said, 'I can't believe you did this.' And by that stage she was really crying. And then HE said something about a granny flat, which I thought was so strange because we didn't have a granny and hadn't had one since I was really little. His voice got louder and louder, until I could barely hear Momma's voice at all and I knew that she was giving in.

When Momma told us we were moving, she said we were not to worry, that it would be exciting and a fresh start. But she looked worried, and when Aunty Ida asked her about it – 'Is it a bit of a wrench do you think, Tess?' – she didn't even answer. Momma said she would drive us back to Laburnum Wood to see our friends, but I knew that she would not be able to. I worried so much and I wished I could tie a huge rope – like the ones they use on the fishing boats in Howth to stop them being dragged out to sea in a storm – around Momma's waist and fasten us all to the other end.

Merci, Monsieur

'It's only Easter,' HE said, 'not Christmas. We don't have to invite the whole world.' 'But,' said Momma, 'we only have Ida so far, and poor Gertie and Ronnie will be so lonely on Easter Sunday.'

Easter. From my bedroom window I peered down at their car reversing up our driveway that was much longer and twistier than our old driveway. Gertie's yellow sponge feet, spilling out over her wide-fit brown shoes, landed first on the gravel. One foot, then the other, her hand grasping hold of the roof of their new green Ford Cortina ('It's olive green,' Uncle Ronnie had told Momma). Her huge, crooked, heavy-ringed fingers spread and locked on hard to the roof before she dragged the rest of herself out of the car. Uncle Ronnie pulled the door as wide as it would open to give her sufficient space. She had grown fatter since Christmas. Momma was not the only one being fattened up.

Then they fussed about at the boot, lifting out reused blue and white striped Switzer's bags straining with their contents. Though only the tops of Easter-egg boxes were showing I could identify every one, since Cissy and I had stood so long studying the bright pyramids in the supermarket: small Smarties eggs with red-coated toy soldiers on the box, and the black packaging of one large Mars egg standing out against the coloured packaging of the small eggs. The Mars egg would be for Tom, like last year.

As Aunty Gertie started slowly up the gravel path, Uncle Ronnie reached into the boot and brought out an enormous Milk Tray egg with a big yellow ribbon tied around the box. And I knew at once: it was for me. I would stay upstairs all day if that's what it would take to avoid having to accept that egg.

Then Aunty Gertie stopped, seemingly out of breath, and set down the bags. They exchanged a few words and went back to the boot of the car. Uncle Ronnie opened the boot and they returned all the bags of eggs to its dark insides. She was talking and talking – saying something like (it seemed to me): 'Take them out, put them back, take them out, put them back,' because that is what they were doing, taking them out and putting them back, taking them out and putting them back. Finally, they slammed the boot shut with only half the amount of Easter eggs in their arms now, or so it looked to me from my bedroom window. And they walked again lazily up our little gravel path, their crunchy, heavy, sinking footsteps sending our gravel sliding sideways to reveal patches of bare ground, and I could tell that he was annoyed about something. As they passed directly below my window, I pressed my forehead harder against the glass and peered down into the bags and could see that all that remained were the small Smarties eggs and Tom's large Mars egg. The enormous egg with the yellow ribbon was not there.

I stayed as long as I could in my bedroom. For a long time, I considered the Easter egg that Aunty Ida had brought me, turning it this way and that. I read its weight, its carton number code, its packing code, its expiry date, and finally removed the egg in its golden foil from its cardboard casing. *Quality Street Large, Chocolates and Truffles with a Milk Chocolate Egg*, I read. Between my cool palms, I caressed the egg in its shiny golden dressing. How beautiful it looked and felt, how lovely the little indentations where the gold foil slipped into the little criss-cross river crevices of the chocolate beneath. How perfect.

But things cannot stay perfect, so I slipped off the golden foil and cracked open the egg and lay on my bed biting into it, determined to eat only half. Then I decided to eat only half of the second half. And perhaps just to lick the surface of the second half of the second half. There is not as much in an Easter egg as it first seems. They are, after all, hollow.

Tilly's voice came up the stairs then: 'Jeanne-Marie, *tout est prêt*.' I was already in the second half of my first year of French in sixth class, and I knew that was not what the French would say; they would say, *À table*. But why bother Tilly about such things. She would only call me once. She only ever did, so I could stay where I was for the moment. The table would be cramped. Perhaps they would forget me.

I lay back on my bed, holding the empty golden foil in my hand and smoothing out its creases with my index fingernail, in an attempt to restore its beauty. I could give it to Cissy for her art box. I closed my eyes, my tongue devotedly sweeping the insides of my mouth for traces of chocolate. Downstairs the distant sounds of cutlery and glasses, the brief whirring of the food mixer whipping the cream for the lemon jelly, and chatter rising up. Baby John F. crying for a moment, in protest probably at having to sit in his highchair, and then happy again, placated most likely with a teaspoon of butter or a drop of Easter Sunday lemonade in his little plastic spill-proof cup, the bubbles removed by Momma.

I had just retrieved, with some regret, what I knew was the final trace of chocolate from the roof of my mouth (though I still had the little bag of sweets in shiny coloured foil paper for later) when I drew in a sharp breath, sensing that someone was watching me. Someone had come into the room. From where? Through my closed eyelids, I felt a shadow suddenly cast directly over me. I dared not open my eyes. I did not want to see. I had heard no steps on the stairs. Not one. Had I been so carried away with the Quality Street chocolate that I had forgotten to listen? 'Ah, there you are,'

Uncle Ronnie said. 'Come on down for your Easter dinner. Did you not hear Tilly calling you?' My eyes flung themselves open and I jumped straight to my feet. *Get out of my room, get out of my room, get out of my room, get out of my room.* 'Coming, Uncle Ronnie.'

I walked behind him across the landing, keeping as much distance as I could in the narrow space, but then he stopped to look at some photos on the wall so that I was in front of him now, just like that, in a jiffy. As I walked along the landing, gathering pace, my hand already poised to grab the banister and hurl myself down the stairs, I felt my bra strap being pulled and snapped lightly by his sharp claw. 'A little bra now — isn't that lovely.' And then he pulled me towards him by the strap of the bra which I had only been wearing for two weeks and which I found very uncomfortable and depressing. He wrapped his arm around my chest and he pressed himself into me, leaning downwards, bending his knees into me, so that the impact was at my bottom. He pushed into me and then he said, 'Wait till you see the lovely big egg I have in the car for you.'

'Found her,' he said as we entered the dining room together. Aunty Ida looked over at us. 'Isn't she getting very pretty, Edmund?' she said. 'And big,' pitched in Aunty Gertie. At the table I was stuck between Gertie and Ronnie. Her odour swept across me every time she lifted her arms. It crept out from under her armpits, and when she turned her head towards Momma to address some comment to her — 'That's a lovely bit of lamb'; 'I can't manage those carrots, too hard with these teeth'; 'We have eggs for good children, only for good children' – her noxious breath seemed to invade the inside of my own mouth, annihilating the lovely smooth aftertaste of Easter-egg chocolate. And on the other side, Uncle Ronnie's elbow dug into my side every time he sliced a piece of his lamb. His forearm overlapped with my body, pinning it in, and Aunty Gertie's did the same on the other side, so that I was hemmed in until finally Gertie pressed her knuckles into the table, straightened her arms, raised herself to her feet and left the room. Slyly I tried to edge my chair away from Uncle Ronnie's, even an inch would have been worth it, but there was no space; the chairs touched each other around our crowded Easter table.

Then Aunty Gertie returned. She had only been going to the toilet. I had heard the bang as she dropped the toilet seat down with her foot. She never liked to get her hands dirty. When Uncle Ronnie got up to get another bottle of wine (which made HIM sigh and light a cigarette and say under his breath to Tilly, 'Some nerve'), I whispered to Tom, who sat opposite me, beside Cissy and Momma, 'Swap places?' 'You must be joking,' said Tom.

But my chance would come. I knew it would come and this time I would take it. I would not have that Milk Tray egg with its yellow ribbon. I helped Tilly to stack the dirty plates while everyone else went into the good room to watch telly and pass around boxes of Dairy Milk and Black Magic (which none of us, except Momma, liked). Tilly hummed the usual French tune about Père Noël, which was not even an Easter song. 'I think I'll go out on my skates,' I said. '*Non, non,* Jeanne-Marie. Look, it's raining.' Then Uncle Ronnie was beside us. 'Come on, I'll give you a hand, girls.' '*Merci, monsieur*,' said Tilly, giving Ronnie a kind of fake curtsey. 'Many hands make light work,' he said, 'isn't that right, Jeannie,' and he began to clear plates. Here was my chance. I slipped from the kitchen and up to the good room.

There was space on the sofa between HIM and Tom, a space I knew was reserved for Tilly, but I sidled up to it and lightly, sneakily, sat down. 'Hey,' HE said, 'it's too cramped. Sit over there.' 'Yeah,' said Tom, 'you're squashing us, fatty.' But I would not move. I did not move. 'Stop that, Tom,' said Momma. 'Let her sit there, Edmund.' HE sighed crossly and lit a cigarette, and though the smoke kept blowing into my eyes, I did not mind.

The film was a James Bond. I could not follow the story at all, but the colours were bright and vivid, and the chocolates kept going round and round, and I ate as many as I could, even the chocolate-covered jellies which I did not like at all but which eventually became the only choice. Uncle Ronnie had an armchair to himself and I could feel him glancing over at me from time to time. But I did not look. I would not let him catch my eye. Then Baby John F.'s little snore made us all giggle softly. It was so sweet. His face was chocolatey and his long blondie fringe was wet and curled from sweat. 'Bring him up to the cot. There's a good girl, Jean.' But I did not answer Momma. I pretended to be completely absorbed in the James Bond film. Some men in suits and ties picked up a girl in a bikini and threw her out a window. Luckily she landed in a swimming pool and did not die, but James Bond was still angry and disapproving and looking for revenge. 'Jean,' said

Momma in a loud whisper, not wishing to disturb the other viewers, 'bring John up to the cot.' But still I did not answer. I did not move an inch. Then HE elbowed me in the side. 'Did I hear you being asked to do something?' I could feel Uncle Ronnie's eyes on me, though he pretended to be as absorbed in the film as I pretended to be. 'Sorry. I didn't hear. I'll be back in a sec. I just want to get a drink of water.' 'I'm not surprised,' HE said, 'the way you're after stuffing yourself.' So I crept off, not wishing to disturb the other viewers.

Only a fool would hide in her bedroom, so I crept out through the kitchen door into our back garden. I shut the door like a thief in reverse, breaking out instead of in, quietly pressing the door shut behind me. It was not dark yet, though already the moon was waiting behind the great dark fir tree at the end of the garden whose trunk was strangled with dead brown ivy and whose branches always shuddered in the wind instead of swinging like the branches of our old laburnums swung. I crept along by the garden wall, my feet on the soft edges where the lawn met the hedge, the earth moist and soft and silent, quieter and creepier than our old back garden. On into the unkempt part of the garden, the secret garden, as Cissy had taken to calling it. Then to the shed behind the big cluster of hydrangea bushes, still wintry and brown and dried out, and in behind the shed; the narrow gap between it and the wall would conceal me completely. I had discovered this spot when I had hidden there after I had accidentally stood on one of HIS Frank Sinatra records. Another time I had hidden there when HE had had a bad fight with Tilly. I had learnt how to be comfortable there.

I braced my back against the shed wall and sort of walked up the garden wall to the height of my waist, making myself a kind of suspended throne by keeping my back pressed firmly against the shed. I had no book, but it would not have been worth the risky journey to my room to get *Little Women*, even though I had just started a very worrying-sounding chapter called 'Dark Days' that made me worry for Beth and for Jo and which I was very anxious to read. At least I had some sweets in their shiny foil in my skirt pocket. I could make them last for ages if I was careful, and afterwards there would be the paper to smooth out with my fingernail. I could wait. I was in no hurry.

It grew darker. Sitting on my strange throne, I cast an odd shadow on the wall in front of me, but I was not afraid. It became cold. I felt a chill through my new Easter clothes which were meant for warmer days, and I stretched my cardigan sleeves over my hands. I had folded the foil papers into tiny squares. There was nothing to do. Somewhere high overhead I heard an owl and I twisted and turned this way and that to try to see it, but the space was too confined. I could not see it, so I closed my eyes and listened to its hooting. *Tu woo, tu woo, All by yourself — out here in the dark? Tu woo, tu woo.* And I opened my eyes with a great start because I had not expected its hooting to sound so unfriendly.

Then the sound of the back door opening: 'Jeanne-Marie, Jeanne-Marie.' Then the familiar sound of the door shutting, and she was back inside.

Without warning, it suddenly became almost completely dark: a black cloud had passed across the bright moon. It began to drizzle, and a sort of mist drifted through the gap between the shed and the wall. I thought of Dracula. Conditions seemed ideal for the Count: the obscured moon; the watching owl; the girl alone, cast out into the darkness. I kept my eye on each entrance to my hiding place, looking to the right and then to the left, and I determined that Count Dracula could only enter from one side of the back of the shed, so that on first sight of him, I could make a dash to the gap at the other end and run to the house. As long as – as long as someone hadn't turned the key in the back door!

It was time to move, to get inside, out of this increasingly scary night – if I could. First I needed to get closer to the house to see if there was any sign that Uncle Ronnie had left. I crept to the weeping copper-beech bush, which sat crouching against the drizzle in the middle of the garden and served in the daylight as a den for the little ones. I crouched down with it. The big fluorescent light in the kitchen came on and suddenly a twenty-foot-tall shadow sprawled across the lawn. First I thought it was the Count standing behind me, but then I realized that it was my own shadow and that if I did not crouch down even lower and move further back someone glancing from the kitchen would spot me. I peered around the wet branches to see Uncle Ronnie and Aunty Gertie gathering up their coats in the brightness of the kitchen. He shoved her handbag into her arms. She must have misplaced it and he had gotten annoyed and impatient. They were leaving. I was overjoyed. I could go in. I was so cold in my summery clothes. I could go in any minute now.

The kitchen light went off and the garden grew creepy

again. I peered through the branches behind me to make sure that the Count was not about and then I looked at my watch and decided to wait precisely eight minutes. But when eight minutes had passed, I thought better of it and decided to wait another four. I held my watch between my thumb and my index finger, watching it like James Bond waiting for a bomb to detonate. But then I thought, *Better to wait another ten, to be on the safe side.* So I did. I watched the long hand of my watch crawl to the 8, making it 10.40, and then I crept along the side of the garden on the soft moist earth where the lawn met the hedge, and finally to the back door where I slipped inside, leaping the step up to our back door.

Uncle Ronnie and Gertie had left. I was sure they had because the porch light was turned off. I crept up the stairs, silently opening Momma's door to check on her. Only a soft bedside lamp draped in Momma's silk scarf with the robins on it was lit, and Momma was snoring lightly. She had started snoring ever since she had begun taking the medication. I heard her nightly through the walls and then I would hear him creep off; disturbed by her snoring, he would creep off to sleep elsewhere. She was at the early-evening snoring stage now, so it was soft and musical in its way, a sound I had grown to like. Away with the birds was Momma, safe and sound.

I crept into my bedroom, not wishing to disturb Cissy, and I sat to undo my shoes which were wet from the dew and the drizzle of the spring night. I glanced over at Cissy. What? What was she wearing on her head? What was my sister wearing on her head? I moved closer to see. I moved the bedside lamp closer in case I was hallucinating. Tied around Cissy's head was the yellow ribbon from the huge Milk Tray egg that Ronnie had taken out and put back in the boot of his new olive-green Ford Cortina. I shook Cissy. She did not want to waken and grumbled back at me. 'Cissy, Cissy,' I said, shaking her harder, 'where did you get that ribbon?' 'Stop,' said Cissy grumpily, so I pulled her up into a sitting position. She was startled and annoyed. 'Tell me now, Cissy, please. Who gave you that ribbon?' 'Uncle Ronnie,' she said, and she flopped back down. 'When, when?' I said. 'When did he give it to you?' But she would not answer and had fallen immediately back into a heavy, chocolatey sleep.

I leaped to my feet and raced down the stairs and into the good room. I threw open the door and I did not care that Johnny Mathis was singing about himself and Mrs Jones and I did not care that HE and Tilly were sitting so close together on the couch. 'Tilly, when did Uncle Ronnie give Cissy that Easter egg?' Tilly looked confused. HE just stared at me, looking as though he was about to lose his temper. 'What are you talking about?' asked Tilly. 'When – when did he give her the egg?' I asked again. HE stood up and took my arm for a moment to turn me around, and with the palm of his hand pressing into my shoulder blade he ushered me to the door. 'Go to bed, for God's sake. You had enough chocolate. Don't be such a fat little piggy. You weren't around when they were leaving so he gave it to Cissy. Get over it. Jealousy is a nasty thing. Out now – bed.'

And so I went to bed that Easter Sunday much relieved, though only momentarily, for as I lay listening to Cissy rolling over and smacking her lips, I grew very, very worried indeed and I vowed that the next time Uncle Ronnie brought an Easter egg with a big yellow ribbon, not only would I accept it, but I would run out to the driveway to collect it. As soon as their car reversed in, and even before their feet disturbed our gravel, I would be there and waiting.

Thirteen

A Great Muddlement

You can only get away with so much for so long. That is what Momma said one day when they were watching the news and a man got caught for stealing money in his job and had to go to jail, with his poor wife coming down the court steps crying out of shame and because she would have no money now and no one would play with her children. And that is true, you can only get away with so much for so long. So although I did escape on that Easter Sunday when I hid in our back garden, I could not hide every time they came and I definitely could not hide in the back garden, not in the dark anyhow, not now that I had become afraid of the dark.

It had happened suddenly when I became thirteen, just when I expected to be afraid of fewer things: I had become afraid of the dark, of Momma dying, of Baby John F. getting cancer, of going red when people spoke to me, of winning the prize for English in school and having to go up onto the stage to receive it, of getting my period suddenly and people seeing blood running down onto my white school knee socks, of getting cancer myself and dying, leaving Momma and Cissy and Baby John F. behind with no one to keep a lookout for them, of going to hell and being covered in snakes, of getting a brain tumour and going mad and telling Momma about Uncle Ronnie because I had gone mad, and she dying the minute I told her because that was what Ronnie had said: 'Don't ever tell your mammy because this would kill her – you letting her down like this.' And I knew what he said was true. I realized that as I got older I was losing courage instead of gaining it.

Aunty Gertie and Uncle Ronnie did not have all the channels on their TV, and so every Saturday they came to watch *Opportunity Knocks* on ITV and then they stayed to watch *The Late Late Show*. 'We might as well,' Ronnie would say. From my window, I waited and then watched as they came reversing in slow motion up our driveway, he with his arm spread over the back of her seat. And then I would watch as he reached into the back seat for the bottle of whiskey he always brought. Then their heavy feet breaking on our gravel. I could not see his face from where I watched them, upstairs at my bedroom window, but I could always imagine it. And I could always smell his breath. Even if someone just mentioned his name, I could smell his breath. Another Saturday night.

It is not so easy to hide in your own house, especially when you are thirteen and are not supposed to hide like a little child. The music of *Opportunity Knocks* was the moment when I needed to make a decision. Where would be the best place for me to be? Going to bed was no good because Cissy was there. I had to make sure Uncle Ronnie never came upstairs. I would perch on the little winged armchair near the door, and if he left the room where we were all sitting, I would cock my ear to listen for his heavy foot on the first step of our stairs and I would jump up and run out to the hall.

But one Saturday night, long after HE had left to go to the other room to watch the football and a little while after Tilly had gone out, I was in the middle of pouring the ginger ale into Momma's and Aunty Gertie's whiskey when Uncle Ronnie must have slipped out behind me. When I turned around to find he was gone, I ran out of the room and straight up the stairs. There he was at our bedroom door, his fingers already wrapped around the handle. Then the most amazing thing happened to me: I became a tiger. 'You're not allowed in there,' I said, and I said it powerfully, as though I were armed with a knife or a gun. I felt strong. But then as soon as he turned to me, grinning his sly grin, my legs turned to jelly. 'Well, there you are,' he said. I turned away and began down the stairs and I heard him follow me. And although I was shaking all over, and although my heart was thrashing inside me, I felt proud that I had drawn him away from Cissy.

At the bottom of the stairs, he put his hand on my shoulder. 'Have you heard this one? What did the bra say to the hat?' I did not turn to look at him at all and tried to lean away from his grasp, but he held my shoulder in his hand and I felt not like a tiger now, but weak as a little kitten. 'You go on a head and I'll give these two a lift.' That was the punchline. The punchline of a joke is the moment when it becomes funny.

'Come on out to the car. I want to show you something.'
Or will I go back upstairs to your little Cissy??????????????? Or

149

will I go back upstairs to your little Cissy?????????????? Or will I go back upstairs to your little Cissy??????????????

And there I was in his car, in the front seat again, and I would be there again and again and again while everyone was inside watching *The Late Late Show*. Again and again I got into the back seat of his car but he always made me climb into the front in the end. Afterwards he would say, 'Go in now. You're a good girl, Jean Kennedy, so you are.' And do you know that in all those times when I sat in his car, we never went anywhere. I was just a passenger stuck in the same place for the whole journey.

Every Saturday night after the car I went upstairs to the bathroom and locked the door. Then all the tears fell out as they did every Saturday night. I stuffed a corner of a towel into my mouth to keep the noise down in case Momma passed outside on her way to bed and heard me and realized and then died within a second of realizing, and where would that leave me and Cissy and Baby John F. and the others? Poor Momma, lying on the floor of the landing, and me shaking her – *Come back to me, come back to me* – but it would be no use, and we would all be alone. So I took the precaution of sucking on the towel, which helped a lot, and I could barely even hear myself crying. I washed myself, rubbing hard where he had been, and then rinsing in really, really cold water, again and again until it felt cleaner and the parts of me he had touched and the parts of me that I hated were numb, and then I covered myself like I always did in clouds of baby talcum powder. The smell of it always reminded me of Baby John F. and helped me to breathe slower.

One of those Saturday nights, a terrible muddle came to me. It was just a dark, dark feeling. I sat on the floor in the bathroom and tried to block out whatever terrible thing was bashing away at my brain, trying to get in. I stuffed the towel in my mouth and bit down on it really, really hard and when that didn't work I got up and ran my hands for ages under the icy cold tap until they were so sore that they were almost the only thing that I could think about. But it got in, and once it started coming, I could not stop it. What if those things that Uncle Ronnie did made me have a baby? I was not sure exactly what you had to do to have a baby, but I had an idea that it was something like what he did to me, what he had always done to me on Saturdays since that Easter when I had defeated him, because, as Momma says, you can only get away with so much for so long. I was thirteen, and I knew that meant you could have a baby. Mrs Simmons had said in Africa girls as young as thirteen had babies and that was why we needed to do the sponsored fast. This was the worst thought I had ever had. I would need to ask someone. Who could I ask? There was only one person. That was Uncle Ronnie. I had to wait the whole week, for the next Saturday, to ask him, and all week I kept checking my tummy to see if it was growing bigger until finally Saturday came and for once I was glad it came.

I never normally said anything to Uncle Ronnie at all, and I never ever looked at him. But now I had no choice. I asked him in his car. I started crying as soon as I began to ask because I could not stand speaking to him and because each word was such a terrible word and my voice was shaking. He thought it was very funny and said, 'Do they not teach you anything in that school?' But then he seemed worried that I was crying so much and told me to sneak inside and go to the bathroom and stay there for a while. Well, that is what I always did anyhow. And then, when I was getting out of the car, he said, 'I'll leave you alone now.' But he didn't. And because I did not believe anything he said, I worried about having a baby until I could hardly speak at all.

I hated *The Late Late Show*, especially the music, which was a pity because it was Momma's favourite. It was the only time she really sat still for a long time and watched the telly.

Some Pain Is Private

And then it came, blood. And somehow, even though other girls in my class had had their first period, and even though I had heard them in the locker room speaking of it almost boastfully, and even though Tilly had warned me that I should expect it any day – and when she had said that, I hated her so much – I felt that it was all Uncle Ronnie's fault. The pain was fierce and unrelenting. It tore across parts of my body that until now I didn't even know existed. I was too ashamed to tell Momma, and I would not tell Tilly because I could not bear that she had turned out to be right, and in any case I could not trust her to whisper. I bent my body in two on the floor by the bath, and that helped the pain. And the worst was that everyone would be able to tell, as soon as I left this room everyone would know. I would disgust them as much as I disgusted myself. And then I remembered hearing the girls in the locker room speak of warm baths and so I filled one and, without removing my pyjamas, I carefully lowered myself into the water because I felt myself suddenly delicate, like I might break. I shut my eyes and lay back, and it was true, the pain dulled. But when I opened my eyes, to my horror, the water had turned bright red. There was too much blood – it could not be normal – this was Uncle Ronnie's fault. I leaped out, almost skidding on the tiles, and tore off my soaking pyjamas and wrapped myself in Momma's bath-robe that was hanging on the door. I scrubbed the pyjamas in the handbasin. The sight of them made me want to die with hopelessness. No matter how hard I scrubbed, the blood would not shift, it just spread. Panicked, I considered the possibility that I might hide here until everyone was in bed and then creep to the end of the back garden to stash the bloodied garment behind the shed. I considered waiting until the house fell silent and cycling to our old road, sneaking down the side passage of Caroline's garden and shoving them deep down into Mr Whyte's incinerator. In the end I waited until I was certain that everyone was asleep and I rushed with them to my room, poured everything out of my school bag and buried them in there.

I returned to the bathroom and sat against the bath. Nothing could soothe the dull aching, and then the sudden tearing deep inside my tummy. It had invaded every part of me. I knew that now this had started, I would have to suffer it until I died, this ripping and tearing of my insides. I hated God. I made no effort to petition him for a reversal of this terrible misfortune, because was it not he after all who had invented girls and all our bloody workings. At last the house fell completely silent. The strip of landing light that had been showing under the door disappeared. In the darkness, I tiptoed to the airing cupboard and reached up high and then far behind the stacks of bed linen for the monstrous pad that Tilly had said she had hidden for me there, though I had pretended not to hear her.

Back in the bathroom I could not stop crying. I leaned into the warm radiator and after a while some relief came. I loathed every inch of myself. Quiet as a mouse, I gnawed on the cuff of Momma's bathrobe. Bite the towel. Stuff it into your mouth.

Africans

On a dark November evening, when a soft drizzle that had been falling since morning turned suddenly into heavy rain and drove angrily against our front windows, Momma got a very bad headache. The doctor came and feared viral meningitis. He closed the curtains and left me and Momma alone in the darkened sitting room. Outside the door I heard him tell Tilly that I really should not be in the same room in case of infection. But that was the only room in the world for the long days that followed.

There was no fire in the grate, and the sight of its coldness frightened me. I felt that a great darkness was to come over our house. Momma lay on the sofa and she could not warm up, even though I had covered her with blankets and tucked two hot-water bottles in at her feet and her tummy; even though I had fed her hot Bovril from a teaspoon and stroked her forehead for so long that my arm ached. 'That's lovely, Jean,' she had whispered. And though I did not have the knack of building a fire, I eventually worked out how to arrange the firelighters to get the briquettes burning. At last, after I had knelt blowing into a tiny flare for some time, a pale flame flickered and licked and waved about, and brought some light into the darkened room.

I sat on the floor, my back against the couch, by Momma's feet, and whenever she budged, and the blankets slipped off, I carefully spread them over her feet again. I listened to her breathing; first it was loud and rasping, and then it grew quiet, and now and again when I thought I could no longer hear it, I held the palm of my hand in front of her wide-open mouth to check that she was safe. I was more afraid than I had ever been before that Momma was going to be taken away from us. I was afraid that if the Angel of Death came calling on her as she slept, she would give him her hand without hesitation and just disappear, for it seemed to me that Momma had passed everything she did over to Tilly, so that there was nothing else for her to do but lie in bed most of the day, as she so often did now. And when she did get up and sit at the table with us, all that came from her were sighs, as though she had swallowed something very sad indeed that was buried now deep inside her. And I knew that this November weather was the weather Momma hated most of all, for she used to say, even long ago when I was little, 'I do not care for November at all, Jeannie, not for these short damp days – all of this darkness is too much for us.' And if Aunty Ida was there, she used to say, 'Roll on Christmas. Isn't that right, Jeannie.'

The day after the doctor's visit, I had a very dark feeling. I felt somehow that Momma had already crossed over, for when I stroked her forehead she said nothing, and when I held the warm Bovril to her lips she turned away as though it were something noxious. To distract myself I turned on the telly and there they were in front of me: starving Africans. And then, everything suddenly seemed to fit together. I came to an arrangement with God: he was to make Momma well, and I was to starve like the Africans. Until Momma got better, I would eat only one bowl of food a day. I chose Sugar Puffs with a cup of warm milk. Ten more days passed and still Momma lay deathly still. I knew that I needed to renegotiate: I vowed to continue eating like the Africans even after Momma recovered.

When Momma stirred, and asked for tea and some cream crackers, I blew kisses up through the ceiling to God.

The first days of hunger were hard. *All beginnings are hard*, that was what I had read in the Chaim Potok book I had just started. But within a few days I felt as light as I had felt skating down the hill at Laburnum Wood with Caroline hot on my heels, when she and I had both been only nine. By day forty, when I stood sideways in front of the mirror, I was straight as a plank, flat as a boy. There was nothing left of me to grab on to. I was ecstatic with these unintended consequences of my sacrifice, and when Uncle Ronnie came, I thought he looked confused. For two months after that there was no blood each month. I knew that I had fallen in love with this hunger, that it would sustain me, and I knew it to be the only thing that was really mine.

Fourteen

Am I a Mouse?

Perhaps it was from skipping breakfast, perhaps from skipping lunch, but it was not easy to concentrate on algebra, not when your seat was by the huge Victorian window, three storeys up, overlooking the sea. I was aware of Miss Something-or-Other, there at the blackboard, smartly dressed, silky red blouse matching glossy red lipstick, high-heeled shoes and wavy, blow-dried hair, as she tried to keep everyone's attention on the xs and ys and digits and brackets arranged according to some pattern that I could not comprehend because it had been weeks since I had been able to concentrate on anything. Even in English class I lost track of stories, missed the jokes in 'The Confirmation Suit'. Sometimes I came to for a moment to find Miss Barrington staring at me. I could find nothing to say when she asked me what I understood by the last lines of 'Fern Hill':

> Time held me green and dying,
> Though I sang in my chains like the sea

Helplessly, again and again, I was borne away over the tops of the cedar trees whose swaying branches waved me out to sea. I knew that at any minute Miss Something-or-Other might turn round and catch me drifting away, I knew that if this continued I would never balance any equation, but I could not divert my attention from the sea to the digits on the board. The waves swirled and curled and raced towards the cliff edge on which sat my school. I had to watch, it was vital that I should see what would come from the waves, for there was no doubt that something awful was taking form out there in the wintry sea, something that concerned me and only me.

And then one day, the sea talked. Speech bubbles appeared out of the charging waves and rose and sat on top of the swirl. It was a message – a terrible message that I did not want to hear, that I dared not think about, and that no one else must ever hear. But I could not look away. It was too late and somehow I knew that if I did not read it, someone else would. The words were taking shape, they were something black and oozing and terrible invading my brain and I would never be able to utter them to another living creature. *Keep your eyes on the dialogue bubbles. Read them in the correct order. They do not come out sequentially so you must adjust them – bring one over to the right side of the equation – bring the other over to the left.*

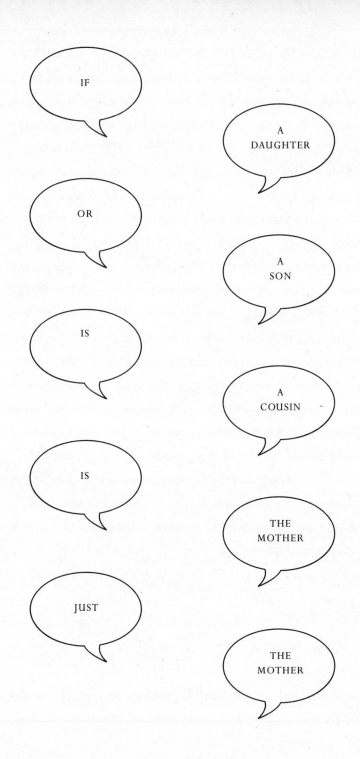

That is a difficult question. Expressed as an equation its variables would be unspeakable variables. Now, Miss Something-or-Other, can you help me balance that one?

'JEAN KENNEDY, is there something more interesting outside that window than on this board!' roared Miss Something-or-Other.

Everyone was looking at Jean Kennedy. Everyone had turned in their seat to look at her, delighted, smirking, because Jean Kennedy's red glowing face was funny.

'Speak up for yourself, Jean Kennedy,' demanded Miss Something-or-Other.

But Jean Kennedy could not. She was stuck drifting all alone in the middle of a very dark sea.

Miss Something-or-Other could not understand the silence. 'JEAN KENNEDY, are you a mouse?'

Am I?

Cars

Getting out of the school building before anyone else at the end of the day was the most important task. If I failed, I would be seen walking home alone when everyone else was in two-somes and threesomes and foursomes. And if someone tried to speak to me, I would have nothing to say. I would only blush.

But the more important reason for getting ahead of every-one else was so that I could enjoy looking down at the sea from the school's driveway, a sight which could only be enjoyed if I was certain that I was alone. The driveway crept around the headland and was full of twists and bends that concealed me. So if I ran the first four hundred feet or so, I could safely slow my pace to look out through the gaps between the giant cedar trees, down towards the scintillat-ing sea below. I loved it most of all in spring term, when on fine days I could pretend it was the California coast. I always walked right at the edge of the pathway and the wooded area, so that as I disturbed the soft cedar needles beneath my feet their scent rose up to me.

Sometimes the cedar trees were a bit eerie with their low, outstretched arms almost touching the ground, and I had to force myself to resist looking over my shoulder and into the dark woods to see if anyone was spying on me.

From time to time I might hear voices begin to trickle towards me as a twosome or a threesome came closer and I had to quicken my pace. Sometimes I had to break into a run to get away. A couple of times Anita Gleason and her threesome had caught up with me and quizzed me about going to discos and whether or not I liked boys and if I had friends outside school and why my hair was always tied back and never loose and flowing like everyone else's.

Did I want it that way? Was it a style choice? Or was it a lice issue?

Sometimes when I looked out to sea, I thought of Stephen Squirrel and Mr Whyte and Caroline and the trips to Silver Strand, and the songs Mr Whyte used to play on his little cassette player would come into my head. Then I could smell the sand and the marram grass. I could feel the warm golden dust on my feet, its warmth radiating up my body, lighting up my insides. And I thought of how Mr Whyte always went for a walk along the beach when Caroline and I were changing out of our swimsuits, and I hadn't even understood how nice of him that was until later. Sometimes while I was changing or struggling to hold the towel around me and my fingers had started to tremble a little, I would look up to check and there he would be off at a distance, his back to us, the bottoms of his beige trousers rolled, his hands clasped behind his back, wading at the water's edge. And now I couldn't even remember if I had ever thanked him for those trips. I ought to have offered to pay for the 99s, at least a couple of times. Why hadn't I thought of that when Momma had always made sure that I brought plenty of money in my pocket?

How unusual Mr Whyte was, a man of contradictions, always cleaning his car but never minding when Caroline and I dripped our ice creams on the back seat. But HE didn't allow food in his car, especially now that he had his new Mercedes that he loved to drive around in and even just sit in at the weekends, listening to the radio and smoking, sometimes just sitting in our driveway for hours until it was so dark that all I could see of him from my bedroom window was the flare of his cigarette.

The Mercedes was black and the bumpers gleamed, and Momma said it was almost presidential. She always said, 'Not at all, Edmund, I don't mind sitting in the back,' whenever HE said that he needed arm room to concentrate on the complex controls on his left-hand side. Uncle Ronnie said that he'd rather be car-less than buy a German-made car. At first, I had thought that was because of the Nazis and the war, but that was not his reason. 'Ford is quite simply superior,' he said. There was nearly a big row over it, even though Aunty Gertie tried to get them to simmer down by saying things like: 'To each his own' and 'It's easier for a camel to enter the eye of a needle.' Aunty Ida had left early to get her train because she did not like arguments, especially between men, and I felt the same as her about that and had slipped away with her to walk her as far as the train station. Ronnie and Gertie had not stayed as long as usual that day either, and it was weeks before they came back to visit. By then they had got BBC on their telly. Tilly was always asking when they were coming, but I knew that was not because she missed them, but just because I always let her take the money that Ronnie left for me under the fruit bowl in the kitchen, the money he said was for helping Momma.

One day, when the sun was bright and glistening on the waters of the California coast, I spotted the olive-green Cortina in the school's overflow car park, through a gap in the cedars. After that, the olive-green Cortina turned up many times. One day, as I walked along the driveway, it pulled up beside me. I did not turn my head. The window rolled down and he called to me, 'Long time no see. Come on, hop in. It's going to lash. I'll drop you home.' *Come on, hop in. Come on, hop in. Hop in and we will drive past the Wall's Ice Cream sign tilting in the breeze, past the cat indistinct in colour . . .*

I had a brainwave. 'Thank you, but I can't. I'm going to my friend's house. Bye.'

I quickened my pace, so that my knees kept banging against each other, and I kept my head down and bent forward like a propeller. I turned out the gate and down the narrow winding road, so narrow that only one car at a time could pass. He was behind me again, and then was rolling along slowly beside me. 'Oh, are you now? Come on, hop in. It's going to lash.'

Poor Uncle Ronnie has no children, it is so lonely for him . . .

'Come on, hop in. It's going to lash. I'll drop you to your friend's.'

'I'm already here.'

I pointed to the gate of a house and then, to my surprise, I opened the gate and walked through. He called out to me, 'Next time.' I heard his engine speeding off down the narrow road. The house looked as though no one was home: there were no cars in the driveway. I waited, looking at my watch, having decided twenty minutes should be long enough. I did not want my uncle to know I was a liar.

Fifteen

What Kind of Bird Am I?

Of all the rooms I dreaded and hated to my core, I dreaded and hated the locker room most of all. But it was unavoidable. I had to go there at the start of the school day to hang up my blazer and get my books before morning assembly, and then again to change for PE, and then finally to retrieve my blazer at the end of the day. But without doubt it was the first visit of the day that I dreaded most, because that was when it was fullest. There were two solutions I could see:

1. Be early for school, say about 7.40.
2. Be very late for school, say 9.15, 9.20.

I made a list of pros and cons in my secret little notebook with the red cover:

Pros of 7.40 arrival:

- Locker room empty
- Avoid everyone
- Make way early to assembly hall

- Sit on the bench along the wall reading a book.
  Ideally a school book: people will think you are
  studying – do not disturb the swot, the square
- Avoid questions such as:
  Do you ever go out?
  How come you still wear vests?
  Why don't you let your hair down – is it because it's so thin?

Cons of 7.40 arrival (= pros of late arrival):

- Won't be able to dress Baby John F. before leaving –
  he will be left standing about freezing cold in his
  pyjamas for ages and will be late for playschool.
- Won't be able to cycle as far as Cissy's school gate and
  get her across road safely. So will worry all day.
- Will be hungry by 10.30 and stomach will growl so
  noisily that everyone will hear and Francesca Mooney
  might turn in her seat and say, 'Oh my God, Jean
  Kennedy – was that you?' (like she did that last time)
- Those early morning builders will be having their
  breakfast, drinking their tea sitting on the wall and I
  will have to pass them. So far they have shouted:
  'Ah cheer up, it might never happen.'
  'Give us a kiss.'
  'Are your knickers wet?'
  'Why the long face?'
  'Any chance of a kiss?'
  'Nice bike.'
  'I suppose a ride is out of the question.'

I decided on the 7.40 arrival option. But my bicycle got a puncture just as I was cycling out our garden gate and there was no choice but to walk. I'd have to walk past the builders, and it would take much longer than cycling. It would give them more time to think of things to shout at me. I could:

1. Cross the road and walk on the other side. But that would look stupid because there is no footpath on that side. They would see I was afraid of them.
2. Run past. Look at your watch when you get close to them and then break into a frantic run – *I'm mad as a hatter, so late, late, late, it shall take all the running I can do to make this date.*

I went with option 2.

I arrived not at 7.40 as planned but at 8.40 – into the bustling locker room, sounds of tinny locker doors slamming, keys being driven into locks, chatter and exclamatory cries; scents of Spanish sprays brought back from summer holidays (*You can't get it in Ireland. Oh God, yeah, I know, I always bring it back when I go*); girls changing for PE if that was their first class after assembly, parading around the locker room in perfectly fitted bras, small waists, small lady-shaped knickers (mine were still child-shaped, as I wanted them to be, and reached as high as my belly button); girls brushing their long, sleek, electrified hair with expensive horsehair brushes, throwing it over their faces, pulling it behind their heads and mysteriously twisting the long braids around sticks like chopsticks, and those who lacked chopsticks proved just as expert with pencils. Perfect girls. 'Excuse me, excuse me. Sorry, sorry, excuse me.' Making my way, graceless, through the long aisles of open locker doors, girls reaching in for books and PE clothes, scents of their deodorants and Spanish sprays rising as they lifted their long, lean brown arms and I shoving through heavily with my straight, unruly body, unscented. It took a long time to reach my locker, last on the left at the back of the room. I reached it hot and sweaty. Now I had an odour too, and once I removed my blazer it would rise into the air.

There she is, there she is. You can smell her.

And the worst then to come. The very worst. PE was first after assembly this morning. So I would have to change now, there in this tight spot, in this room brimming with life and beauty and friendships and Spanish perfume.

At the back of the locker room, I had become aware that sitting on one of the long wooden benches were Margaret Collins (who had a private driver to bring her to school) and Stephanie Long. A conversation was going on between them. Unusual, because Margaret was immensely popular and hugely confident – and even ticked the teachers off, telling them how her family had been donating to the school since 1896 – while Stephanie was not popular at all, a middling girl, middling at everything, not academically weak or strong, not bad at sports, not good, not hated, not liked.

When I shut my locker door, the room had almost emptied and Margaret and Stephanie sat, no longer chatting, out of words I would guess, having so little in common. They were bored with each other, with the morning in general.

And then there I was, just appearing from behind the locker door. 'How are you?' asked Margaret. Was she speaking to me? We had been in this school three years, her locker next to mine, three years and she had never spoken to me before, although she had looked hard at me and stared at me, mainly when she was bored. 'Fine, thank you.' Why was she speaking to me? *Because there is no one else to speak to and because no one but Stephanie is here to witness this.* What should I do? Turn and leave, or stand in case she wished to say more to me? 'Not going to assembly?' she asked. I shrugged, believing non-committal the most acceptable response. She stared at me. She was chewing gum, which was completely against the rules. Stephanie stared at me too now. Then she got up and, adopting an odd physical stance – rounding her shoulders, bending her head forward so that it jutted out like a chicken's, hanging it towards the ground – she took half a dozen lolloping strides. Margaret watched her, grinned and turned back to stare at me. 'Guess who?' she asked. Although I did not wish to offend her, partly because she was so powerful and had been since 1896, I turned to leave. 'Hey, Jean,' called Stephanie, 'what kind of bird are you anyhow?' I did not know, but it sure gave me something to think about.

My Own Private Driver

One October morning at assembly, a few days before Halloween, Mrs McKnight was making her announcements, enunciating each word perfectly as always, rounding her lips and then spreading them widely. Although I watched her lips with great care, I did not listen. I did not hear anything she said until I heard the words: 'Olive-green Ford Cortina.' 'If anyone sees an olive-green Ford Cortina near or parked any-where inside the school grounds, they are to keep away from it and to report it to us immediately. And in the meantime, until it is sorted out, no one may walk along the main drive-way but all must use the back gate entrance.'

A Diary for the Sea

Miss Emily Barrington, my fourth-form English teacher, assigned us a summer project. 'Make a record of your feel-ings,' she urged passionately, assuring us that she intended to do the same.

2 July, Loneliness

I ought to be glad to lie in the grass at the top of the garden, out of sight behind the copper-beech bush, not to be at school, in that deeper pool of loneliness, where I am all the time torn between humiliation and flight. I am strange there. But I am strange here too, in the grass alone, listen-ing. I am somewhat compensated because against my ears tiny creatures hum. This morning a black and red ladybird scaled a blade of grass, gripped it expertly, only twice fall-ing, uninjured, pedalling herself upright, and setting out again. If I was not so gigantic, and my fingers not so clumsy in that world, I might have assisted her, though I think it is her privilege to do her own work. And it is a kind of privilege to lie here and watch her. When I gaze up into the sky and follow the jet streaks, white and fluffy against the blue, I know that somewhere else life is going on. I don't mind. It is peaceful here.

But the creatures are not with me at night when the loneliness is most profound.

It is bizarre, but sometimes at night, unless John F. has come to me seeking comfort from a bad dream, I begin to long for home. It is the most absurd of longings because I *am* home. Momma is here, and Cissy and John and the others, but still I ache for home. It feels like a great emptiness, so vast that there is a danger that I will cave in on myself, because I am hollow. Perhaps it is that I long to go back to our old house and the laburnum trees. Vaguely, I know that there is someone there whom I miss, but I cannot work out who it is. I try to get a grip on myself. I say emphatically, repeatedly, in my head, in those cold hours when I wait for dawn, *You are home, this is it.*

4 July, Lost Cause

We are strewn about. Cissy is off all day at the stables earning 50p an hour for grooming ponies. A boy there likes her. She is worried because he is only eleven and she is twelve. I tell her not to fret, that if they are meant for one another, nothing will divide them. In the evenings Tilly tears off in Momma's car to collect her, with the radio blaring. HE takes Tom to the office with him on Mondays and Fridays, as a kind of apprentice executive, Momma says. The little ones don't need me any more. Not like they used to. John F. is big and five now and runs up and down on the road all day, stays out until it is dusk when I call him in. It is only at night, and only when he is afraid, that he comes to me, settling himself in beside me, and I tell him a story until he is no longer afraid. He is my great comfort. I am his.

Momma seems a little better. She seems to prefer these summer days. She needs me very little now. It seems such a long time ago that the doctor took her from us that I am afraid I imagined it, and I don't like to think of it, and Momma never mentions it.

Sometimes I hear them talking to each other. They hardly ever fight and often their chat seems pleasant. I can't work out exactly how Momma has changed, other than her appearance, but she is not as she once was, in our old house. Sometimes, I find myself staring at her in the warm afternoons when she is dozing. I don't know what I am looking for – who – but so far she has not come. Perhaps I am trying to make out the face within the face, that one that is now surrounded by the loose flesh that billows around it like an oversized skirt.

Sometimes I brush her hair, the way Cissy used to brush her old doll's hair until it looked as well as it had done on the day that she got it. But it does not restore anything of her, and just at that moment when it seems we might start chatting, she shuts her eyes and drifts away. I don't know what to say to

Momma any more. She doesn't seem to know what to say to me either. I wonder if that's why she shuts her eyes. It is as though there is something that we each know we ought to say to the other but we must not say. We both seem to be drifting, parallel to one another, like jet streaks in the sky.

Today she was sitting out on a deckchair in the garden. When I had laid down my poetry book to brush her hair, she said, 'I'd like to write some poetry.' My heart shot up to my throat, but I held back; to react too enthusiastically might frighten her back into that place where she has been so long settled. So I waited a minute or two, wildly imagining how her name would look in print, and then as casually as I could manage, 'I could get a ribbon for the typewriter in the garage. I'd type it for you, Momma.' A smile across her beautiful mouth, warm and loving, but there was defeat in it and I saw it straight away. She reached over and patted my hand. 'No, I don't think so, Jeannie. I wouldn't be up to it. Every thought I have seems to stay with me for only a second and then it's gone.' And she smiled sweetly, as though she thought it no great loss. I wanted to protest – now in that moment when I thought I had glimpsed her – *It's the medication, Momma*. But I knew the cause lost.

'It's too hot,' she said. 'I think I'll go inside.'

7 July, Visitors

Our only visitor is Aunty Ida, and her visits are infrequent. These hot days she finds the steps to the footbridge over the rail tracks too steep, the walk from the bus stop too long. When she does come, she asks me in a whisper, 'Am I very flushed-looking, Jean?' I shake my head because I cannot bear to lie to her outright. I know that she doesn't believe me. I wonder if she has fallen in love again with someone unattainable. 'I think I'm better off with winter,' she says.

Ronnie and Gertie make no appearance. They have been absent since the third Saturday of June, spending the summer in Gertie's family home. They are not on holiday. Her father is dying – somewhere in Roscommon. Aunty Ida reported today that Gertie's sister has joined them with her children. 'It must be close,' she said philosophically. 'Are they boys or girls?' I asked. She isn't sure. Aunty Ida says farmers are the wealthiest people in the country. Momma says, 'It's well for some.' At that moment HE passes on his way to the granny flat. HE enlightens them: 'It's a pig farm.'

It is cruel, perhaps evil, but I hope Gertie's father takes as long as it is possible to take an old man to die.

12 July, Spy

If this house leaves us strewn about, one from the other, at least it is near the sea. When the cloud is not too low and it is not too dark, you can stand on the back garden wall and catch a glimpse. Sometimes you can see the mailboat glide snail-paced across the bay. It is a ten-minute cycle to the sea. Almost every evening I go down. There is no reason not to. Momma dozes happily and never finishes the crossword before the new puzzle arrives in the newspaper the next day, when she starts afresh.

I sit on the wall at Seapoint, a packet of cigarettes and matches beside me, in case I need to look nonchalant should any threesome or foursome from school come along. Though my book is always open on my lap, I never read while I am at the sea. I am too intrigued, watching groups of teenagers jumping off the rocks. Sometimes I worry that they might look in my direction, to where I sit on the wall slyly surveying them, my book open, the cigarettes ready on the wall beside me, but they never do. Why should they? Life is over there with them. I am grateful to be able to watch them. Sometimes I am certain I can feel the cool water hitting my skin as they dive beneath it.

But today the sea came to an end. Distracted by a little fishing trawler chugging towards the harbour, I let down my guard. They came up behind me and must have been standing there for some time before a girl's voice shouted, 'Boo!' I started so violently that *The Grapes of Wrath* almost flew out of my lap. Margaret Collins shouted, 'Spying on us, are you?' And then they disappeared over the rocks with only one more comment, delivered, it seemed, as an afterthought: 'Pervert.'

In bed it is too hot to sleep. The pillow is hard as rock and beats my skull. And I can't stop thinking. I wonder what is wrong with me, why I can't blend into the fabric of everything that is around me: school, the swimmers, home. I know I cannot blend in because I am too strange. I am tainted or scarred or torn somewhere. There is a gash or a wound, across my cheek perhaps, that I cannot see but everyone else can. I am like a bad apple, a grim reaper. I possibly spread melancholy. I contemplate the name they have called me: *Pervert*. It is almost light, and still I haven't fallen asleep. I think I know the meaning of the word *pervert*, but I need to be certain. I go down to the kitchen where the dictionary is kept for Momma's crosswords. My fingers are trembling as I open the heavy volume that harbours the stench of stale coffee and bears the fingerprints of sticky cake. The seagulls who nest in our chimney are wakening up and squalling; otherwise the house sits silent.

Pervert: a person whose sexual behaviour is regarded as abnormal and unacceptable

This diary ends here. Tomorrow I should take it to the sea and throw it in. That is what the sea is for.

Whirligig

In August, when the heatwave ended, hailstones the size of gobstoppers fell and ricocheted off the lawn and dropped down our kitchen chimney, the huge, round pellets flushing out the seagulls and landing on the stove to sit for a moment before melting. The wind lifted the deckchairs and sent them fleeing across the garden to land collapsed and sodden against the hedge. It lifted the summer leaves from their sun-beaten branches and tore out blossom wherever it was still to be found.

Everyone stayed inside and mourned in her or his own way. Tilly refused to drive Cissy to the stables. John lost his temper with Cecil and tore down his Lego skyscraper, sending its debris flying across the room. The twins intervened, taking Cecil's side, and John had to be rescued. The house was over-stuffed and it seemed as though already winter was laying siege to us. The little sulphur-coloured clouds seemed to be returning to Momma's eyes.

And then light. On the 23rd, we heard Aunty Ida's distinctively gentle knock on the front door. She stood in the hall soaked to the skin, her cheeks pink from a fresh hail shower, laden with sopping parcels and a saturated cake box. John tugged at her bag and retrieved a whirligig. In a crazed fit, he liberated himself to the garden and ran around in circles, the wind spinning his new toy. The kettle was boiled, the cakes set out on plates, the kitchen table suddenly alive again.

But the news was bad. Aunty Gertie's father had finally succumbed.

Uses for a Baggy Jumper

Momma had worried that there would not be enough space for all of us round the Christmas table, now that we had all got so big. She said she half hoped that Ronnie and Gertie might find somewhere else to go. But they didn't, and that was how our Christmas dinner table became lopsided. Had it been a boat, it would have capsized. No one had wanted to sit beside Aunty Gertie or Uncle Ronnie. There had been a scramble to sit beside Aunty Ida or Momma. HE and Tilly sat at either end of the table, playing their usual game of never looking at each other when they spoke. John F. asked to swap places with me so that he could have Tom on his other side. I tried to dissuade him, but his pleading became insistent and louder: 'Swap with me, swap with me.'

'Oh, for Christ's sake, Jean, swap with him.' HE continued to glare at me until Tilly set his main course in front of him and he twisted his cigarette out in the ashtray.

So that is how I ended up sitting opposite Uncle Ronnie on Christmas Day. There is something intriguing about a plate of Christmas dinner, and I found myself looking into it, cutting its meats and ordering them by colour, and then by texture and then by colour again. I could feel his eyes boring into me from the opposite side of the table, seeking my attention as he chewed and as I arranged the Brussels sprouts and carrots according to their size. In an attempt to have me look at him, he cleared his throat, but I would not look. I felt satisfied by my own canniness at having chosen to hide behind a long, baggy jumper, though I was burning up with its heat. Determinedly, I stared at my plate and the Christmas conversation at our table washed over me, until:

'Have you a boyfriend, Jeannie?'

Tom, hearing the question, looked at me sidelong, then turned back to his plate. This was not the kind of talk he liked.

'I wouldn't be surprised if you had,' Uncle Ronnie persisted.

Though I still had not looked up at him, I felt his

penetration. When I cut into the stuffing it fractured sharply, sending a dozen peas spinning across the table to land at the edge of Ronnie's plate.

He grinned and turned to Cissy. 'What about you?'

'None of your beeswax.' She said it not rudely but lightly, in an almost sing-song tone: she might be joking, she might not be joking. Why couldn't I do that?

John F.'s boredom was on the edge. He had begun to swing his legs under the table.

'I've a girlfriend,' he declared boldly to Uncle Ronnie.

'Have you now.'

I couldn't resist looking over at him. I did not want to, but he had drawn me in somehow, like he always did; like the way you are drawn to look into a cage in the Reptile House, and you keep looking, though you do not have to. Nothing compels you to find that gloomy, cold corner where the creature lurks, but you do because it has dark powers that have been working on you since you entered.

As though fuelling himself for what he was about to say, he took another large sip of wine, swilling it around in his mouth for a moment.

'Tell me about this girlfriend of yours, John.'

John F. could not speak: he too was topping up with a great glug of cola. Instead he pointed to me decisively, masterfully.

Aunty Ida smiled at me and then looked at John F. 'Very nice, John. Isn't he lovely, Ronnie.'

Ronnie ignored her, as he always ignored her. 'You can go to jail for that now, John, so you can.'

John F. set his glass down heavily on the table and burped. 'I'd love to go to jail. I'd get a gun and break out.'

'Would ya now?' Uncle Ronnie said. 'And where would you get yer hands on a gun in a jail!'

John, still looking defiantly at Uncle Ronnie, his cheeks glowing from the heat of the Christmas table, two selection boxes, the overly warm red, pure wool Christmas jumper, his eyes sparkling and powerful, fuelled by his passion for Christmas, professed his trust in me: 'She'd bring me one.' He pointed to me again.

'Yer girlfriend?'

John nodded. Was he going to grow bored and abandon this argument, or would he see it to the end? He did not like Uncle Ronnie. 'Oh no, not them,' he had said when he had caught sight of the olive-green Ford Cortina reversing into our driveway. And he had slapped his hand against his fore-head and looked at me compassionately.

'If she did that, she'd end up in the jail with ya.' Ronnie was chuckling. Chuckling yet aggressive, dangerous. He needed to punish me, that was his right, for I had failed to meet his glances all day.

John F.'s legs were swinging more violently now, his feet tapping the table's centre pedestal.

'So what – she'd like to be in jail with me.' And then he pointed to Tom with his thumb. 'He'd bring us a gun.'

Tom glanced in Ronnie's direction. But he would not be sucked in. Ronnie was chuckling, some would have thought him merry, but I saw that his eyes had grown smaller and dark and mean.

'I don't think Tom would do anything as foolish as that.'

With every swing of John's legs, the turkey platter was vibrating, tapping against the Waterford cut-glass bowl of sherry trifle. No one else had noticed yet, but they would.

'Yes, he would so,' said John F.

Ronnie shoved a stacked forkful of turkey, ham and potato in through his wine-blackened lips. He chewed and sneered and swigged back his black wine all at the same time, and it seemed as though he had eaten something alive.

'You look like Dracula with blood on you,' my brother declared triumphantly. John and I can read each other's minds.

'Isn't he lovely, Ronnie,' said Aunty Ida. 'Gorgeous blondie hair. Will it stay blond, I wonder?'

'I'm very surprised Santy gave you all those things the way you behave.' Suddenly Gertie had come to her husband's defence. Her mood had turned because her plate was empty. She had filled it twice already and she was angry because to fill it a third time would perhaps be outrageous.

At that point John F., in his genius, exploded. Our Christmas table, already in danger of capsizing, suffered a tremendous barrage of kicking from its hull. Conversations halted. Wine slipped over the rims of glasses onto the white linen tablecloth. Within seconds HE was dragging a scream-ing John F. from the table. I was on my feet in his defence, though I knew I must hold back and would only be of use afterwards. 'You're a bitch,' John F. cried out to our father, still kicking wildly, seeking contact. He took a last glance at Uncle Ronnie before our father lifted him, kicking and screaming, and took him out of the room. 'You're a bitch as well. Why did you come – you bitch.'

I love my brother John. He and I can read each other's minds.

I followed behind them, keeping my distance. Uncle Ronnie chuckled. 'That's the last we'll see of public enemy number one for tonight.' Momma did not seem too disturbed. The medication was designed to calm her.

With all of my being, I wanted to tear John F. away from HIM. I wanted to kill HIM. I wanted to kill Ronnie. But I held back, for otherwise I would not be able to comfort John F. afterwards.

I watched from the foot of the stairs, in the candlelit hall. John F. was distraught, his hair wet with sweat. HE had begun to thump him, slyly, surreptitiously, lifting his fist only a little before planting it in John F.'s thigh. Then HE opened the door of the downstairs loo, threw John F. off his shoulder to the ground, pushed him inside and pulled the door shut, causing the Christmas bells that Cissy had pinned to the door to jingle, and turned the key.

HE did not turn to look at me as he walked back up the hall, but he knew I was there. HE was about to enter the dining room when he had second thoughts. HE opened the front door, fished for something in his trouser pocket and flung it outside. And I knew that it was the key. HE knew that I was watching. The key was for me, it was for John's rescue.

It was almost dark outside, but the ground was bright with frost, and I hoped that I could find the key quickly. The winter lawn was bumpy, and in places hard tufts of grass stuck up out of the ground. I ran back inside, to reassure John F.: 'I've nearly found it – the key.' He was sobbing badly now, his fury turned to sorrow. 'And I have a big surprise for you.' And then I added in a moment of inspiration, 'Santa's left it for you.' The sobbing stopped. 'What?' he said. 'Yes,' I said, 'upstairs, and I've nearly found the key.'

I got on my hands and knees, onto the frostground, and raked my fingers through the crisp tufts of grass. It might have been the most perfect day: the frost, John F.'s red jumper, Cissy's retort – *None of your beeswax*. Instead I was distraught that John F. was crying on Christmas Day. And then my ice-cold fingers met the metal key.

I freed the little captive and held him tightly to me. Though he was heavy now, I picked him up and carried him to my room, pressing my hand into the back of his hot head. We almost toppled over on the first landing and he laughed and then rocked about to try to unsteady us again. I set him on my bed as though he were a baby and I lay beside him, smoothing his sweaty hair off his forehead. I began to sing 'Rudolph', his favourite Christmas tune. I replaced Rudolph with Ronnie and gave him a very snotty nose. 'Covered in wee and poo,' John added, laughing heartily now at his own joke.

Then he remembered the surprise and sat up excitedly, gazing down at me, his eyes wide and clear from the tears and the anger and rage of love and his innate passion for just-ice. My boyfriend, my hero. 'What's the surprise?' he asked. I struggled to think of something, and then I remembered.

I got up, opened the bottom drawer of my chest of

drawers, and pulled aside my school blouses and jumpers. There sat fifteen Mars Bars, twenty-one Kit-Kats, eleven Bountys, six tins of Coke and two small boxes of Maltesers: all the little gifts that Aunty Ida had brought to me on her visiting days, stretching back to the commitment I had made to the Africans in exchange for Momma's survival.

'Jesus Christ,' exclaimed my eloquent boyfriend. 'How did they get there?'

'Santa must have left them. They must be a special surprise for you – because you are so good.'

He looked up at me. 'Am I?' But already he was reaching into the drawer, trawling through the chocolate bars as he selected his feast.

We sat back on the bed. He insisted that I join him, and I did. After all, it was a celebration, a victory of sorts, for I knew that John F. would remain in my room for the rest of the night, long after Uncle Ronnie had gone home. Watched by John, relieved at last, I stretched and removed my baggy jumper. 'Oooh, nice dress,' he said. 'Very Christmassy.'

Sixteen

The Members of the Wedding

As soon as I opened the door to Aunty Ida, I saw the consternation on her face. Barely greeting me, she enquired abruptly, 'Where's your mammy, Jean?' And then, although still out of breath after her long walk from the train station, she seized the banister and propelled herself up the stairs.

I fetched her a glass of water and made the ascent myself to find her standing over Momma, who had propped herself up on her pillow to listen.

'Well, I can hardly go,' Momma said, looking around the room as though hoping to spot something that would help her demonstrate the impossibility of attending her cousin Adeline's daughter's wedding. Then she was out of bed and pulling through the clothes in her wardrobe, throwing some out on the bed and saying, 'No that wouldn't do, that couldn't do.'

The following Saturday afternoon, Momma and Aunty Ida and I found ourselves spending two hours in the changing room in Arnotts. With their coats piled high on my lap and the handles of their handbags wrapped around my wrists, I sat ready to offer opinions. Momma emerged and re-emerged from behind the curtain at least seven times, turning and twisting in front of the mirror, sighing as I tried to offer reassurance about how slimming an outfit was. After a few rounds of this, Aunty Ida emerged from her dressing room for the very first time. I could see immediately that she was in trouble, for Momma turned from her own dilemma to focus sharply on her sister's. Again and again, deep sighs and whispered exclamations of 'Oh my divine Jesus' could be heard; and again and again, each time she emerged, Momma said, 'No, no good. Too ordinary, too everyday. You need something bright.'

Unable to find anything for Aunty Ida, we left Arnotts and sat together in Bewley's on Westmoreland Street, Momma's new cream coat and lime-green maxi-dress tucked against the leg of the table. Asked by the waitress what she would like, Aunty Ida pronounced straight away that she would have a jam and cream doughnut, a fried egg and chips, extra vinegar and a pot of tea. Because it was a Saturday and I had decided that on Saturdays I would eat as much as I could fit in, while focusing on the Africans' suffering from Sunday to Friday, I simply said, 'The same, please.' Momma ordered only a cherry bun, of which she would eat just half, the other half to be divided between me and Aunty Ida, for Momma had been slimming since the arrival of the wedding invitation.

For the first half an hour or so as we sat there, I felt as happy as I had ever been and ever could be, for there we were, the three of us, me and my two best beloveds in the world. I looked from one to the other as they chatted, and I did not need to speak at all for they let me sit, as though I were a child.

But the plates emptied, and the tea became too strong, and Momma raised the issue of Aunty Ida's wedding outfit again. I had seen it coming, for she had been watching Aunty Ida with a deepening look of consternation as she cleared the crumbs of the cherry bun from her plate with the tips of her fingers, then delicately deposited them on her tongue. 'Wasn't that very tasty,' said Aunty Ida. But Momma only nodded, leaving Aunty Ida to repeat, 'Very tasty indeed,' and I knew she was in trouble.

'There's two weeks to this wedding, Ida. We'll have to make a decision.'

'Oh yes, Tess.'

And I could detect the despair in her voice as she glanced at me and gave me that wide sock-puppet smile of hers which always meant that she was hopeless and defeated.

'Will we go back and get the rust-coloured skirt and the cream blouse?' Momma said.

And so we did, before we finally threw ourselves into the back of a taxi and headed home, all three of us worn out, and silent by the time we were passing Sandymount Strand, except for when Aunty Ida asked, 'Are we crushing you, Jean?'

As I helped Aunty Ida climb exhaustedly out of the taxi, I wondered if it would be ethical to privately advise her to fake illness on the day of the wedding, for I felt that in front of her lay a very miserable experience.

On the morning of the wedding, as I helped Momma to get dressed, all of a sudden I felt a terrible darkness fall about her. She asked for a cup of Nescafé, to buck her up a bit, but when I returned with it, she was already sitting on the side of the bed, staring towards her open wardrobe, the tears pooling in her eyes. In desperation, I held the Nescafé to her lips. 'Have this and you'll be fine, Momma,' I said. 'You look lovely. You're getting so slim.' But not even Nescafé could prevent what was already well under way.

Aunty Ida was in despair when I broke the news to her, and in desperation she stood in front of our hall mirror and with a trembling hand drew pink lips upon herself. She was still trembling as she held her black patent handbag with both hands, pressing it against her chest as though it were a shield. HE descended the stairs then, the scent of Old Spice preceding him. Clearing his throat loudly, he called out, 'Tom, come on – get dressed, you'll have to come instead.'

But Tom would not come. And that is how I ended up at my second cousin Yvette's wedding, completely by accident, completely against all my good instincts.

Aunty Ida had climbed into the front passenger seat of the car, but she ended up beside me in the back, for HE said, 'No, get in the back. I'm putting the present there.' As we turned at the bottom of the road, HE glanced at us in the rear-view mirror, then lit a cigarette. 'It's a pity you never learnt to drive, Ida.' HE took a pull of his cigarette and threw the match out of the window. 'I could have drank myself unconscious.'

'Oh yes, Edmund. Sorry, Edmund.'

'All I need now is a chauffeur's cap.'

'Oh no, Edmund, not at all.'

And we sped off. I was in despair. Not having any wedding

outfit, and without the benefit of Momma's advice and her natural feel for glamour, I had had to resort to wearing my school blouse, which at least was white; Cissy's blue wool crocheted poncho that was too short on me; and Cissy's Easter skirt, which was long and embroidered at the bottom with little pairs of clogs and rectangular houses that looked Dutch. I wore my school shoes, for nothing else would fit comfortably. How strange they looked over Momma's nylons instead of school socks. 'My God,' HE had said, as I had descended the stairs, 'it looks like she's wearing a pair of canal barges.'

As we got closer to the church, he cheered up a little. 'Well, Ida,' he said, 'is there any sign of a fella for you in the office these days?'

'Not at the moment, Edmund.'

'So we won't book the Gresham yet.' The old punchline.

The church part was not as bad as I had feared. There were no moments of participation, no speaking other than when Aunty Ida leaned into me and said, 'Isn't she lovely,' as the bride, beaming at the congregation, made her way up the aisle on her father's arm. The church part was con-cluded. Outside, I drew back behind the confetti throwers and stood by Aunty Ida clutching her black patent handbag. The look of dread on her face unnerved me even further. I vowed to stick beside her for the rest of the day, for both our sakes.

Later, as we walked in through the hotel lobby, HE glanced back at me traipsing behind with Aunty Ida and looked embarrassed by us, and although he did not say it, I knew that he was wishing we two had stayed at home. I was wishing the same. Soon, though, at the bar, HE shook hands and drank heartily and bought generously, and twice sent a bottle of Coca-Cola and two bottles of Babycham to the little table where I sat with Aunty Ida. We two did not talk at first. It was as though we were in shock, paying our respects at a funeral instead of celebrating a wedding. And then endless Babychams and Cokes began to arrive at the table from various corners of the lounge, their delivery by the waitress prompting a friendly wave from the generous relative who had seen us sitting alone. And soon Aunty Ida was sparkling with Babycham and commenting on how good the telly ad for Babycham was, and telling me that it was very flavoursome and I would find that out myself some day. Aunty Ida's waving to relatives became more energetic and friendly, while I just kept drinking back the Cokes.

Just as Aunty Ida had whispered to me, 'I think those ladies are a bit tipsy, Jean,' a group of hatted ladies came over to us and led Aunty Ida away to join them on the sofas in the lobby. I did not feel utterly alone until the barman cleared the empty Coke and Babycham bottles from the table, and perhaps not utterly bereft until he returned to take the ashtray. 'You won't be needing that,' he said with a bitterness that made me wonder how I might have offended him.

I had no book. Even the beer mats had been removed, so that I could no longer slip them beneath the tabletop and peel away at their edges. I was utterly alone, while all around me crowds of back-slapping men grew drunker and clusters of women grew tipsier, and as they all closed ranks, the more visible I became.

I lamented the loss of Aunty Ida. I had not expected that the Babycham would emancipate her, that she would leave me alone at the table. Then within the space of only a few minutes, the lounge emptied. Only the barmen remained, and a lounge boy went about the tables clearing away glasses. He looked at me, concerned: 'You know they've all gone in for the dinner?' I blushed and nodded and he picked up the glasses and went on about his work. And then I spotted it, a folded newspaper under the bench where Aunty Ida had been sitting. When the barmen were not looking I retrieved it with my foot and spread it over the table, bowing over it, my head in my hand in feigned concentration. For the next hour or so I read and reread the *Daily Mirror*'s Sports supplement, which reported on the Benson & Hedges Gold Cup, the Northumberland Plate and the Magnet Cup, and with every utterly perplexing word I read, I regretted more and more ever having come to this wedding.

Eventually the diners began to return in dribs and drabs and it was not long before the little round table at which I sat was surrounded by the grey- and navy-pinstriped suits of men who had pushed back towards me in order to make room for their comrades at the bar, and soon the backs of their long legs were pressing into my little table, pinning me in.

I felt the air grow thicker and smokier. My left foot had gone to sleep, and I wiggled my toes, but then my right foot got pins and needles. Occasionally one of the tall, suited figures turned round to set an empty glass on the table, and occasionally one or two caught my eye and regarded me as though to say, *What are you doing here?* Another one looked me up and down, and I seem to have made him feel ill, for he turned away quickly as though he regretted ever having caught sight of me at all.

In a moment of ingenuity, I seized one of the dirty glasses and pretended to sip from it. The strong whiff of whiskey reminded me of Saturday nights. I began to feel sick.

I also began to lament a missed opportunity: when the lounge had been empty, I could have taken the opportunity to go to the ladies. Then, the feeling of needing to pee had been vague and unobtrusive. Now it was urgent, now that I was pinned in on all sides by jolly swilling gentlemen, now that from a distant corner a tinny piano was accompanying some lady demanding an answer to her question: '*Has anybody here seen Kelly?*'

When I was little and needed to wee at night but felt too afraid to get up, I used to distract myself by thinking about whatever book I was reading – becoming the sixth member of the Famous Five, or the mysterious new girl in the first form of Malory Towers. I tried that again now. I set about becoming Little Dorrit, just as Mr Arthur Clennam was realizing his feelings for her. But suddenly I became alarmed, in fear for my life, for I felt my insides swelling up and demanding to escape the tight waistband of Cissy's Easter skirt. I had heard of burst appendix, of exploding bladders and spontaneous combustion, and I feared now that my life was to end with all of my entrails exploding onto this round lounge table. And I knew the solution was so very easy, for only eight feet away was the door: *Ladies, Mná*. I examined the circle of suits around me but could see no way through. And I thought, *What an embarrassing way to die.*

While my vision had been entirely obscured by such merry clusters of gentlemen, a band had been set up and were now singing 'Isn't She Lovely'. Now the men were being dragged by ladies to the dance floor. My passage to the toilets had been cleared. This time I would not miss the opportunity. I headed straight towards the toilets. Since reading in the *Evening Herald* of herpes and its potential to leave a woman unable to have a baby – if not kill her entirely – I no longer sat on toilet seats. I hovered in great relief and with deep gratitude as my bladder emptied.

When I exited, I saw in front of me that the table at which I had been sitting had been taken over by a little huddle of women. Attempting to look decisive, I walked straight past it, out into the lobby and through the great double doors we had entered four hours earlier. I walked across the car park and tried the door of our car, but HE had locked it. It was dusk, and chilly. I pulled Cissy's blue poncho around me and went in search of some place where I could wait for it all to be over.

Around the back of the hotel the music pulsated from the ballroom. I peered through as I passed the French doors to catch a glimpse of Aunty Ida drinking her Babycham with two similarly aged, similarly comported women on either side of her. She seemed content, participatory even. To be truthful, I felt a little betrayed.

I walked across the lawn, ducked in behind a great stone lion and sat on his pedestal, following his gaze out across the bay. He seemed to be guarding the great occasion from sea invaders, or perhaps he was simply turning his back on it. It was almost dark, but the sky was still dappled here and there with pink salmon scales. Settled at the great creature's feet, I began to warm up a little, and we two stared out across the cold-looking bay, back inland towards the Pigeon House, and onward to Sandymount and Booterstown, for we had travelled all the way out to Sutton. Around the bay, more and more lights flickered on, and as they did so, I took great satisfaction in my ability to identify landmarks and rail tracks.

And then something exceptional, extraordinary. A boy came. Immediately he recognized, as I had done, the great lion's purpose and he ducked in behind it. He glanced at me and said, 'Hiya.' Though he wore a suit that seemed intended for a man, he was every part a boy. Every part of him knew of the wedding what I knew of the wedding. Every part of him objected to it. He was in fact, it instantly struck me, one of those boys who seemed to object to everything. He leaned against the lion's huge stone paw and lit a cigarette. It was only with that momentary and sidelong illumination of his face that I caught the brightness of his eyes, and in them his whole demeanour. Though we said nothing at all to each other, I felt that we were sitting together, in flight from something, he objecting to everything, but not, I felt almost certain, to me.

After he had lit a second cigarette, he climbed up onto the pedestal, reached up and stuck it into the lion's mouth, then jumped down and looked up admiringly at his work. I thought it brilliant, and my admiration must have shown on my face, for next thing he had begun down the sloping lawn that lay in front of us and was beckoning with his hand, glancing briefly over his shoulder in my direction to indicate that I should come along. Although uncertain, for I feared perhaps that gesture was not towards me – although it could otherwise only have been to the lion – or that I was misinterpreting it entirely, I rose and then found my feet to be slipping down the slope of the manicured lawn.

It was so steep that I had to look down and concentrate on my feet to ensure that I did not slip, and it was only in those moments that I loathed my school shoes and wished I had agreed to suffer the pain of wearing a pair of Momma's, as Cissy had so strongly advised. But how was I to know of the excitement of this sloping lawn? Once or twice the boy called back to me, 'Grab the bush here,' and then, 'Slow down, we're coming to the rocks.' This advice was offered in secretive tones, and I felt that we were two strange birds – perhaps even the last two of our species – fleeing from a terrible hunter hell-bent on our annihilation.

Before we reached the end of the increasingly steep slope, I heard the water, the waves lapping against the rocks, then the rattling of the shingle. We descended a broken stone staircase flanked by a rusty handrail, and there he warned, 'The whole step is missing here.' He sat first while I held back a few feet from him, gazing out across the water. We had arrived at the most perfect of beaches on which I had ever set foot. It was so tiny that it seemed carved into the cliff face for only two people. A full moon fell on the water so that it seemed a perfect screen.

He sat with a freshly lit cigarette hanging from his lips, and then began to pick up handfuls of pebbles and cast them into the water, but he did not do so like an ordinary boy; he did not draw his arm back and fling them, like Tom or the twins might have done. Instead, he swung them artfully into the water as though he were feeding some delicate animal. When he had delivered two full handfuls of pebbles, he gathered a third and without turning around to me, he stretched out his open hand and offered them to me. I hurried towards him, my canal barges slipping on the stony, shifting foundation beneath my feet. I was shy about touching his hand, so I just skimmed off the top layer of pebbles, but he continued to hold his palm open to me so that I had no choice but to accept the fullness of his gift, and my fingertips slipped along his open palm. I began in imitation of him to swing the pebbles just beyond the water's edge, and he watched as each little pebble hopped against the shallow, slow-moving water.

When I next turned to him, he was swigging from a pocket-sized bottle of vodka. And I don't know if it was that that made me do it, but I sat beside him, a little below him on the flat rock, and next thing the bottle of vodka was hovering in front of me as an offering, an act of sharing, of recognition, of communion. This was to be my very first drink.

The burning in my throat excited me greatly. I felt bad. For the first time in my life, I felt bad. Apart from everyone. I felt that I had, with that swig from his bottle, separated myself out from the others, even from Momma. After the second swig, I held the bottle neck at my lips moments after I had already swallowed, for I could taste the boy's lips, though I had not yet looked upon them.

I returned the bottle to him and stretched my legs in front of me, then discreetly discarded my canal barges and pushed them aside so that he could not see them. I regarded my feet in a new light, quite favourably, as they sat one on top of the other in the nylon stockings. How comparatively small they looked, neat, like a girl's, perhaps like Momma's had looked when she had been slim and when her thick chestnut hair had sat on her shoulders like Natalie Wood's.

When I looked out once more across the water, the great silver screen seemed to shimmer more cheerily, and even dark patches of sea bore nothing foreboding or worrying. It occurred to me that this little beach was a film set constructed to contain only me and this boy, for it was too small for even one more person. It occurred to me that I was dreaming.

The bottle appeared hovering before me, and on the third swallowing of the magical silver liquid I felt a wonderful rush through my entire body. It began in my shoulders and seemed to pause in my elbows as though it were an engine revving up for a final surge, then gushed even into my toes. Next came the cigarette, already lit, hovering before me, another irresistible gift, another instrument of my separation. I drew on it and almost choked from an urge to cough but I fought through it, and blew the smoke out, expelling it as far from me as I could. I glanced at the cigarette between my fingers, and it seemed to me that it looked elegant, that I was holding it in precisely the right manner, perhaps like

Gloria Gilbert in the book I was reading – *The Beautiful and Damned* – whose elegance so captivated Anthony Patch.

By then we two had laughed at something, but I did not know at what; perhaps at nothing, perhaps because he could feel the energy surging from my elbows through the rest of me, perhaps because he knew, though I did not tell him, that this was my first drink, my first cigarette. And then he slid down the rock and was beside me.

'Aren't you freezing with your shoes off?'

I regarded my slim, elegant feet and shook my head. And then perhaps too obviously and immediately regretting it, for I saw him search them out, I said, 'They're not my shoes anyhow.'

'Whose are they?' he asked after a few moments. 'Your grandad's?'

And then we were both laughing helplessly, and he had retrieved one of the shoes from where I had concealed them, stood up, drawn his arm behind him and flung it into the water. I thought his gesture brilliant and within seconds I was on my feet and had flung the other one into the water to meet its mate. The sight of the shoes bobbing on the water's surface, coming towards us on a wave and then being dragged out again, was hilarious and we both doubled over and collapsed to the ground again with our sides aching. 'Oh my God,' was all that I could say as I began to recover. But then the laughter began again as he said, 'I'd do the exact same with mine if they didn't . . . didn't . . . belong to my' – and at this point he could hardly speak, anticipating the hilarity of what he was about to say – 'if they didn't belong to my granny.' Well, that was the finish of me, and I rocked with laughter and my cheeks ached and only slowly did our laughter die away and leave us again watching the sea.

And then out of the blue, he asked me a strange question: 'Do you believe in evil?' The question seemed to puncture everything, to slash through the smooth silver screen.

'What do you mean?' I asked, pretending the need to consider the question.

'W. H. Auden said that those who suffer evil pay it back with evil.'

I felt something inside me deflate. I wanted to say to him, *Don't say such things, for we two are separate. I am at last separate.* For a second it occurred to me to tear off one of his shoes and fling it out across the water to see it float with my two barges, but a darkness seemed to have descended on him and I dared not, in spite of the courage of my drunkenness. All that I could manage as I gathered up some pebbles with my fingertips was: 'I hope not.'

'Yeah,' he said, and then it was my turn to swig and this time I took too much, perhaps to obliterate the preceding seconds, and I coughed and gasped and that set him banging on my back and the two of us howling and choking with laughter again. And when I was quite able to breathe independently again, he left his hand placed on my back. Never before had I sat so still, for I feared any movement, however slight, any jerking caused even by a single heartbeat, would cause his hand to slip away.

We were quite still for some moments, the moon providing us with an excuse for our stillness as it performed a disappearing act, only to reappear and cast its spotlight onto the silver screen again, ending the intermission. I felt the urge to cough and prayed fervently that I could suppress it, for surely the racking would cause his hand finally to slip away.

'That was some escape we made,' he said. When he said that – using *we* and not *I*, or *you*, or *you and I*, a gush of warmth swept through my whole being, and I felt as I had once felt so long ago when I had been eleven and Stephen Squirrel had said, 'You can play.' Here were the words of a second anointing. And thus anointed, and without thinking about it, I looked up into the boy's face, and at almost exactly the same moment he turned from the sea to look at me. Strangely I did not feel shy or afraid. I did not think, *He is going to think me ugly*. I did not think of my own face at all, I thought only of his. I looked at it deeply – his wide, thin, pale lips, the marvellous and dramatic curve they took under his nostrils, his wide-set pale eyes which were perhaps blue, perhaps grey, twinkling at me darkly, his hair – even in the moonlight – discernibly light in colour, long and flopping across his forehead. I wished I was a camera so that I could capture that image and take it into my brain never to forget it. And then he leaned in and he set his lips over mine, barely touching, almost hovering. And then our lips touched, ever so softly, gently, and then we were both looking out across the screen again and it seemed no longer scarred and torn.

'No,' he said, 'I'm only asking you that question because I'm doing Auden for the Leaving.'

I nodded, not really listening because I could not believe that a boy had kissed me, that I was normal.

He asked me, 'Are you doing the Leaving?'

'Next year.'

'I don't really care about it.'

'Neither do I.'

'It's just for the parents.'

'Yeah,' I agreed, but did not know what he meant by this remark since neither of my parents were, as far as I knew, aware that I was supposed to be preparing for it.

'Yeah, for my father mainly,' he continued, and again I felt his darkened mood. Then out of the blue, he leaned in and kissed me again, as though he were experimenting, testing something, but I did not know what. He withdrew, touched his lips and looked into the distance.

He asked, 'Where do you go to school?'

My eyes scanned the outline of the dark bay in the distance, my hand tracing the outline of the headlands: out past the Pigeon House, along the low lights of Sandymount, out past the harbour at Dun Laoghaire, and then my hand halted and I pointed to the cliff on which my school perched. My method amused him and, grinning, he in turn raised his hand, traced the headlands, then raised his finger to point towards the mountains beyond Bray Head. 'I used to go there – a grim old hole of a place.'

'Not any more?'

'Nope,' and he patted his blazer breast pocket where I noticed for the first time the deeper colour of the fabric where the school crest had been removed.

He lit a cigarette and we stared for a while across the Bay.

'Can you do this?' he asked. I turned to see that he had

pulled up his sleeve and was holding the lit cigarette on the back of his arm. For a moment I was too shocked to do anything but then I pushed his hand and he let the cigarette loose and it flew across the rocks. He was laughing.

'I don't think you should do that – hurt yourself like that.'

He laughed again and then pulled up his sleeve to reveal a track of cigarette burns running up as far as his elbow. 'Why do you do that?' I asked, horrified, as though I did not immediately know.

'A present for my father,' he said, and he pointed to one and then another burn. 'That was for his birthday last year, that one was for the previous year. See that little cluster? That was for his fiftieth birthday – a big celebration – we had a massive party for that one. So I did three – a trinity – Father, Son and Holy Ghost.'

Though he was laughing again, I feared he was about to cry. And then he turned into me and placed his lips on mine again, withdrawing again quickly. 'I don't do that well, do I?' So I felt the only assurance I could give him, the only consolation, was to show my strong approval, and this time I leaned into him and placed my lips softly upon his, resting them long enough so that mine began to tingle.

Once more we sat quietly. Some lights in the great hotel behind us seemed to have been extinguished, for the flicker of one that had sat out on the water all that time while we had been sitting there was suddenly gone. He had grown so silent that it occurred to me again that he might be crying, so I looked at him, but he was just still and watching the water as I had been. He tapped the crestless breast pocket of his blazer. 'Do you know why I got kicked out? Well, there's two reasons – maybe two, maybe one. The first is not the worst, so I'll tell you that. We were out on a cross-country run – which I loathe, by the way. I jumped into the river and fished out a guy who'd gone in.'

I was impressed and suddenly imagined him thrashing across the river, his skin glistening, bent on rescuing his classmate. I said, 'Wow,' but I didn't think he heard me since I had only mouthed it, for already I had anticipated a bad ending to this story.

'He'd already gone under the water when I decided to leap in. Yeah, anyhow, then they found out – my father found out and he went and told on me.'

I looked at him quizzically. He turned away from me.

'Guess what they found out?'

Though desperate to make any attempt, I could not think. I could not think of a single theory.

'That I was the one who'd pushed him in, in the first place. Yeah, and I knew he couldn't swim.'

He looked far out across the water. 'He'd pissed me off so much – too many times – know what I mean?'

I did not know what to say. I would like to have said, *Well, that doesn't matter*. But it did matter; it would have mattered if the boy had drowned. Sensing my discomfort, he began laughing and I couldn't help thinking of Momma that night when she had spring-cleaned our kitchen in a final attempt to get rid of all the filth. After a while, it came to me to ask, 'Well, did anyone drown?'

'Nope.'

'Then no harm done.'

He turned to examine me. 'You're strange,' he said. 'You're not like a girl – I mean in a good way.'

But I felt there was no good way in which he would not see me as a girl.

'We need more booze,' he said after a few minutes, during which I had got up and looked out across the water, pretending to search for my shoes. I needed to be alone for a few minutes since I could not find any way to recover from his comment. I thought I might kiss him again. Perhaps that would do it, but I was too afraid of the second terrible thing that had caused him to lose the right to wear his school crest.

As we ascended first the rocks and then the sloping lawn, I felt drunk again, and the grim feeling that had descended on this boy seemed lifted. All my thoughts became focused on not toppling back down the slope and onto the rocks. He reached back for me, pulling me up the steeper parts, and giddily offered to carry me by piggyback through the prickly undergrowth that led to the lawn, since I was barefooted, Momma's nylons torn to shreds by the rough ground. He offered three times, and three times I refused, wishing after each refusal that I had assented, for it would have been splendid, to let him bear my weight, to sink into him. To feel like a girl.

He pulled me over the last part of the undergrowth, and we were on the soft lawn again. At the top, we leaned once more into the gigantic paws of the great lion, out of breath. He glanced up at the great, noble face as he pulled out another cigarette. 'Got a light?' he asked the lion.

This boy was magnificent. In all his grimness and his sadness, his burnt, tortured arms, he made my heart sing and soar and I loved him.

And then, invading the quiet night, I heard HIS voice calling out from the direction of the hotel, ricocheting around the body of the great stone lion: 'Jean, Jean,' and then slightly lower, 'For fuck's sake.' And then Aunty Ida's genteel voice: 'Jean, oh Jean.'

The boy looked at me. 'Is that you?'

'Jean, for fuck's sake.' HIS voice came again, and I guessed from its agitation that he had already been drunk and had sobered up for the drive home and was overall disappointed by the wedding.

'I'll come and collect you at your school. Top of the cliff – yes?'

As I turned to run off, he grabbed a corner of Cissy's poncho and pulled me back to him and said, 'Don't be afraid of anything.' It did not strike me as odd that he would say such a thing, and once he had said it, I felt that I would never again be afraid of anything.

HE was standing at the car. Aunty Ida was already in the back seat, her head fallen back, her mouth agape. She had drifted off with the Babycham. She looked content, at peace, for once not worried, and I forgave her betrayal. I plunged into the car as though I were diving into deep water that would render me invisible. HE was raging and shouting at the rear-view mirror: 'Where the hell were you?' It made me laugh.

And then, just before we reversed, I saw my boy coming

from the back of the hotel and climbing into his father's car, and although I strained, I could not see his face and they too pulled away.

Paradise

On the second occasion when he arrived at my school gate, they witnessed him. Margaret Collins, powerful since 1896, and Stephanie Long, now more integrated into that circle of six that now, by fifth year, seemed to entirely run our school. He was sitting on his bicycle, his shoulder braced against the gate pillar for balance. As I came closer to him, he drew himself back a little on the saddle and opened his arm for me to take a perch on the crossbar. He had offered me the same perch on his first visit, but I had declined, in spite of wanting so much to be his passenger. This time the penetrating eyes of that little cluster only feet behind me seemed to inspire me and I sat on his crossbar. His arms immediately enclosed me and, with surprising ease, he sped off.

Though the crossbar cut into me agonizingly, I was elated. I knew myself to be smiling most ridiculously, unnaturally, so I turned to face in front so that should he happen to glance down at me he would not see, for my pleasure would surely strike him as being excessive and he would know that this was the best thing that had ever happened to me, and it might have seemed to him so little.

We sped along the narrow roads, high up over the sea, and then descended at great pace towards the tiny harbour.

I ought to have been concerned about us taking a tumble, and about the blowing of horns as we veered onto the wrong side of the road and took corners at an immense pace, but I felt his strength, his competence, his ability and determination to bring us to the little harbour of which he had spoken on that first occasion when he had been waiting for me at the school gate. That he had arrived again one week later was an answer to every petitionary prayer I had ever made, since long ago, even when I had not known for what I was petitioning.

The first ever glimpse of my boy had been in the light of the salmon-pink dusk by the great lion's paw, the second against the moonlight screen of the sea. In those days before his first visit to my school I had had to imagine the colour of his hair, the precise colour of his eyes, before I saw how accurate my projection had been, for it was indeed dark blond, and his eyes pale blue, almost grey, seeming to change colour just with a tilting of his head. And as I had imagined, his skin was pale and smooth with only a smattering of freckles around his nose.

Now on this second meeting, as we two sat on the soft, sandy grass of the little harbour, I drank his beauty in once more, attentive to every detail so that another week of school would pass with my thoughts of nothing other than remembering every second of his visit, every movement of his hand, every draw he took from his cigarette. Since I had first encountered him, even before he had turned up on that first occasion at the school gate against all my expectations, I had felt grounded in the world, as though I were firmer on my feet. Things that would usually have upset me – 'Jean, what the hell happened to your school shoes? Do you think I am made of money?' – now just left me slightly amused. And although I still sat each evening by Momma's bed, and though I still stroked her hair whenever I sensed her fretting, I no longer felt in the same danger of losing her.

Though it was only early April, the sun had warmed the rock against which we two sat. He discarded his crestless blazer and flung it aside. The book he had been reading slipped out of his pocket and I rescued it and read the back cover.

'Is it good?'

'So far, but not his best. It was his last – it had to be finished for him. I despise him for drinking too much and dying too young and not writing enough stories for me.'

This boy was brilliant.

'Have you read him?' he asked.

'Just one: *The Beautiful and Damned.*'

'The only one I haven't read is *The Great Gatsby*. I won't read that because it was on a reading list in fourth year. I never read anything recommended to me. I make it a rule.'

'Yeah, I know what you mean.' But I did not, for there seemed to be nothing of a rebel within me, and the long list of novels furnished to me at the beginning of each summer by my English teacher, Miss Emily Barrington, I faithfully read.

He reached for his blazer, rooting through its pockets for his packet of cigarettes. He lit two in his mouth at the same time and passed one to me.

I dreaded a coughing fit that would give away the tremendous extent of my inexperience. I expelled the smoke as far away from me as I could. Though we had kissed at the wedding, we had not kissed the week before when our visit had been hurried and more dominated by discussion of the great distance between his home and mine, since he lived in Howth on the other side of the bay. How we would overcome that distance seemed to be the subtext of our brief conversation. Now, it seemed, it had been overcome.

We sat quietly, listening to the water lapping, watching the distant turquoise waves foaming against the miniature island that was close enough to swim to. The sun slipped behind a cloud and I shivered. He stretched his blazer around my shoulders, but I insisted that we share it, and so we moved closer together. 'Men don't feel the cold like women,' he said. 'I know,' I said, but I did not know, not until a few moments later when his arm and shoulder, pressed into mine, began to radiate the loveliest warmth – penetrating, soothing. And I thought to myself, *If I do not move, if he does not move, paradise will be confirmed*. I thought, *Let this be the day from which I never move on*.

But paradise is not for everyone. It began when he kissed me. Differently this time. Now his lips were parted. The wetness was nice, warm, metallic-tasting, a certain sweetness that I could not compare to anything. After a while he stopped and I knew it was my turn to re-invite him, so I leaned into him and with parted lips I kissed him softly. My kiss was briefer than I had perhaps intended. Some kind of worry had come into my mind, something very distant, yet almost commanded of me. Then he came towards me once more and began to explore my mouth with his tongue. I felt a tingling and a warmth, my heartbeat seemed light and rapid, but somewhere again that vague worry, still distant, yet a little more menacing this time. He withdrew. He had sensed something.

'Are you okay?'

'Of course.' But his question had prompted only more worry, for now I knew that he sensed something rising in me, yet even I did not know what that was. He leaned into me again and this time draped himself over me. The blazer slipped from our shoulders, and I thought, *I should really pick it up. It will be destroyed if its edges drip into the little rockpool.* I thought of telling him, but it was too late. And then his hand began to slide along my leg and up beneath my skirt. Although I felt joy that he had fully recognized my girlhood, a vague but demanding panic was stirring. I let him continue and I tried with all my might to calm myself, but the harder I tried, the faster my heart raced, the harder it was to breathe. Something was demanding my attention. I had begun to sense something terrible nearby. In confusion, I pushed him away from me and sat up, my heart racing, barely able to breathe, so smothered and stifled did I feel. And I stared at him bewildered and I wanted to beg him – *Say your name, say your name* – and I must have said it, for he said, 'What's wrong with you? Roger – you know it's Roger.'

I stood up, humiliated, ashamed, terrified. He could not forgive me; I knew that he would not. He would think I had forgotten his name. Of course I had not. I had just momentarily, terrifyingly, found myself in another place, as someone else's passenger.

A glance out across the water revealed it to be calm and blue and empty. There was no evidence to which I could point, nothing to explain.

He cycled me back to the school gate, my face throughout the reverse of what it had been on our outward journey, now swept by the wind into what I imagined to be a face turned inside out, exposed grotesquely to the world and to him, my beautiful boy. I alighted and he pedalled away. He did not look back, and it was only when he had disappeared around the corner into the village that I realized he must have thought my forgetting of his name just that, a forgetting of his name, and have concluded perhaps that only a girl who had had many boyfriends could forget something so vital.

My feet on the ground lost that sense of firm foundation, only so recently won. I was foundationless again. I collected my bicycle from the bike shed and wheeled it all the way home. I had no strength to pedal, my bones hung broken about me, incapable of bearing me, disassembled. I did not want in any case to arrive home, or anywhere. I wanted only to disappear under those foaming turquoise waves we two had watched.

The weeks that followed were the emptiest of days. He did not return to me. I returned to my ration of one bowl of cereal per day, and the hunger brought some solace to me. I thought of him all the time. I composed letters and cards and postcards of explanation to him. But no words could apologize, and in any case it was mysterious to me how I had suddenly lost my bearings, not knowing where I was, who I was, who he was, as he had draped himself over me.

For my last English homework of fifth year, we were required to write on Gerard Manley Hopkins's 'No Worst, There Is None': *What does the poet mean when he writes 'O the mind, mind has mountains; cliffs of fall / Frightful'?* Miss Barrington read my essay aloud to the class, another betrayal. Afterwards Margaret Collins, powerful since 1896, asked, 'How's your boyfriend?' She knew. Somehow, in her canniness, she knew.

PART THREE

Seabird

(1980–1981)

Seventeen

Demons! What Demons?

I entered my final year of school with a great hunger. And perhaps because of the hunger, I took an unexpected interest in Jesus. When *Jesus of Nazareth* was shown on telly a few weeks before Easter, he enchanted me with his kindness and his blue eyes. But more than anything, I was enchanted by the exorcist in him, by his power to drive out demons and provide instant emancipation to possessed women. After that I kept seeing him spinning in the summer skies, in the weeks just after my Leaving Cert, when dusk came slowly in unnameable colours, and lingered a long time in the sky, and no dusk was ever like any that had come before it.

He appeared in the woods on my evening walks. Only his voice of course, not his body. He had already given that away. 'Take it,' he had said in what Miss Barrington had once described as his most profound act of selflessness, the act that had inspired John Donne to plead with God to batter his heart. And Jesus said nice things to me, like: 'Demons! What Demons? I don't mind about all that business.' There in the woods, I felt less like the sole member of a strange species of bird, just for that hour or so of walking in his company. It was one hour of the day when I fitted well into the company

I was keeping. But he was to vanish, never to return. I had wanted to ask him one thing: *Excuse me, Jesus — am I supposed to give away my body too?* But he was gone. Perhaps he would have thought me very forward, not being used to modern girls, so it was better that he vanished before I had the chance to say anything.

Sometimes, I believed in God too much. It was like being sick. I feared that if Jesus was to come again, he might ask me — might even command me — to become a nun, which I certainly did not want to do. I did not want the outfit, which horrified me, the shared living quarters, the obedience I would be required to show the priests when I myself would never have that magical moment of turning water into wine, the hours and hours on my knees in a musty chapel beside other nuns on their ancient knees. And more than anything, nunhood would have stood in the way of what I wanted most in the world — some day: a baby like Baby John F., to sit on my hip as Baby John F. had once sat on my hip in those happiest of days. So although perhaps it was unfaithful of me, I was relieved that Jesus made no more appearances. The sickness of faith departed.

One evening I had left it rather late to go out for my walk. I had hung about, waiting for Tilly and HIM to get over some kind of an argument they were having which had arisen as a result of John F. playing with his car key and losing it, meaning that Tilly would be late because now she would have to walk to the train station. Declining HIS offer to call her a taxi, screaming about how waiting for a taxi would make her even later, she left, slamming the front door and stomping up the gravel driveway and out the garden gate. She'd be back of course. They were always having little tiffs like that, the causes never entirely clear to the rest of us because the two of them seemed to have their own language, their own rules. Momma never got involved. No one did. But HE was always in a foul and mean mood after such rows. So I waited a little longer, half reading my book, half listening, until John F. had gone to bed. Just in case.

When he was safely tucked in, I was hurrying to the front door, knowing that I had already missed the dusk and the summer-evening skies, when HE roared up the hall, 'Where do you think you're going at this hour of night?' 'Only a quick walk – like always,' I responded, turning towards him with my hand already on the front-door handle. 'A walk,' said HE, 'do you really expect me to believe that? At this time of night?' I was puzzled. Why would HE not believe that? Did HE know nothing about the summer-evening skies? I began to open the door. 'I'm only going for a walk,' I said. But HE came up behind me and pressed his hand firmly against the front door to prevent me from opening it. 'Do you think I'm stupid,' HE roared into my face. 'You can't do whatever you like here you know – you little . . . hussy.'

Oh, Daddy, I thought. *I would love to be a hussy, but don't you know there are monsters in the sea.*

And then HE roared some other things like: 'What kind of a fool do you take me for?' and 'Who do you think puts the food on your plate?' and I knew he was just in a rage over Tilly.

Momma came out to the hall, and then Cissy. 'Just leave

it now, Edmund,' said poor Momma, who hated any kind of altercation. She said her medication made noises come into her louder to her than reality. I tried to walk back down the hall. But HE grabbed my coat sleeve: 'You're not leaving this house tonight.' Well, I knew that. That was why I had turned around and was heading towards the staircase. I pulled away but HE reached out and grabbed me again: 'Don't you walk away from me. Don't you dare walk away from me.' Cissy came towards us: 'Stop it, Daddy, let her go.' And HE swiped at my precious sister Cissy so that she fell against the grand-father clock and it rattled and chimed on its old legs as she hit it. 'You hypocrite liar,' I shouted, and I barely recognized the sound of my own voice and had no idea from what secret place inside of me it had come. 'You're a horrible man. A horrible lying man.' HE was pulling me about by my coat sleeve now, rattling and shaking me about, his eyes rabid and dying to steady me so that he could hit my face. HE really wanted to hit my face; his eyes burned with passion.

'I know what you do with Tilly. I know about you and Tilly.' And it was only when I said that that I realized I did know. There – slap-bang across the side of my head. Fine. I didn't mind any more. As my head was lashed sideways, I caught a glimpse of Momma's horror, her hand clasped at her mouth. Horror, disgust, shock. 'Jean, how dare you use that language with Daddy. How dare you.'

Sorry, Momma. I hardly ever say the things I want to say, but sometimes, Momma, they just shoot out. Like demons evacuating the body of a possessed woman.

'You hurt Momma so much. I hate you. We all fucking

hate you.' Poor Momma clasped her hands over her ears, her poor ears scorched by my obscenity.

HE pulled me up the hall to the front door by my anorak sleeve, opened the door and shoved me outside. Outside my own front door. His front door. Tilly's front door. I stood there in shock with a throbbing head and a trembling body, a trembling that I knew to have been caused as much by this new, unfamiliar rage as by fright. I stood at the door for ages, so that I would be ready to walk in when Momma opened it. But she didn't. Eventually I crossed the garden and sat on the wall, facing the house, staring at the front door, like a dog waiting to get in out of the rain. Like a dog with no human sense of time.

Later I saw Tilly return through the garden gate. She stomped angrily up the side passage to her granny flat, her high-heeled steps sending the gravel flying. Eventually Cissy came, hours later when the house was in total darkness, beckoning me to come in, and we crept upstairs to our bedroom and climbed into bed. 'Oh my God, Jean, why did you have to say that?' she said. I shrugged because I did not know why. *Maybe hate. Maybe love.* 'All you've done is upset Momma.' 'I know,' I replied. 'Sorry.'

Sleep would not come to me, of course, for I had done a terrible thing, a terrible angry thing. I had spoken and I was terrified that I might be seized again by this new evil speaking spirit in me, and I would speak again; flames would roll off my tongue, burning up our house. What would happen then to Momma? I lay with my eyes on fire, staring at the wall behind which Momma lay sleeping, my eyes hostage to it again as I listened like a safecracker for Momma's feelings to seep through. Then, just as I heard the canny milkman slip in and out of our porch and the jackdaws and the crows begin their taking of their territory, I heard a car reversing towards the gate. I leaped up to see Momma's car pass through the pillars and turn away from our house. Had I driven her away? Would she drive off Dun Laoghaire pier or into a brick wall? You stupid girl, you featherhead. What madness possessed you? I lay back in bed to hide from myself and to listen for Momma's return and to pray to Jesus that she would not drive off the pier.

I lay in bed all day, to avoid everyone, even John F. I did not help him with his reading. I lay in bed all day in case I was pushed outside the front door again. *Come on, Momma, forgive me. Forgive me.*

In the evening, when the movement about the house and the sounds of dinner had faded, Momma's car scratched across the gravel. Not off the pier, not smashed into a brick wall, not tangled in a bombing, not abducted by trees in the mountains past the heather and the Wall's Ice Cream sign. Thank you, Momma.

She was in our room within moments of her return, standing over me in the bed. 'Now, Jean,' she said, quite strong-voiced – Momma could be quite strong sometimes – 'I have gone and asked advice today, from a number of people, professionals, and they agreed that the best thing for you is to move out. To get your own flat. You're ready for university anyhow. Untruths are untruths. Daddy is Daddy and I can't have the younger ones hearing that language and . . . these things. I have to keep this family together for everyone's sake. That's my job. Now I have a place for you – very nice and not far. And you're old enough now – and the truth is, Jean, you never got on with your daddy.'

And that is how I got my own place. The very next day.

All Girls Should Dance

After all that business, I suddenly found myself alone and reflecting on the terrible blunder I had made, on how things once said cannot be taken back, and with many things to work out, such as how to remind Momma that I needed rent each week, how to get a job when I had never worked before. Although I had been given some money to get started, and although sometimes Momma did call by to leave some money for me, when she did call by she cried and cried and was really quite angry with me, asking why I would have made up such a thing. She persisted in asking me the same questions over and over again: *Why would you say that? Do you realize the problem you have caused? You have said a very low thing, brought the family very low.* And sometimes she telephoned in the evenings, and I had to stand in the hall listening to her, with other residents passing me and giving me hard looks. Strange expressions for a strange girl. Momma would keep me on the phone for ages, just asking over and over why I had said such a thing. And she cried and cried, and again and again I said I was sorry and agreed with her that such a thing could not be true. And people opened the doors of their flats and looked down from the landings, or peered around their doors to see how much longer I was going to be on the telephone. They threw their eyes to heaven, slammed their doors, tapped on their watches, for they did not know that on the other end of the phone was poor Momma in a terrible state because of her very own stupid girl. And listening to her sobbing, demanding evidence of me, I regretted down to my very core ever having said anything about Tilly, for what did it matter, as long as Momma did not cry. Perhaps I had imagined it all, or perhaps I didn't understand. But what is said cannot be unsaid, what is done cannot be undone. We can only hope it might be forgotten. I had not said it for revenge or for spite, as HE had told Momma; I had said it because somehow I knew my days at home were drawing to an end, and because I was angry and because I was hated and because I am not a saint, and because he had pushed Cissy, and because Momma had become so fattened up for roasting. She had to be warned. Though I knew that in truth my warning had come too late, that I had achieved no good, only harm, abhorrent harm.

So that is how I had ended up alone, in a bedsit in a nice house on a pleasant avenue not far from the Martello Tower on the Strand Road. 'Lovely walks for you,' Momma had said the day I left. Momma knew how I loved to walk. Through the elegant, Edwardian six-panelled door I entered the ground-floor bedsit, having carefully avoided looking either left or right at the doors of other tenants. I had brought very few of my things with me. There had not been time to gather up much.

The room was high-ceilinged, wide and airy, with two windows, one overlooking the side passage to the back garden, and the other overlooking the long back garden. A little kitchen area crouched in one dark corner, and the bed was set into a recess that was screened off by a thick, musty green curtain that hung from the ceiling to the floor. I arranged those of my books that I had chosen to bring – the two dozen or so that I loved best – in piles beneath the small melamine-topped table that sat with its single chair in that window that looked out upon the old, overgrown garden. I telephoned home and asked Tilly to bring John F. to see me. 'Oh, come on, Jean, you know he'll refuse to walk that far from the bus stop. You come here.' But I knew that it was Tilly who did not want to make the journey.

One day, having collected my laundry from the clothes-line, I almost crashed into an American artist on the narrow pathway of the side passage that led to the garden. It was a deeply embarrassing moment, for when I raised my head to look at him, he turned out to be very handsome, and my underwear was sitting on top of the pile of clothes. 'Whoa,' he said, 'slow down.' And he reached out and held me by the shoulders, as though to prevent a violent collision. Then he glanced at his hands as he removed them from my shoulders. 'Excuse the paint,' he said, 'I'm an artist – as you probably guessed.'

He peered intently at me for a few moments as I reddened deeper, and then pronounced his love for Dublin Bay. 'I guess you're wondering what I'm doing here – in this strange house. It's the light from the Bay, do ya' see – nothing like it anywhere, nothing as spiritual. That's why you'll always see me painting outdoors – the light in this garden is superb.'

I was instantly impressed by this spiritual painter. He asked if I would like to see his paintings. Well, of course I said yes, for who would not want to see an American artist's paintings? An artist who knew so much about art that he had come all the way to Dublin Bay for the spiritual light it held and cast. So I accepted and was flattered, and he asked when I'd come to see his paintings, and I replied, 'Next time,' without any sense at all of what that meant.

Next time came only two days later. After a walk on the strand, I was about to insert the key into the door of my flat when he came through the front door on his return from cleaning his brushes in the back garden. 'Hi,' he said in a lovely, charming, lilting accent. 'You busy?' 'Oh no, not really,' I replied. 'So come up,' he said. As I followed him up the elegant Edwardian staircase – slipping my hand along the rosewood banister rail, just for something to squeeze so that I would feel less nervous – I told myself that this was not a stranger in the real sense; he was an American and that put him in the category of enlightened, as far as I was concerned. And a painter, an artist, so undoubtedly there would be a sensitivity in him, unusual in men. For all I knew, I might have been following the next Van Gogh up the stairs to his little garret, and his hair after all was the brightest orange, and the freckles, on his face as wide as Van Gogh's.

The room was a good deal smaller than mine, a tiny bedsit, but a double bed occupied practically the entire floor space. I stood just inside the door, and he went into the little kitchenette that, like mine, was tucked away in a corner alcove. 'You'll have coffee?' he asked. 'Yes, please,' I replied. Of course I would accept his offer of coffee; there was nothing more American than coffee. A little battery transistor sat, among many jars of paintbrushes steeping in colourful water, and dozens of used mugs and plates, on a sideboard which ran the length of the room as far as the open window. He came out of the kitchenette and switched on the radio. 'I like background noise,' he said, 'it relaxes me.' He fiddled with the stations until he came to 'Fly Me to the Moon'. He moved a little to the rhythm, very coolly, very American. 'Do you dance?' he asked me. 'No, not really,' I said, shaking my head and blushing. 'Too bad,' he said, 'all girls should dance,' and he slipped off his sneakers and danced for a few minutes, holding his arms out to an imagined partner. Was I supposed to watch him, his hips swaying, his arms waving to the swing rhythm, his head rolling, his eyes shut? Or should I show that my interest was truly in art and instead begin to examine the paintings on the wall?

The song ended, and he returned to the kitchenette. I heard the tapping of the teaspoon as he stirred the powder into the cups. I glanced over to see an open jar of Nescafé, its lid sitting on the counter. 'Milk?' 'No, thank you.' I immediately regretted my hasty response. I should have said, *No, thanks. No, thank you* sounded like a child. 'Good, yeah, I don't know why you Irish always put milk in coffee.' 'I know,' I said, 'I don't know either. It's terrible really.' Again, that sounded wrong, too regretful, as though it was tragic to put milk in coffee, instead of just un-American. He passed me the mug, which was scalding hot and instantly burned the palm of my hand. I should have taken it by the handle, but it was too late now. My hand turned red and slippy. And I thought, *My hand looks like a farmer's*. 'Hey, sit down,' he said. I felt stupid. 'Take the load off your feet.' I felt fat.

There was only the bed to sit on, so I sat on its very edge, the edge of its edge, so much so that I had to be very careful that I did not slide off onto the floor. The edge on which I sat was just beside the open door. I was still wearing my coat and had begun to sweat heavily inside it. Soon I would smell. 'Come on, come on, off with the coat,' he said, as he stood over me with his arm held out, ready to unburden me of the winter coat on this summer's day. He took the mug from my hand. To assist. 'Jeez, that's hot,' he said. 'You must be thick-skinned.' And then I lowered my coat from my shoulders and let it slip down my arms before I reached to take the mug back from him. 'No, no,' he said, 'don't sit on your coat. You'll crease it. Get up – give it to me. Come on – up, up, up. Give it here.' So I did, and now we were standing in the same square foot of carpet and his eyes were peering at me impatiently. I really did not wish to annoy him. He tossed my coat into a corner, and I watched its flight as though in slow motion. It caught the edge of the sideboard and slid onto the floor, and I got the distinct impression that I was still in it.

I sat on the side of the bed, and he moved back a few paces, leaned against the wall, stooped to set his own coffee mug on the floor, folded his arms and then began staring at me. I did not know how to respond, but it was clear that I had annoyed him. I shouldn't have made such a fuss over the coat. Now I did not know where to look and I was melting beneath his stare. So, I thought, since this was all about art, that would be the place to look, away from him: at the paintings that covered his walls. First I turned to those on my left, and then to those on my right. I spent a good while gazing at each one, until I became startlingly aware of my blinking. I thought my eyelids had begun to make a clicking sound, like an old clock. My neck began to ache. Eventually, I looked over at him to find him still staring at me. His eyes were impatient, he appeared to be cross, and I felt a little rush of panic, of confusion, until I realized precisely how I had offended him. And it was obvious: I had made no effort to look at the paintings behind me. Of course! How stupid of me. Artists can be so sensitive, so vulnerable, so spiritual. The brilliant Van Gogh had cut off his own ear, so much in doubt of his own genius, so much in agony had he been. So I stood up carefully, and he watched me – every muscle, every bone of mine as it unbent and screeched and straightened.

The back wall was entirely covered in seascapes: the Pigeon House chimneys; rocky, dark coastlines; detailed studies of deep-green and black seaweed-locked rockpools; and some seabirds – a gull, a cormorant, a heron perched on a rock on one leg. 'So . . .' he said. 'Oh, they're amazing,' I responded, 'you're so talented.' And I hesitated before saying, 'You'll probably be very rich.' 'Would you like that?' he asked. I looked at him quizzically. 'Would you like if I was rich?' he said again. I was puzzled. What did he mean? More importantly, what was the right answer? 'There's more there in the corner, stacked up against the wall.' I glanced to where he was pointing. 'Go on, it's fine, take a look. Just be careful not to put your fingers on them – I don't want the fresh ones smudged.'

It was difficult to make my way to the corner, through the narrow gap between the bed and sideboard. Once or twice, I had to grab on to the cluttered sideboard to avoid falling onto the bed, and my shoulder almost swept the wall so that I had to tilt myself away from it to avoid brushing against his oils. Whenever I moved – now, and when I had first sat down and first stood up, and when I had turned my head to see the paintings behind me – he grew very quiet, which made even my slightest movement sound out across the room, as though my body was made of a crumply paper whose sound cannot be concealed. Like a crisp bag.

I wondered why he was watching me with such attention. Did I have something odd on my face – jam, or a giant oozing spot, or was it my clothes? Were they particularly dorky today? Or masculine? Or comical? Perhaps he was watching me for fear that I would try to steal a painting? Or perhaps it was just that he was so artistic and consequently was watchful and contemplative? And I thought for a moment of Van Gogh's self-portrait: how cross he looked, and frantic, and how fiery his red hair. Yet behind that maniacal stare was a man who had never hurt a fly; an artist, a martyr to his zeal, a loving painter of peasant women in their toil, their round bodies, full-skirted, stooping over; he had watched them for hours and hours, perhaps for days, to get the folds of their skirts right, to tell the story of their bodies in their labour. Yes, that was what was going on here, something like that, and here was I in my paranoia blushing and trembling and losing my balance and scalding my hand.

I proceeded to leaf through the stack of paintings that leaned against the wall, but without really seeing anything, other than for a split second reading the signature – *Joshua Urt* – and gaining a vague impression of indistinct splashes of colour. Because I had suddenly become nervous again. It was all very well to be stooping in your long skirt under the Provence sky with the golden fields swirling around you and a big yellow sun-ball on the horizon, and Vincent Van Gogh standing some distance away on a hill – straw-hatted, freckled, innocent – but I was in a room not much bigger than a shoebox. A quiet room with only the occasional inhaling and exhaling of the summer day through the net curtains, and the occasional hard whack of a racket on a tennis ball. Calm down. The door is behind you. Did Van Gogh's subjects need to sign a consent form? Of course not.

Then came the click of the door as he shut it quietly. Perhaps I should think of that as the whack of the tennis ball as it hits the racket. Just another sound of summer. I had reached the end of the stack, so I began again from the beginning. This time I would scrutinize them with greater care, so that I could provide comment. Comment and compliment. Comment and compliment. But now I could not even make out any colour, my fingers alone worked, feeling the tiny bumps at the edges of each canvas and the slight stickiness. And now I sensed his body, his breath, his stare. I wished he would move. I wished he would not move. I wished he would say something. I wished he would not say anything. I tried to be logical, to work it out. He wished me to say something. Something about his art. There were so many things I might have said – simple things, such as *good*, or *brilliant*, or *amazing* – but I could not see what I was looking at. I had become blind and evidently dumb as well. 'Your hands aren't sticky, are they?' he said. I turned slightly towards him and, holding my hands up to him, I said, 'No, they're clean.' And I turned back to my browsing. And I knew that my response had sounded ridiculous, like a child's.

My coffee mug sat at my feet on the narrow strip of floor between the bed and the sideboard. The song on the radio had changed – 'If I Can't Have You'. But the volume seemed lower now. And suddenly I was terrorized by the prospect of a sneezing fit, provoked by the dusty carpet and mattress, the heavy dust of the room so evident to me now that I was kneeling on his floor.

Things felt suddenly very bad. And I could not get out because he stood with his back to the door and the room was filled almost completely by the double bed, save for the two narrow gaps on either side. He could have said something – *Do you like the pictures? Would you like more coffee? Would you like me to paint you?* But no, he would not say anything.

How stupid of me. He wanted me to leave. That was what he wanted. Over the last couple of days, since I had first encountered him in the garden, I had thought of him during my long walks on the strand, or while lying in bed dozing, half asleep, half awake. I had reflected on his attention to me – our brief garden conversation had somehow made me feel redeemed, re-catalogued, reassessed. Hopeful. And whenever he passed my window, coming and going to the garden, he had waved to me. I had even contemplated the possibility that I had the kind of looks he actually liked.

And then he was beside me, sitting on the bed. 'Gee, you really like those paintings, don't you?' I nodded. 'Gee,' he said in what might have been a humorous tone, 'you're an uptight girl, aren't you? Come on, leave those for a minute. Tell me about yourself, relax.' So I sat up straight, like I used to in senior infants in order to be counted as good, and I ceased scrutinizing his works of art. He dipped his head and looked up at an angle into my face, and his eyes had lost that darker, impatient look and they seemed softer and perhaps a bit amused. 'Does this girl speak?' he asked. I knew that I was meant to find that funny, so I smiled as though I had, and said, 'Of course.' 'Okay then, talk.' That was not so funny.

More silence and his hand sliding along the side of my jeans, then lightly stroking my leg, 'So how old are you anyhow?'

'Eighteen – in eight days,' I announced, with a precision and volume I had not intended. I knew the right answer to a question he had asked. Surely, he must be pleased.

'You're very mature – intellectually, I mean.'

I watched his hand. His fingernails were long and full of dirt which I surmised was oil paint. It was dirty, sticky stuff, unless on canvas. 'So . . . what do you think of my art?'

'Really, really good.' I glanced down at my hands, which lay at my sides, settled on the bed; my fingertips raked very slightly over the furrows of the potato fields of his yellow bedspread. I moved them onto my lap, decisively, perhaps decisively: *These are my hands.*

'Do you like the seagull? That's my favourite.'

I nodded.

'Hard to mix the paint for the beak — you know, so that it wouldn't stand out as his only part. Know what I mean?'

'Yes.' And then my hand was on his crotch, on his American Levi'ed crotch, and it was hard and throbbing a little, like a trapped animal. He held it there, where he had assigned it.

'Do you like the feel of that?'

I knew that I was supposed to. I was not so stupid that I did not know that, so I nodded, but he seemed unconvinced, so much so that he took my hand and put it inside those American Levi's.

'It feels good, doesn't it?'

I nodded, and vomit surged to the back of my throat and I was not sure I would be able to contain it. But I knew that I ought to like this. I should just get it over with. This was love. This was romance. This was womanhood.

Fortunately, he did not appear to have noticed my alarm, and good-humouredly and encouragingly said, 'Come on, relax. I can teach you so much. You should take advantage.' And he began to slide his hands inside my jeans. 'Are you wet?' he said. 'No? I'll have to work harder.' And there was that vomit now, pressing harder.

Come on, I coached myself, *it's not so bad. It's a beginning — a brown-eyed American, hair the colour of Van Gogh's, an artist — and after this he'll talk to you about America and he will invite you over there, and you can lie in his arms, and he'll stroke your hair and he'll comfort you. And you will be normal. Joyously normal, at last. Enfin! Normale!*

But that was not how it would end. I was evidently becoming increasingly annoying. If I was not clear about much that was happening, I was clear about that. 'Come on, relax, come on. Jesus, loosen up.'

I was desperate to loosen up, so that he would not see my fear. So that he would not see that I was not normal. So that he would not see that I was not really someone he might invite Stateside in gratitude for services rendered.

He seemed to need this badly. What difference would it make to me, he was just another one come along, and this body was not really part of me anyhow. It was just something I had been dragging along for years. Something someone occasionally took a fleeting interest in. Here it was, one of those moments when it might just possibly be of use to someone. What was it Christ said? 'Take this, my body.' But my body would just not be given; it simply would not loosen up.

'Jesus,' he said, 'you're uptight, but don't worry, that's kind of sweet. I get tired of all these liberated easy women.' If I could just get this pulling motion right then he would be pleased, and it would be finished. What I could not stand was his hand inside my jeans, so I pretended to be getting deeply involved in the pulling, and at the same time with my other hand I tried to work out a way to draw his hand out of my jeans without offending him or making him cross.

Then I felt his hard American private part shrivel in my hand. And I thought, *What's going on now? Is it finished? Am I done?* 'For fuck's sake,' he said, as he rose to his feet, fiddling with his fly. 'Now look what you made me do.' He took long strides across the room, passing through the narrow strip between the bed and the sideboard – long, raging strides, all the time pulling at his zip. 'I'm going to the can – stay there – don't move – two minutes – don't move.' And he left.

But after a couple of seconds of absolute rigidity, I moved, moved just as I became aware that my heart was racing, my body pulsating. I got out of that room and light-stepped down the stairs, my hand slipping along the rosewood banister for balance.

A trembling, uncooperative set of sweaty farmer's fingers held the little key to my bedsit. *Turn the lock slowly, as silently as you can. The lock might not turn this time – the door might jam – listen, there is the flush of the toilet upstairs – hurry – he has finished – turn the lock, you stupid farmer's fingers – listen, the long flush is over – there's the sound of the water trickling down the pipes behind you – turn the key – it's the other way – remember – what do you want – do you want to die – turn the key – it's the other way – don't you remember – head like a sieve – get inside – the key is stuck in the lock – don't pull it out with such force – it slides – don't you remember – it's a knack – have you forgotten everything about your own door – this is not my own door – yes it is – it is now – this is your only door. Quickly – into the little bed – Va faire coucher, mes enfants.*

In the little bed, I lay still. Nothing moved but the blanket that bounced against my heartbeat. *Distract yourself. Make still that trembling. Think: what shape is this house? Whose floor is your ceiling? Whose footsteps are those moving about now on the floor above you? Come on, think.* The footsteps again as someone – shoeless – pattered across the floor, then came to a halt, directly overhead.

Be Generous or Dry Up

For a couple of days after I had viewed his oils, the American artist knocked at least three or four times a day, calling out, 'Come on, open up. I know you're in there.' A sort of good-humoured voice on the first few occasions, like in a game: *Come out, come out, wherever you are.* But then his annoyance increased, and he banged harder and raised his voice: 'Come on. Open up. What the hell's wrong with you?' Would he huff and puff and blow my house down? But I was lucky. I had the strangest little bed in the world, screened off from the entire world, so that if someone had entered the room, they might never even have discovered me.

After a few days of relatively polite knocking, he began to huff, and he began to puff. He pounded on the door with his American artist's fist: 'If you don't use it, it will rot, you know.' That was worrying. Sometimes he stood at the door repeatedly pounding and outlining my flaws – *cock-teaser, frigid little bitch, dried-up pussy, little cunt.* That was how I knew it was the weekend, that the country bankers had all departed on their Friday-evening trains and would not return until late on Sunday evening. Sometimes he would just give one big fistful of a bang as he passed the door, presumably on his way to the back garden to clean his brushes. And then, once outside, as he passed by the window of my funny little bedsit, its curtains now permanently drawn, he would thump on the glass a couple of times and the delicate Edwardian window frame would shudder as he shouted insults. But my dried-up pussy was locked away behind the dusty pea-green curtains of my strange little bed sitting in that alcove, tied up like a little boat in a harbour to prevent its destruction in a storm it was not built to endure.

I lay and I watched as thousands of particles left my body, like living creatures off the dead. I watched as they were sucked into the violence of the evening sunshine that slipped into the room through the gaps in the drawn curtains. And I did not mind. No, not at all. There was a comfort and a fittingness to this disintegration. After all, it is not everyone who gets to see their very own bones and flesh broken down in such a silent and mystical manner. Perhaps I too was an artist of sorts.

Well, the American artist turned out to be right when he said, 'You can't stay in there forever, you know.' Afraid to go to the shops for fear of encountering him, for a whole week I only had a box of Sugar Puffs to eat. I crept to it very late at night when the house fell completely silent, when his footsteps overhead, for which I listened all day as I tracked his movements, ceased. And I dipped my hand inside, grasping a fistful and creeping back to my strange little bed, eating the sweet kernels so that the nausea would die. And there was the problem of peeing. The toilet was one flight upstairs on the first landing. I had attempted many times to co-ordinate my need to use it with the American artist's departure to the garden. I would stand with my ear to the door, listen and wait, wait and listen. And as soon as he had thumped the fine Edwardian glass as he passed my window, I would make my way to the door, turn the lock slowly, slide the chain across, holding it between my thumb and my index finger to lay it down quietly against the frame of the door, and slip out the door, up the stairs and into the tiny toilet, where I peed as silently as any girl has ever peed.

On the fifth day, when I was about to flush the loo, I heard the slam of the back door. I heard the American artist whistle tunefully – and I stared at the wooden door, reflecting on how flimsy it suddenly looked. And then my eyes rested on the little metal bolt. How flimsy that was too. *Stay still. Don't move. For how long? Bite your lip. Do you feel how your teeth are chattering? Keep them still. Bite your lip.* A slamming of a door then. The whistling – somewhat less tuneful – grows louder. BANG. The American artist's fist makes the door shudder. A drop of blood on my lip. BANG. 'I know you're in there, little girl.' BANG. But then the whistling again. It seems to be moving away. *Don't be fooled. Stay still.* SLAM – the back door shuts.

Below the toilet window his steps on the little gravel path. *Now. Move now.* But if I do and this is a trick and he turns back, he will make it to the bottom of the stairs at exactly the same moment as I. *Stay. Wait. Listen.* The squealing of the shed door's hinges. He has gone inside. *Has he?* Leap. Run. Like a gazelle. Hold the banister rail. Steady yourself. Should you fall you are doomed, doomed, doomed.

In my room again, my legs take me round in circles, round and round the room. No more risk-taking. No more going upstairs to the toilet. *I am so ashamed, Momma, I am so ashamed that I have to pee in the sink, it disgusts me. I have to drag the chair and climb on it and then disgustingly lower my knickers and lower myself and pee in the kitchen sink then let the tap run to flush it down. I am so disgusting, Momma.*

Shame. Shame on you, Jean Kennedy. You are going down, down, down.

A fortnight passed. I knew it was a fortnight because twice the landlord had knocked looking for his rent, and twice I had lain still until he went away. There was nothing I could do, for Momma had forgotten to send money. On the second occasion he turned the key and pushed the door to discover that the security chain was fastened. Through the crack, he called, 'I'll come back,' and he said it rather gently and went away quietly. But I knew this accumulation of debt could not go on and I knew that one or other of my debtors would finally lose patience. So one night, abandoning my belongings, I left in the darkness, silently, trembling. I pulled open the great Edwardian front door, with its slight sticking sound that was like the peeling back of Sellotape. *Don't run. Don't run yet.* The gravel would be a problem, I had forgotten that, but it was 4.30 a.m., the house sat in darkness. I took the six or seven steps across the gravel to the sandy grassy bank at the side where the hedge grew, and I moved quickly along it. Through the garden, out the gate. *Now run. Run now.* I ran against the half-darkness, half-light of the early morning. I ran home. But there, of course, I could not stay.

I crept into the bedroom that I no longer shared with Cissy, that was no longer mine. My old bed had been removed, and Cissy was sleeping in a double bed. When I slipped into the bed beside her, she sat up with a start and then embraced me, and we bent into each other like spoons in a drawer, just as we had always done when we were afraid. Lying next to her, sleeping and not sleeping, I enjoyed the warmth of Cissy's body and the sound of her smacking her lips, so familiar to me. And then I was fully awake, listening to the empty milk bottles being removed as fresh ones were set down by the canny, creeping milkman. I lay on my back, and as the room brightened I could see that Cissy had covered the walls in posters of horses that she had cut out of her equestrian magazine. They seemed to stare at me in protest, as though I had invaded their space, wandered into their wild places, rather than they into mine. I had not seen Cissy for weeks, and when I had imagined her, I had not imagined her sleeping in this room, as it was now.

Cissy stirred. 'I'd better go,' I whispered. 'No, please don't,' she said, and sat up, seizing me round the shoulders. 'I haven't seen you for ages – you have to stay with us. They'll forgive you when they see you.' That was Cissy's dream speaking, her child's view of the world, and foolishly I went along with it.

Cissy dressed as we whispered to each other, and giddily she told me about her boyfriend, who worked in the stables in Enniskerry after school, of how they had just celebrated their second anniversary – though in months not in years, she laughed – and then we went downstairs to the kitchen. For a moment I seemed to have forgotten that I ought not to be here, in this house. Cissy served me cereal and toast, she told me where the sugar was, where the spoons were, as though it were not my home, as though I were not at home. We ate silently, glancing across the table at each other, wondering how much more time we would have together.

Momma came first, wrapped in her dressing gown that could barely close around her middle now, so large and round had she become. Her face was flushed and her hair cropped short to her chin. She had new pink-rimmed glasses. When she saw me, she came straight over and pulled me into her warm clasp and she wept and wept and said, 'My Jeannie, my Jeannie.'

Cissy made her tea and Momma and I sat hand in hand, but we said nothing. I did not expect this to last long, so I just held her hand while I could, knowing that soon she would withdraw it, that she would remember, that she would be angry again. 'Can she stay?' asked Cissy, and that set Momma crying again. 'Oh, I don't think so. I don't think Daddy would like it after what happened.' And I felt neither grief nor disappointment, for I had already grieved for them all for a long time now. And this house had become a strange place to me. In so little time, a strange and stifling place where I no longer knew how to be anyone who might belong in it.

HE came to the door then and after only a very brief glance at me, he drew in his breath, muttered, 'Christ,' and then, 'Get her out of my sight.' And then HE left, and I saw him pass the kitchen window in the direction of Tilly's granny flat, where he would no doubt be fed with Saturday-morning croques monsieur.

Momma spent the day with the *Evening Herald*, making phone calls to arrange a new home for me. That night she sent me in a taxi to stay with Aunty Ida. She gave me a white envelope with lots of twenty-pound notes so that I would not have to worry for a while if I did not find some kind of a part-time job, and anyhow, she assured me, she could always send me more money. I was not to worry.

Aunty Ida seemed of the opinion that I had created a bit of a mess, unnecessarily. Compassionately and philosophically she counselled, 'We can't always say what we want to say, you know. Some things should just not be said. Better not to. Life's too hard when you do. And anyhow,' she said, 'your daddy makes a great living. Where would your mammy be without him?'

The next morning, my new flat arranged, Aunty Ida blew me a kiss as I drove off in the taxi. I turned in the seat to look back at her, and then I turned away, overwhelmed and brimming as I was with absences, and now hers to top them up.

Presences are warm and they land on you here and there, in your arms, in your hands, in the warm part of your tummy, in the small of your back. But absences occupy every part of you, every inch, every bone, every muscle, every cavity, and should you hesitate at a mirror, viciously and mercilessly they stare you down. Absences are loud. They are as loud as

when the teacher calls the roll and the loudest child present
is the child who does not answer, the child who is absent.

The Mischief of the Lugworms

The new flat was one storey up, so at least I did not have to
worry about anyone banging on my window. It was not far
from the last one, so when leaving and coming back I would
have to keep an eye out for my two creditors: my old landlord,
for I owed him a good deal of money, and the American artist.

The taxi driver dropped my boxes of books at the bottom
of the front steps. I dragged them upstairs to my new bedsit
and shut the door, fastening the chain across it. Suddenly
faint and drained, without removing my coat and without
putting a sheet on the bed, I fell upon it. Immediately the
odour of damp and must rose up and seeped through me.
The mattress sagged, wet and cold against me.

For endless days a long silence fell. I stopped phoning the
house because I had been so often disappointed by Tilly's
report that Momma was sleeping. And Momma didn't call
me. And no one came. I was vaguely aware that I ought to be
waiting to hear if I would get my place at university, but I
was not waiting, for I did not care. I began to fear that the
melancholy that had taken Momma from us so many times
had come to take me, for I became as still as she had become,
and as silent. And every time I woke – in and out of what
seemed a constant slumber – I determined each time to fall
asleep once more. The days stacked up against me and the

nights were filled with a stiffening grief that I could not account for, for no one had died. The strange bed, uncomfortable and chilling though it was, held me captive, and I was as helpless as though caught in a great iron claw. I did not fight but instead permitted the claw its victory. The days passed like nights and only when it was dark and silent did I make my way down to the sea.

One evening, sometime in early August, just after darkness fell, when the great house of bedsits sat at last still and hushed around me, after a three-night absence I decided to go to the strand. As always, I left the house in silence, fearful of disturbing the other tenants, all of whom I had managed to avoid in the three weeks since I had moved in. I turned out of the village with a vague sense that something was taking shape in my mind, something from which I had been shielding myself for some time, but which now would insist on being heard.

Too weary to walk out to the water, I sat on the strand wall, gazing across the sands broken here and there by pools of shallow water that shimmered under the moonlight. From unseen places, birds of varied song curled across the distance. For a while, out towards the Shelly Banks, I watched three figures, bent and digging for fishing bait. I watched them, thinking, *What is it that they are feeling, that I am feeling?* After some time, they walked back towards the road. I watched their car glide silently towards the city until it disappeared. I wondered what those bait-diggers might say to one another on that journey. But I could imagine no conversation. And it occurred to me: loneliness is something more than a feeling on the inside of yourself. You can see it also on the outside of yourself, for no matter where you look, it reflects back to you.

A thick cloud shifted in from somewhere far out at sea to block the moon's light so that the shallow pools no longer shone and the darkness landed solid. I began to consider the position in which I found myself. I began to wonder what I might do. As I sat staring dumbly at the horizon, I made some calculations: *The distance between where you stand at any point on Sandymount Strand to where the unreachable waves flatly glitter like a field of furrowed metal is the definition of infinity. And the sum of absences, felt in every muscle, bone, cavity and scale of the skin, is the beginning of the end.* There now. Something of a victory over absence, if only in an equation.

So the ending was imminent. It had not been my decision, but no part of me seemed ready to object. And with this realization came insight and a full comprehension of the destruction I had caused, of the trouble with truth. Truth did not matter. It was not, after all, the thing that keeps us whole. It was, as all along Momma could see, the thing that would break us apart.

And there I sat, and I sat, until the cold chill of the wall had burned up into my thighs. The sky darkened, lightened, darkened. Lightened to exhibit at some incalculable distance a rectangular ship with no bottom, only barely connected to the water – like all ships off Sandymount – nearly motionless, trying to enter or exit the bay. Run aground on a sandy bank, perhaps? But no. Watch closely. It was moving. It was I who was still. Boats never seem to move in Dublin Bay, but when you turn back to glance at them once more, they have always disappeared. That is just the way it is with this bay. Is it the tides, or the mischief of the lugworms, or is it just because this is a disappearing place?

Long past the midnight chimes of Star of the Sea, I gazed across that desert. What was I to do with this sense of an ending, pushed upon me by the choking absences which had filled every vacant part of me? It would happen without me, though it was to be my very own ending. I would be its instrument and yet also a bystander. And another equation came to me: *the inhaling and exhaling of a summer breeze through a net-curtained window is the equivalent of one's participation in the inevitable ending which sometimes comes to one, which is at all times equal to the swinging of a Wall's Ice Cream sign in a summer breeze witnessed only by a cat indistinct in colour.*

That equation balanced, there seemed no reason not to give up entirely, but I was not afraid. Something was going to happen, something inevitable. I was powerless against it, for it had already overtaken me. Numbed by this new knowledge, I retreated to my bedsit to await my ending.

There in black sleep the claw held me, merciless in its grip, for many days, each one nameless, as slowly, slowly, I disappeared. *I am so ashamed, Momma, so ashamed that I have given up.*

Nevertheless . . .

Yet, quite mysteriously, one evening, perhaps a week or so later, something lifted in me. I had determined to go to the strand no more, vowed that I would turn my back on that disappearing place that had somehow flattened me. But then I felt again a longing for the sea. I opened my eyes, unbound myself from the foetal position and lay on my back, contemplating rising from the claw, which had loosened its grip. My hand had been dangling to the floor, my fingertips just about brushing the cover of my Leaving Certificate poetry book, *Soundings*. And then – I picked it up. I turned to those lines that had for so long perplexed me: 'O the mind, mind has mountains; cliffs of fall / Frightful . . .' I understood in that moment that what had happened at the strand was that I had fallen. And if I had fallen, I could get up. In some 'selfyeast of spirit', I rose from that black sleep; and in search of crashing waves and of a wider sea, I set out for Seapoint.

By the time I was freewheeling down Seapoint Avenue, the evening sun was in its last half hour. I hid my bicycle behind the bathing shelter and headed past the Martello Tower to the ramp to the sea. The tide was out and the small beach teemed with life. Little parties of sandpipers and wagtails foraged for delicacies left behind by the tide. Out on a distant rock a singular long-billed, white-bellied cormorant stood confident on his stilts, gaping out across his fishing grounds. Half a dozen times I walked the length of the short beach. I knew it impossible, but I was certain that I could hear not just the water's lapping, not just the seabirds' song, but the sounds of crabs no bigger than my fingernail, creeping and living, and the swishing of the tails of those shoals of minnows.

The last couple of evening bathers retreated, disappointed

by the water's shallowness and the sudden darkness. Occasionally a dog-walker strode up the beach, but soon I found myself alone. The tide was coming in. The water set about rattling the shingle, lifting the sea plants that swirled about. Unperturbed by my presence, and while there was still time, the parties of little sanderlings intensified their foraging at the water's edge, anxious to feast on what they could before the beach was taken again, to disappear beneath the shallow waters.

I climbed back over the rocks and sat on the bench by the railway footbridge whose pillars rose darkly above me, high up towards the deserted road. I was contemplating removing my tennis shoes and wading for a while when something distracted me and, for no reason I could detect, I felt an uneasiness, an urge to make haste as the sandpipers were making haste, to get off the beach before the tide came. But I resisted because I knew that if I left, I would be defeated and I was so relishing those moments of communion with those sandpipers.

Perhaps it was the change of mood that I witnessed high over my head that changed my sense of that place. Two gulls, first heard squawking overhead, suddenly swung down on wide wings and skimmed the water, their white wingtips almost brushing the spray. At first, I thought them partners, united in their hunt for supper, until without warning of any shifting mood, one of the gulls banked, turned and lunged at the other, who screeched and, panic-struck, flew in confused circles overhead. The other pursued him, screaming accusations. Out of nowhere a band of gulls, in investigation of the commotion, screamed and swooped down at the feuding pair, immediately took the side of the pursuer, and lunged violently at the guilty party until he fled far out to sea. Though I did not know the cause of the row, I felt somehow the injustice of that condemnation by the mob. I wondered sadly whether the offending gull would survive. I wondered whether he had been wrongly accused.

So distracted was I by the court of the gulls that I hadn't noticed a new arrival at the shore. A man in a dark overcoat was striding – with little thought for the sandpipers who on his approach scattered in low flight up the beach – towards the water's edge. He stopped, turned around, put his fingers in his mouth and produced a long, sharp whistle that pierced the night, whose sounds until that moment had hovered in such perfect balance. Moments later a large black dog, barely visible against the darkness, bounded up to him, made towards his ankles playfully, then changed its mind and entered the water where it waded for a moment and then galloped, barking angrily as the waves broke and crashed. Without warning the man pivoted as though suddenly aware that he was being watched. Caught out, I turned away quickly and tried to appear as though I had been gazing beyond him, out to sea. A strong instinct told me to get up quickly and leave the beach, but I was afraid that such a swift departure might draw the man's attention to me.

It had grown chilly. I zipped up my anorak and sat on my cold hands. In a moment, I determined, I would leave. I checked the man's position to find that he was nowhere to be seen. He and his dog had left the beach. I decided to sit another while, now that the little party of sandpipers had moved up to the cover of the rocks and were only a couple of feet from me, now that they seemed calmer and were feasting on dead crab claws that lay scattered on the rocks.

For how long I sat, I could not say, but out across the distance even those two ships that had been sitting in the bay all evening had vanished. I became vaguely aware of my isolation, of the lateness of the hour, that I ought to leave, when, suddenly alarmed, the sandpipers abandoned their feasting and all at once flitted away. Suddenly the man was behind me. He and his dog, two black shadows, two dark exhalations into the empty salt air. The bay had seen this kind of thing before. I had never felt such darkness, but when it comes, you know it; there is no mistaking it.

I dared not move. The dog wandered onto the rocks and panted and snuffled and peered into the shallow rockpools. I heard the chain of its leash clink as it dragged on the ground behind him. And then the dark was all around me. Two great hands, warm and fat-fingered, grasped about my neck and began to squeeze. The pressure was even, controlled, calm, firm but slow, like when you want to squeeze some sauce from a bottle, but just the right amount, not too much so as not to ruin your meal.

I was caught. My only thought was, *So this is inevitable*, the end of the absences at least. I had willed this through my calculation, my equation, nights before when I had sat at Sandymount Strand, unwittingly admitting dark forces. I have never felt such strength and conviction in a pair of hands as I felt in those about my throat now. I was a sparrow with a sparrow neck. I would fold. But then suddenly out of the blue, Momma came to mind, and it struck me that Momma would hate this. She would really hate this ending. My hands reached up and seized his great forearms, just above his great wrists. I could only grip them; I could not move them or pull them apart to release even a little of the pressure on my neck. As I pulled with no effect, my legs began to kick out in front of me, up and out and back against the wall. The right, the left, the right, the left. As furiously as they could, they kicked out, beating the chill salt air, back and forth, like a girl on a swing trying to slow it down by interrupting its momentum, and all that time I was thinking, *Momma would hate this ending.*

Then his hands were off my neck. I felt them opening and felt him draw back a little from me. I fell forward from the bench onto my knees, and I crawled a little towards where I could hear the dog scrapping about in the rocks. Then I was on my feet, and I was running.

I ran onto the sand, my feet stumbling on the uneven ground. As the sand became wetter, deeper, my feet changed direction, back towards the bathing shelter. I could feel the man's dark figure in pursuit behind me. How far behind, I could not tell. Then suddenly I became aware of his lack of firm direction. I felt his incompetence, his stumbling. He could not run as fast as I. He seemed to be losing heart and I could tell that he did not really hope or expect to catch me. I sensed him slowing.

'I'm sorry. I'm sorry,' he yelled. 'I didn't mean to. I'm sorry. Jesus I'm sorry. I only want to say sorry to you.'

But I kept running. *See, Momma, see how fast I can run now.* And then I was pushing my bicycle before me up the steep avenue that led down to the sea; leaping upon it at the top, pedalling frantically along Seapoint Avenue, and then with every bone of my body trembling I tore through Blackrock village, past the bird sanctuary at Williamstown, over the railway crossing, until at last I was behind my bedsit door.

The man had failed. And something about him told me that, a bit like me, he hardly ever did anything right. *But there you are anyhow, Momma. It's all right, I am still here. And I am so ashamed, Momma, so ashamed that I almost gave up.*

After that terrible turning of the tide, I became afraid to go down to the sea. I missed the sunset, the sandpipers' delicate feasting, even the courts of the seagulls. I felt the injustice of it; considered disguising myself as a boy; abandoned the idea as foolish, it having failed me once before. And in any case, I was reminded of the words of Anthony Patch in *The Beautiful and Damned*, those words which upon first reading had offended me, but which now seemed finally indisputable: '*Most girls are sparrows.*' The evenings grew longer, the days shorter. There was less to miss at the sea. Gradually, I felt less deprived of it.

Eighteen

At the University

Summer passed. My hunger was restored to me. I was, as I wanted to be, plank-like, Sugar Puffs my mainstay. Twice a day, morning and evening, their sweetness was sufficient to quell my appetite, and the two boxes a week that I consumed fell well within the small budget I allocated for food. I got a job covering the lunch hour of a woman who worked in the bookshop in Sandymount Green. Aunty Ida had arranged it. I had been fearful about it, but unnecessarily so, for no one came in for the entire two weeks I worked there. I did not speak, except to say hello when I entered to relieve the woman for her lunch break, and to say goodbye when I left. If I was careful and did not bend a book's spine, I was permitted to read it. I read *Jude the Obscure*. I feared I was becoming him. He seemed unfortunate, plank-like. When I read about his failure to be accepted into the university, and then of his son's ending – the children hanged – I went home and crawled into my bed. I wept for Jude and with him. Well, who would not? That was the end of my career in the bookshop. I would not return, for there on the shelf sat Jude's ending waiting for me, and I could not bear to know it.

Momma phoned on the 10th of September at 4.30 p.m. I was lying once more in the grip of the claw. The girl from the top landing banged on my door for ages. I was pretending to be out, but she knew. She did not cease banging until I gave in.

My place at the university had come in the post. 'You don't seem excited,' Momma said.

'No, I am. I really am.'

Poor sad Jude. I am a plank, Momma, silent and creeping. You should see me. You have not seen me for weeks. I am plank-like, straight-bodied, flat, hard, silent. I won't speak again, Momma, I promise you. Your love has won my silence, for love conquers all.

All Beginnings Are Hard

The first morning came. I lay in bed, heavy, my eyes stinging from sleeplessness. *Must I go?* I thought. *Why should I go?* I thought. *My books are here about me. I am a plank, shelf-like — these books sit well upon me. I am alone. It is good to be alone. It will be the same as school, I know that, because I am the same. Girls from school will be there. They will see how I continue to be alone. It will amuse them. Why is loneliness so visible, so shaming? Why can't it be concealed, like bad teeth, behind lips?*

I could lie here. I could just lie here. But HE has paid the fees. It is too late. Momma will phone and describe his anger. 'Poor Daddy,' she will say, 'poor Daddy.'

Then I seem to have left, for I see myself pulling the door of my bedsit behind me. It is early October, but it is too warm. My brown anorak encloses me. I am steaming inside it. I can smell my body, but I need it to cover the plank, for it has grown brittle. I fear it might snap.

I have deep worries. I do not know where to go. I pass the Nassau Street entrance, follow the wall that curves to College Green. Through an archway, across ancient wooden tiles. I almost slip: wet leaves on the tiles. I emerge into grey autumn sunlight.

Immediately assaulted by a fairground: *Roll up, roll up. Sign up here for archery trigonometry chess horses boats thespians hockey.* A couple of roaring student ambassadors catch my eye, but they are instantly embarrassed and their eyes dart away. A plank in an anorak cannot belong here. I pass through them with deliberation: my head juts forward, my eyes on the rounded cobblestones that glisten from the early-morning shower. How must I look? *Hey you, what kind of bird are you?*

I burrow on through the tunnel of student-society stands, trying to look as though I am intent on my purpose. At last I exit the human tunnel. I see a library. Books visible through its long windows. Books to the ceiling. There, that is my society.

All beginnings are hard. I searched out Freud in the library; I had heard that he had answers. I selected *The Psychopathology of Everyday Life*. It seemed relevant, though difficult. Long before the designated time of my first lecture, I went to the room listed on the noticeboard. I went early to be first, so as not to have to make my way through rows of students. To be there first and seem perhaps as though I was in command.

I brought *Daniel Deronda*, because it looked impressively large. Not Freud, of course, for I did not want them to see me reading psychology. They might be led to conclude that there was something wrong with me. That I was mental.

No one came: no professor, no students. I got up from my seat numerous times, checking the number on the outside of the door. I wondered what kind of place I had come to, no one turning up to learn. And then I understood the meaning of Freshers' Week. Everyone else was where they were supposed to be, outside in the fairground.

By the second Monday, I knew how to enter. I knew how to walk: with a folding of my arms across my chest, not too tight, not too limp, my head downcast, my old school satchel thumping my rear.

Hey, leave her alone, she's thinking, she's one of those — you know what I mean, one of those.

I arrived at my first lecture before anyone else. Then a girl, not knowing my reputation for silence, sat beside me. She crossed her legs. Her leg-warmers were striped, pink and purple. Cissy had the same ones. Should I say something — about the leg-warmers?

'Hey,' she said. Did I detect a Californian lilt? In my first lecture had I found an American? I tried to emulate her casual tone, but it was beyond me. The word, the single word *hey*, got stuck in my diaphragm. She turned some pages in her folder. They were empty, the pages divided by pink subject dividers. She stooped into her bag. I thought she must be thinking, *I have to move*. But she emerged from the shallows of her belongings and sat back.

A boy and a girl entered. The girl called out to my neighbour. The boy exuded good humour. He stopped in front of her, clicked his heels and saluted. I had the bad luck to catch his eye at that very moment. He was beautiful. I turned crimson. The couple sat down. I saw that she too was beautiful. My neighbour began to jiggle in her chair, edging away from me. She bent to her bag again, ducked into the shallows, searching through them, emerging with something like a chopstick. She gathered her thick chestnut hair in her suntanned hand, twisted it and pierced the knot with the chopstick. I was mesmerized.

I opened *Daniel Deronda*. She slyly bent her head to see what I was reading. 'Jesus, it's massive. I have no fucking intention of reading that,' she said. She said *fucking* beautifully: *fuck-king*. 'Have you any notes on it?' She seemed friendly after all. Alas, I had to disappoint her: 'Not yet.'

A group sauntered in, chatting excitedly. I thought I detected Spanish perfume. I shouldn't have looked up from *Daniel*, but I did. In the company of three other girls, Margaret Collins, powerful since 1896, breezed across the room. On her way to a seat in the front row, her new set of friends trailing behind her, she caught my eye – *Hey, what are you doing here?* – and moved on. Suddenly the room felt too small to me, the air too close. My neighbour shifted. She knew she had made a serious mistake. I felt her look me up and down. I felt licked by a cat. Cats sense when you are uncomfortable around them; to make it better – or worse – they lick you. She had recognized something in me. She asked, 'Are you cold?' Her tone was incredulous, though not unkind, not wholly. I nodded. My lips trembled — *do not cry here*. She gathered up her folder.

Please do not move. If you had moved four minutes ago it would not have mattered — but please do not move now, not in front of Margaret Collins. If you stay, I will write your essays — all your essays — I will . . .

But it was too late. She had risen. 'Oh, by the way, if you get a chance to make some notes on that monster I'd love to share.' I looked up. I nodded and smiled. I neglected to tell her that it wasn't on the reading list.

That evening I exited through the front arch. My future had been determined. It had begun when the professor entered, when he had stood over my chair, towering, casting his shadow upon me, as he addressed the class. For a moment his fingers had tap-danced on my desk, then scuttled across the cover of *Daniel Deronda*. In those very moments it began. It was like a soft ticking at first, almost a bubbling, but then it gained power and force and momentum and ticked and swung and banged and ticked and swung and banged against my breast. I made it to the toilet just in time, before every-thing fell out of me.

In the library afterwards I sat at my favourite desk, beneath the bust of Samuel Beckett, and thought about that event, about its visibility to the others. I pressed my hand to my forehead, feigning concentration, concealing the reality that my head was about to blow off. Beckett's bust above me, set on its pedestal, without body, his iron eyes penetrating, watching me. *Are you sure you should be here?* I pretended not to hear him. Could Beckett have seen me rushing to the loo?

My eye was drawn to a heart etched onto the leatherette top of the desk, an arrow through it. And next I was drawn to the word *FUCK* penned deep into the desk's wooden border. *Fuck off – I love you – fuck off I love – hate I hate.* I had to tilt my head to continue the story as it continued around the curve of the desk. In the end I could not tell whether it was a tale that ended with hate or with love. And then I planned my liberation. I would exit through the tunnel and I would not return. *Never, Mr Beckett. This is your place, not mine.*

Does This Girl Speak?

But to my surprise, I did return. Trinity College, Year 1, week 4, Michaelmas term, raining. I had missed almost two weeks of lectures but returned with a carefully conceived strategy: sit at the back of lecture rooms, or towards the back; arrive early or just a little late; always be absorbed in a book. Dracula is just about to dig his fangs into the pale-skinned girl who is somehow out in the storm alone; Tom and Maggie are lost in the flood waters – would she do it, would she kill them?

A couple of times I was asked, 'What are you reading?' Or, 'Good book?' All that I would like to have said was clear in my mind as I walked home to my flat in Sandymount: *Jane is magnificent – you must know Jane. You don't know Jane? Let me introduce you to Miss Jane Eyre. Ha, ha. A glass of wine? Yes, I'd love to. Especially because you are so handsome with your thick brown hair and your blue eyes and your lisp which I can see embarrasses you but makes me feel weak when I hear it. And you are so tall and straight and I love the way your jacket hangs on your shoulders and most of all I love the little dog-eared notebook that sticks out of your pocket and the pencil that sits in your breast pocket and the fact that apart from your bicycle clips, that dog-eared notebook is all that you carry, and I love it when I pass you and you are bending to unlock your big, black, old-fashioned bicycle, and all the way as I walk home I listen for you coming up behind me, tinkling your old-fashioned bicycle bell, and when I turn round you grin like Butch Cassidy and you open your arms to invite me to sit on your crossbar, and as I prepare my food in the evening I listen for the flat bell to ring because I know it will be you. Come for a spin, you say. I dream before I go to sleep that you turn round and stand up and you say, Oh hi there, Sleepy Jean — would you like a crossbar home or we could cycle to the sea and eat ice cream? Come on up here on my crossbar and I will spread my long arms around you and tuck you in like a blanket. Come on up here on my crossbar and we will cycle away and I will be funny and make you laugh, and don't worry about that other girl. Sure she is very pretty but I prefer you because you are just my kind of girl.*

But of course, you probably don't know my name, because already it is week 4, Michaelmas term, raining. I have so far been mainly absent, and when present I have not spoken.

I had taken to scrawling inky words across foolscap paper as though desperate to finish writing an essay. Nobody asked, 'What are you writing?' No one approached me, except once when a girl asked me if I would mind moving back a row so that she could sit beside her friend. *Of course, of course. I am so sorry I sat here, I should not have, I should have known better.*

The greatest concern was that the professor would call upon me to answer a question or to give an opinion. I wasn't sure whether it would be better to try to look stupid or highly intelligent and fully absorbed. *How would you like me to play this, Professor Higgins?* He selected students, apparently at random, to give presentations on various topics. The beautiful boy with the notebook in his breast pocket had given one. How beautifully his lisped words had rung out, how fascinating his untidiness had been, his confusion when he had lost his place, not having numbered his pages, which had made him run his fingers through his long, thick hair. How charming his embarrassment, which had made him shift his feet and lean on the lectern this way and that, awkwardly because he was so tall, stooping to rest his elbow. And when class had ended, his friends had gone over to him and patted him on the back, and he had run his fingers through his hair and laughed before they whisked him off to the Buttery for beer, I would guess. *Come back, come back, I will take you. I'm the one who loves you, come back. Look over here, I'm over here.*

The question was, would I be next? And then –

'At the back there – I don't know what your name is – but next week, twenty minutes on memory in Samuel Beckett's radio play *Embers*.'

Yes, Professor Higgins, of course. Now, how would you like me to play this? I could lie on the ground right now and die; I could throw a fit like a woman possessed by demons, writhing about on the floor; I could pay a hitman to cut out my tongue; I could throw myself in front of a car on the way to class. You would run to the window on hearing the screeching of the car brakes and the screams of the crowd.

Would that convince you? See that girl lying under the wheel of the car down there, class, she can't speak after all.

On the other hand, what if I could do this? If I worked very hard, could I do it? Suppose I knew everything upside down and inside out? Once I was up there at the lectern, perhaps I would be fine. After all, the beautiful boy had lisped and been awkward and hardly anything he had said was coherent, and everyone had patted his back and he had laughed about it and they had gone off drinking. Perhaps, perhaps I could do this. And if I stuttered and lost my place, perhaps the beautiful boy would come and take me for a beer, and then I could sit enveloped by his arms on the cross-bar and we would ride off together into the dark evening.

Memory in Samuel Beckett's radio play *Embers* – could I do this? I read at my favourite seat in the Berkeley Library, ordering books from stacks, piling them high around me, making copious notes, using up three ink cartridges – two black and one blue. I read Freud on memory and Jung on memory, I read Jung on Freud on memory, and I selected extracts from the play to demonstrate my point about subjectivity and memory. I outlined the dramatis personae: the father, dead, sitting on the rock in the bay; his son Henry desperately trying to engage him; the wife nagging that angry son about the dangers of sitting on damp rocks ('they're bad for your growths'); the ghostly, distant figure of the little daughter, high above on the cliffs, tormented by her music master ('*smart blow of cylindrical ruler on piano case*'). The daughter who wouldn't let go of Papa's hand: 'Run along now, Addie, and look at the lambs.' Then to the effort of analysis, my analysis.

And all that time that I sat at the desk, dedicated to my task, on the fifth floor of the Berkeley Library, Beckett himself was looking down at me, through his cutting metal eyes, from his pedestal. And when I raised my eyes to glance at him – *I think I've cracked it, Mr Beckett!* – I thought I caught a cynical grin.

I paid to have the relevant passages from the script photo-copied so that I could distribute them before my presentation. *Here, beautiful boy with the bicycle, pass these around, would you? Thank you ever so much. Sorry, what did you say? Yes, it's Jean, though some call me Jeannie. Really, you never noticed me until this moment? Well, here I am.*

And so the day came and I had twenty numbered pages ready, with writing on one side only so that nothing would become blurred or difficult to read, important points under-lined in red biro so that I would remember to emphasize them. And I had read it out loud backwards and forwards all day Saturday and Sunday; the people in the neighbouring flats must have thought I had friends in. I made my way to the lectern and settled my pages on the desk. People were still chatting quietly. Should I begin? Wait until there was silence? And then the silence came and there I was in its net. Should I begin? Should I begin with: *Hello, my name is . . . ?* Why hadn't I worked that out before? 'You can start,' said the professor.

'In this presentation I want to examine the charge of misogyny which, it is claimed, runs through the character of Henry's relationship with his wife and daughter. Critics of the work often comment –'

'I'll stop you there.'

I stopped. What had gone wrong?

'Sorry, I can't hear you. Can you speak up?'

I nodded towards him and began again: '. . . often comment that the work is indecipherable, and in any case bears no resemblance to his actual attitude towards women, but I would argue that –'

'Stop – I still can't hear you. Can anyone hear her?' He looked out across the rows of students, and I looked too, though my head was still bending to the papers. Some grunted, some shook their heads, some stared at me with a vague look of sympathy, some with a vague look of horror. One or two lowered their heads discreetly, pretending to write something down.

'It's not just me, then,' said Professor Higgins. 'Speak up.'

'But I would argue that Beckett is purposefully trying to demonstrate –'

'No, no, go back to the beginning. I haven't heard anything yet.'

Back to the top of the page. *The rain in Spain stays mainly in the plain*. My voice was shaking now, my ears burning. I began again.

'LOOK, I still can't hear you. Can anyone else?' He looked around the room. 'Can you speak louder, I wonder?'

I nodded and began again. 'The imagery of the bay and its two sides might represent . . .' Out of the corner of my eye, I saw the professor stand up.

'I'll stop you again. Let's get this sorted. Right now, first of all, I have no idea why you are wearing that big coat. It must be twenty-five degrees in here. Shall we start with you taking that off.'

Now this was highly entertaining. Everyone was having fun. I wanted to say, *No, Professor, I will not, I cannot. Do you know what is under this anorak? Do you have any idea? If you did, you would not dream of asking me to take it off. Once it is off there will be no going back: particles and particles of dust will sail across the lecture room.*

But there went the anorak, slipping from my shoulders. I folded it slightly and put it over a nearby chair. The sleeve slipped to the floor. *Am I still in there?*

I resumed.

'No, still nothing. Is that the loudest you can speak? Do you have a speech impediment or something?'

I shook my head, still looking down at my pages.

'Because if it's a speech impediment you should have told me, and I wouldn't have wasted the class asking you to present. No, not a speech impediment? OK, start again. Come on, shout, pretend you're calling out across a field or something.' He put his hand to his mouth, making the shape of a megaphone. 'HELL–OO,' he called, aiming his speaker at the back wall of the lecture room. Everyone laughed. 'Go on,' he said, giving me a little smile, 'start again.'

I will be here all day if I keep starting again, this is a time warp, I will be here forever, starting again and again and again; they will be there with their arms folded, staring at me, delighted I am taking so long because the class will be over and the professor will not have time to ask them for their comments.

'Critics of Beckett –'

'Look,' he said, 'sit down. I am sure that what you have there is very interesting, but no one can hear you so there's no point in wasting any more class time.'

I gathered my pages, picked up my anorak, which felt so heavy on my arm – I knew I was still inside it – and slunk back towards my seat. As I passed the others, my head hanging, I began to recognize some of the people sitting on the chairs. There was Uncle Ronnie, in the corner, not paying any attention to anything other than the bowl of yellow jelly he was sucking up between his teeth; there was the American artist with his easel, a paintbrush between his teeth; there in the front row hung a line of builders' boots swinging back and forth, their black leather caked in dirty cement. And there in the very corner was my father holding his stomach, which hurt from laughing so much.

Sunlit Girl

For twenty-seven days, I lay in bed. My only companion, the living mattress. Though I had stretched two layers of sheets across it, it itched me, poked me, probed me with its mean and hard fingers. Unable to find a place to nestle in this strange bed, I felt myself a trespasser, with all the ghosts of former tenants in league to oust me. *Hey, this is our bed of ashes and dust. Find your own.*

My mind flitted about in all directions. I saw things, places, people, ghosts. I heard their voices. Sometimes I was in transit, as though I were a passenger in some terrible vehicle flying over lost days, looking down. I analysed myself. Too much Freud, or perhaps too little. I focused often on the foolishness of my demeanour, of my voice, my voicelessness, my cawing, gargling. I had shown them all my weakness. Vaguely I contemplated my own ending, but lacked the motivation to bring it about. I knew I would be gone soon, like a bluebottle zapped by the electric blue-light executioner. Gone, whoosh, past the Wall's Ice Cream sign.

I rose only to use the toilet and to call Momma on the public telephone in the hall. Often, she could not come to the phone. Once Aunty Ida had answered, and chatted sweetly to me. 'You are such a clever girl,' she had said, by which she meant, *I know your heart is falling out of you, like mine, and that, like me, no one will ever want you.* She went away to get Momma, then came back and said, 'Your mammy's indisposed at the moment, Jeannie. But she said to say . . . she misses you.'

She knew I did not believe her. Instantly she knew and regretted it. 'Do you like the food there – in Trinity?' I reported that they served chips in the Buttery all day. 'All day long?' She could hardly believe my luck. 'All day, Jeannie. Highly unusual.'

Another time Cissy came to the phone instead of Momma, though she could not chat for long. Her horse-obsessed boyfriend demanded all of her time. She told me she had kissed him. I hadn't asked. I warned her about herpes. She said, 'Oh my God, Jean, grow up.'

I didn't seem to be able to – grow up, that is. I seemed to be stuck. Stuck somewhere in an airless box.

Vaguely I knew there was a last humiliation in front of me

that I would have to bear. It was the essay. Not the mark, the inevitable fail, but the humiliation that would result from my honesty. The professor had instructed us: 'Write what you see in the relationships between Beckett and the women in *Embers*.' What I had claimed to see was shameful, and surely in that he would see the real Jean Kennedy. But I would not be caught this time. For as long as I lay here waiting for the inevitable blue light, the electric disappearance – whoosh in a jiffy – I was safe.

Sometimes I was lucid. Panicked lucidly. What had I written, declared of myself? I had commented on Beckett's coldness, hatred, misogyny, captured in that moment when the father wished to dismiss his little daughter. He had dropped her hand: 'Go on with you now when you're told and look at the lambs!' Shaming her. It is shameful to be hated by one's father. No doubt the analysis was entirely subjective, emotional, too much Freud – or too little.

How frail and helpless the professor would think me, mouse-like, as broken as that daughter. Why had I not focused on the majesty of Beckett's language instead of on his brutal coldness? *What brutality?* the professor would say. *What coldness?* the professor would say. How I had let my guard down, and to him, to this man who had drummed his scuttling fingers on my copy of *Daniel Deronda* as though he were entitled to. A man terrible in his suit and his tie and his pointy black shoes. He who had towered over me that day outside his office when I had stuttered and murmured an apology for the lateness of the essay. 'Put it in the essay tray,' he had said, incandescent at my stupidity. To think that he might have sullied those fingers, broken his train of thought for the day by accepting my thin analysis. But then, as I had begun down the corridor, feeling his eyes boring into me, he had called me back in an annoyed tone: 'Here, give it to me – I'll take it.' So I had had to turn back, though really I wanted to run away from him, down the corridor, into the stairwell, out the Nassau Street entrance – never to return. But I had returned to him, crimson-cheeked, sweating in my anorak, head jutting out, shoulders stooped. *Shame on you, Jean Kennedy.* I had held it out to him, my meagre offering, and he had snatched it. I feared I would cry. My bottom lip trembled, twitched. He peered down at me, and he must have seen the twitching for I thought I heard him say, 'You got your hand back, didn't you?' And I knew that he would think my essay foolish, and through it see deep inside me and know me stupid and dark and broken.

Yet, in spite of all that, on the twenty-eighth day I rose again. What raised me from the mattress, I cannot say. It is a mystery. There are mysteries. Perhaps it was that I could not help being curious about the mark which by now I would have been given by the tall professor who had hovered over me, his fingers tentacling on *Daniel Deronda*. Perhaps it was because I needed to retrieve the essay, lest anyone else should read it. Retrieve it and destroy it. Whatever it was, I knew that I could not leave the essay behind in the university while I departed to some elsewhere. I decided to go through the tunnel one more time.

I suited up in my anorak. I felt thinner. Perhaps my muscles were wasting away after twenty-eight days of stillness, perhaps bits and pieces of me were breaking off. Once more my head propelled me through the arch, on through the tunnel, my arms across my chest. I was a creature from beneath the earth, so used to living in the dark soil that the only way I could move was this burrowing, this tunnelling.

I burrowed my way to the English Department, arrived at the empty corridor. The metal basket outside the office appeared to be empty, but when I bent over it, I saw my essay, the only one: *Jean Kennedy, Junior Freshman*. On the cover a number was circled in red pen. I carried it away with me, hurriedly down the corridor, concealing it beneath my folded arms, like a thief. In the quiet sections of the stairwell, I stopped and looked at the number again, and then hurried away, back to my nest.

In my little bedsit I locked the door behind me – *safety first*, Momma always said – and leaned against the door. I opened the last page of the essay, my hands trembling, my heart thumping.

Jean, I have been setting this essay title for more than ten years. This is the best essay I have ever read. It is insightful, perceptive, and demonstrates an independence of mind and a maturity of analysis.

And all I could think of was how I would never get those twenty-seven days back again. All the lectures I had missed. What a fool I had been.

Suddenly I had to see Momma. No matter what mood I might find her in, no matter how she might interrogate me as to why I had let the family down by making such allegations, insinuations, foul degradations. I had to see John F. But telephone first, always telephone first, to check who is there. The sound of John's voice elated me.

'Who's there, Johnny?'

'Momma, Aunty Ida.'

'I'm coming home now.'

'Daddy says you don't come much any more because you're too big for your boots now you're in Trinity College.'

Triumphantly, joyfully: 'He's a liar.' I did not feel that this would disturb John F. in any way, for he and I had always been able to read each other's minds.

I sailed along the Strand Road. Soon it would be dark, but for now the late-afternoon winter sunshine captured every part of me; from every angle it entered me. It penetrated and warmed me. I became aware that I was hungry. Aunty Ida was there: there would be cake. As I turned at Merrion Gates, I raced the train, out past the bird sanctuary to Booterstown Station. Here was I now, sailing, sunlit girl – held though I was by death, green and dying, adrift in my pea-green boat – singing in my chains like the sea.

Acknowledgements

My deep gratitude to my four inspiring children, and to George.

And to those first readers of this book whose devotion to it thereafter was extraordinary and without whom it would not have found its life: C. Samuel DeVeau, Mary-Ellen Nagle, Louise Nealon and Ian Sansom.

And heartfelt thanks to Brendan Barrington for his tremendous kindness, sensitivity towards the text, clarity of vision and pure artistry.